THE A[...]

to lose
YOU

N. ISABELLE BLANCO

Dorian

"I was a God back then. Untouchable. Consequences didn't apply to me. It was my right to do whatever I wanted—I never thought it would eventually cost me the one woman I'd ever fallen in love with."

I should've just told her everything from day one.
Not that it would have mattered. I always knew it'd be too much.
That the dirt of my past would ruin us.
I can't blame her for leaving me. For the pain everything caused her.
If I were a nice guy, I'd let her go.
Maybe I'm an evil bastard, but whatever the fuck it takes, that woman will return to me.

Demitra

"You think you know someone's reputation—then you find out it's so much dirtier than you imagined."

My soul is addicted. Living without him is impossible.
Five months of having him and it feels like I've never lived without him at all.
Now, I'll have to learn. Will have to rip him out of my being.
Or I can choose to suffer through the struggle.
To fight.
To accept the pain in order to keep him.
To go up against everyone standing in our way.
Including my own father.

To Lose You
Allure #3
Copyright © N. Isabelle Blanco

Cover design by Pretty In Ink Creations
Formatting by Midnight Designs

Publication Date: February 15th 2022
Genre: FICTION/Romance/Contemporary

ALSO BY

A. Isabelle Blanco

DORIAN

dorian

PROLOGUE

"You're still mine, Dorian. I don't care if you're in denial about it."

Rage warred with disbelief inside me. Of all the crazy shit to say . . .

Monica leaned on my desk, her black hair falling in waves over her shoulders.

I stared up at her and squeezed the pen in my hand. "You're fucking crazy—"

She pressed her fingers to my lips, shushing me.

I jerked my face away, shooting to my feet. "Don't fucking touch me."

Seemingly oblivious to my dangerous mood, Monica spun around slowly and sat on my desk. "That's not what you demanded the last time we were naked together."

"Which was over seven months ago, in case you forgot."

Shrugging, she smoothed out her hair. "Not the longest we've ever gone without fucking each other." She pursed her thick lips, humming thoughtfully. "You were supposed to come back to me by now."

"I'm no longer interested. And the last time we saw each other, you made it clear you were going to find yourself another stud to take my place."

"Oh please. I came back to you that night. But you didn't even want to let me in." Her hazel eyes narrowed in my direction. "What's her name, Dorian?"

I carefully schooled my expression. "What the hell are you talking about?"

"Someone was in the apartment that night. Admit it."

Like hell. Realistically, I was aware that I couldn't hide it forever. Demitra and I were together. Oh, we hadn't discussed it yet but that woman was mine.

And I'd be damned if I let Monica ruin it in a childish pique.

Eventually, Demitra and I would be out in the open. Soon.

But I had to plan it perfectly. Minimize the damage Monica could inflict. There were things about me Demitra could never know. She would never look at me the same again.

Most people probably wouldn't judge the insane sex life I had before Demitra came back in my life. I was single. It was my right to do whatever I wanted.

Or so I thought.

Then I experienced this entirely new, all-consuming attraction to Demitra. One that eventually morphed into something else.

I was only her second lover. She was barely twenty. How could I ever expect her to be okay with my past when I would go *crazy* if the roles were reversed?

Monica was still silently analyzing me.

Inhaling slowly, I shook my head and smirked. "You're actually fucking jealous. Look at you. How sad is that? Didn't you once tell me only weak women feel jealousy? Yet here you are, so worried about whose pussy my cock is in."

"So there was a woman there."

My jaw ticked. "You're psychotic and possessive. It's sad."

Monica waved her hand dismissively. "I fuck other men. You fuck other women. A lot of the time, we fuck them together. In the end, though, we always go back to being with each other."

"Not this time!" Sheer force of will kept me in place, when all I wanted was to force Monica out of my office.

Violently.

So violently that it would scare her forever out of my life.

"Dorian, whoever she is, we both know that I can fuck you way better than she can."

"You fucking wish," I growled, biting back everything else I wanted to say. The last thing I wanted was her getting any information about Demi. "Stop acting as if you have feelings for me. It's kind of pathetic."

Her tinkling laugh rolled through my office; a perfectly orchestrated giggle. "This isn't about feelings. No one can fuck me like you do. It's your fault for being so damn good at it."

"So, you like the way I am in bed, and for that you want to own me."

"Or share you. As long as you're still around to give me something." She shrugged.

I laughed, making sure to pour every bit of disdain I felt for her into it. Walking to my office door, I placed my hand on the knob. "Monica, what did I once tell you was my biggest turn off when it comes to women?"

"I already told you—"

"Possessiveness. Jealousy," I cut her off. Truth is, I was full of shit. I had *zero* problems with it if it came from Demitra. However, I'd never been okay with it from anyone else.

A fact Monica knew well.

She rose off my desk, smoothing her hands down her skin-tight, burgundy knee-length skirt. "You expect me to believe you just decided to stop fucking me for no reason?"

Couldn't help it; my head fell back and I chuckled at her audacity. "Are you seriously that conceited? Because I need to be honest with you: It was good, but it wasn't *that* good."

She grabbed her clutch off the desk and began walking toward me, hips swinging seductively thanks to her six-inch heels.

And she did nothing for me. Nothing. Just a memory of all the empty sex I had in my life.

"Right." She smiled at me, teeth perfectly white against her tan. "Yet you fucked me how many times in the last seven years?"

The reminder made me sick. Not because I didn't enjoy it while I was doing it. Lord knew I did. Yet, all those moments of meaningless sex with this woman could end up costing me the one woman I did love.

The only woman I had ever loved.

A woman that didn't even know it yet because I hadn't brought myself to confess it to her. It'd only been four months. I was waiting for the right time.

I was still waiting for that time.

Monica stopped before me.

Jerking away, I hurried to put some space between us. "It doesn't matter how many times we fucked. Clearly, I'm done with it."

Her tinkling laugh filled my office again. "Honey, the last time I had you, you were coming all over yourself like a geyser. Actually, every single time I had you, it was that way."

My stomach sank at that. That's exactly the type of shit she would vindictively tell my Demi. Sentences like that could never be overcome. The images they would leave in Demitra's head would eventually destroy us.

Again, I knew this because I wouldn't be able to deal with the tables being turned. I'd gotten lucky with my girl's inexperience. I knew that. The sick, insane possessiveness I felt for her wouldn't have allowed me to live in peace any other way.

"Monica, this isn't about the sex," I said calmly, trying for another tact. Managing the damage was the only option for me. I didn't know the end result, how I would get that brat to let me go without a fight.

But considering I was planning on making it official with Demi soon, I had to find a way.

Fuck. Stephen was going to be angry enough about me being with his little girl. My reputation spoke for itself, but a lot of that was based on just rumor.

That bitch in front of me actually knew a lot of the facts.

Crossing her arms in a way that pushed her fake breasts higher, Monica leaned back against my closed door. "Then what is it about?"

"This attitude of yours is a turn off. I'm sorry. You're the very last woman I ever expected possessiveness from." *Make it all her fault. Keep the focus on that.* It was the only way to keep her from questioning who I was with.

Another eye roll and sigh from her. "I already told you: I'm not possessive." In a flash, she was in front of me, cupping my cock. "I just want you to continue giving me this dick."

I practically flew away from her. "Don't fucking touch me. What's wrong with you? Don't know how to handle the word *no*?"

Her eyes narrowed, this time with a hard edge to them I knew well.

The princess was on the verge of throwing one of her epic fits.

"*You* have never said no to me before," she said in a low, tense tone.

A huge fucking mistake. I realized that now. Damn it, I'd spoiled that woman with my dick. Gave her some false illusion that it would always be at her service. I should have known better, but of course I didn't think about that. I was too busy enjoying every hole on her body whenever I felt like it.

Jesus. I'm a piece of shit. How could I ever be worthy of Demi? I wasn't and wouldn't be, that's the truth. But nothing in the world would stop me from keeping her. I couldn't live any other way.

"I'm saying enough. Seriously. I'm a grown man and have the right to decide who I want to fuck. That person is no longer you." Monica opened her mouth to speak but I shook my head sharply. "And, it has nothing to do with another woman. As a matter of fact, I have just as many at my disposal now as I did in the past. So if you want to blame another female for this, you're going to have to lay the blame on all of them."

Cold, fucked up statement, but it's one the old me would have had no issue saying.

And because of that, it was *exactly* what I had to say to her. I had to keep her thinking I was still the old me. It was my only hope of getting her off Demi's trail until I could find another solution.

Something—*anything*—that could help me in my quest to keep the sordid details of my past from becoming known to the woman I loved.

Fists clenched, I faced Monica fully, wondering what the hell I was going to have to do to get her out of my office and out of my life.

Her eyebrow arched, and she let her eyes trail over me. A slow, hungry perusal.

And for the first time ever, it made my skin crawl.

My hands slowly curled into fists. "What do I have to give you so you'll leave me alone?"

Her analytical stare bore through me, trying to pick up on any clue. Any hidden tell.

Emotionally, she was fucking stunted to an extreme, but that didn't mean she was stupid.

No. She wasn't. God, no.

I almost jerked at the realization; I was officially staring into the eyes of one of my most dangerous adversaries.

She was vicious enough to do it. To ruin me, not only by causing me to lose Demitra, but also making sure this hit the press. A viper, that one. One that struck out the moment it felt a little betrayed.

Over a hundred-years of my family owning this company. Of making a name for itself.

She would take it all from me just to soothe her ego, and she was astute enough to get away with it if I wasn't careful. The only thing that might stop her was the contracts between our companies. And even that might not be enough.

"Is that an open offer?" Monica asked.

"Define open," I countered, thoughts racing.

She scoffed, lips curling in an amused smile. "This isn't a negotiation, Dorian. You would have to prove to me there isn't someone else."

Frustrated, I ran my hand through my hair. "Why the fuck are you so obsessed with this idea?"

"Because you're acting like a man in *love*."

I barely flattened my expression in time. "And you're acting like a *woman in love*. Damn. Didn't realize I'd hooked you like that."

This time, when her eyes flashed, there was no denying the malicious intent in them.

Her phone began ringing from inside her purse. Taking it out, she stared at the screen, lips pursed.

Pick it up, I silently begged. *Please let it be an excuse for you to get the fuck out of here.* She did, eyes on me as she brought the phone up to her ear. "Yes, Simon?"

Her assistant.

On my desk, my own phone began vibrating across the surface. Eyes still on her, I turned to head back toward it.

"Yes. I'm aware. But why isn't Rolland handling this?"

It was fucking creepy how she could focus on whatever issue she was discussing and also keep her attention obsessively on me.

Picking up my phone, I discreetly looked at the screen. Fuck. Fuck. Fuck. It was Demi. My heart thumped painfully in my chest, but I couldn't give anything away. So, I waited for the call to head to voicemail and slowly placed my phone back on my desk, as if nothing was wrong.

"Yes. Yes. I'll be at the site in less than half hour. Thank you, Simon." Monica hung up the call and her eyes immediately dropped to my phone. "It was her, wasn't it?"

Exhaling a rough breath, I placed my hands on my desk and leaned toward her. "Do you even realize how unhinged you sound?"

She just blinked at me, too far gone in her own mind to even be insulted by my comment.

Suddenly, I felt weary down to my fucking bones. "Monica—"

My phone started ringing again.

Demitra's name flashed across my screen along with the picture I'd taken of her in my bed the other day. Her hair was a mess, her light blue eyes shining, and her lips swollen from my kisses.

God, she was the most beautiful, wonderful thing that had ever happened to me. The thought of hurting her with my past made me sick.

Monica began walking toward my desk again.

Impulsively, I swiped my phone off the surface and dropped it into my pocket, where it continued to vibrate with the incoming call.

A triumphant smile tugged at the corners of Monica's collagen-enhanced lips. "You couldn't have confirmed it to me louder than you did just now."

She was right. I'd just given myself away. There was no help for it, though. Better that than letting this cunt see my girl's face and identify her. "Listen to me. We work together—"

"Oh, I *know*." Her smile grew wider.

I swear to God, a cold shiver danced down my spine at how crazy she looked just then. "So you're aware that considering the sheer number of mutual contracts both our companies have, we can't afford a harassment case?"

She laughed at that. "Dorian, are you threatening me with legal action just because you're trying to hide the identity of your new little toy?"

I bit down on the inside of my cheek to prevent myself from warning her to stop. No one talked about my Demi that way.

"You want to know what's the saddest thing?" Her smile grew even wider and she 'tsked' at me. "Whoever she is, you picked wrong."

"*Excuse me*?"

"You heard me. Creatures like you and me, we have a sexual darkness in us. A hedonistic need to be sexually free and to explore that with whomever we wish."

That *used* to be me. I won't lie. But it wasn't me anymore, and the more she described who I was in the past, the more my dread multiplied. "What's your fucking point?"

"That it's obvious that whoever this woman is, she doesn't understand you. She doesn't *know* about you."

The chilly sensation crawling along my skin morphed into a cold sweat.

"And"—still smiling, Monica spun around and began walking to the door, peeking over her shoulder at me—"you're desperate to keep her from finding all of this out."

She didn't say anything more.

She didn't need to.

That Cheshire Cat smile aimed at me, she waved happily and finally stepped out of my office.

Leaving me there, my mind an utter mess.

This bitch knew. She knew I was in love. She knew the woman I loved didn't know about my past.

Worst of all, she knew that Demitra could never understand it.

That no normal woman could ever be asked to accept it.

Monica hadn't said it aloud but I knew: she had just declared all-out war on whoever the woman I loved was. All because I wouldn't sleep with her, nor would I ever share Demitra's body with her.

It would end up being her word against mine, but regardless, whatever she would say to Demi would be the truth.

My twisted, toxic, fucked-up truth. All because I was selfish. Narrow-sighted. I lived my life however the hell I wanted it, and as long as it didn't cause a scandal that ruined my family's reputation, I didn't care about the consequences.

Now here they were, slapping me in the face.

And this was just a taste.

It was about to get much, much worse.

I had no idea how to contain this bullshit, but it was time for some serious damage control. Something I wouldn't be able to do on my own. Pulling out my phone, I selected Luke's number.

"What's up?"

"I need you and Calum to meet me as soon as possible."

There was a pause, then, "Dude, you sound like shit. What's happening?"

"I'll tell you when you get here. Just hurry."

chapter one

It'd been weeks of dealing with the Monica situation. Ever since I got back from my four-week business trip, all she'd done was hound me. Stalk me. To the point that yesterday I had to begin speaking with my lawyers about how we could break our twelve ongoing contracts with her company.

Easiest way? Go legal with my stalking claim. File an order of protection, etcetera. Problem with that? Well, the same problem I faced if I broke my contracts with her another way.

Retribution, plain and simple. The woman would make this a huge scandal, tell the world everything she knew about me.

Including the fact that I'd begun dating my intern—who was nineteen-years-old at the time.

How did she find out? Fuck if I knew. She must have had me followed or something.

Growling under my breath, I tugged on my hair. I'd allowed it to grow longer because Demi loved my curls, but with the way I felt, I was going to end up tearing it all off.

I didn't even give a fuck about my family's reputation anymore. I had no siblings and my parents were dead. What was left were my aunts and uncles, and my cousins. Most of which still carried the Sorenson name.

Yet, that couldn't matter to me moving forward. If the name got sullied, then yes. It was my fault for living the way that I did, for not being more careful who I fucking stuck my dick in.

But the reality was that I had this beautiful, young little thing that I loved, and she had no clue about who I really was. As Calum and Luke told me a few weeks ago, I may not have any choice but to tell her.

Prepare her.

How? Fucking, *how*? Was I just supposed to sit her down and tell her that my crazy ex-fuck buddy was threatening to let her know all the sordid details about our sex life?

Yes. Lord help me, that was exactly what I had to do. I no longer had a choice. Demitra had been stressed for weeks because of this. I'd done my best to hide it from her, but Monica was being so insistent that it was impossible.

Shit. When I called Demi ten minutes ago, she'd automatically assumed I was breaking up with her.

I stopped before one of the large windows in my living room and looked out into the city. My chest tightened every time I replayed the memory of how small her voice had become. Weeks of this shit had taken its toll on my girl.

Nothing in the world could help me forget that I was minutes from confessing things to her that I wasn't ready to confess.

This wasn't how everything was supposed to go, yet the choice had been taken from me.

In minutes, I would have to lay it all out on the table and risk losing her because of it.

My entire body revolted at the idea. I shoved the feeling down. This wasn't the time to listen to it. I had to do the right thing, no matter what it cost me.

Demitra deserved as much.

Whereas I didn't deserve shit. Not from life, not from her. If I lost her, I would have no one to blame but Monica and myself.

Anger coursed through me—anger at my weakness. At my inability to imagine a life without Demitra although it'd only been four months since we began seeing each other.

Anger at my old self for not being more careful.

Anger at Monica for existing in the first place.

God. Where was Demi?

Unused to this extreme level of anxiety, I stormed over to the door and peeked through the peephole. Within mere seconds, the elevator doors opened and I saw her step off.

Demi.

She looked as stressed as I felt. Just as afraid.

I'd never felt my stomach drop as it did then. *Don't be a fucking pussy. Just face the situation.* I told myself that over and over, but it didn't help shit.

Demi raised her hand to knock—

I practically tore the door open, grabbed her arm, and yanked her inside. Without saying anything, I closed the door, knowing damn well that I was probably hurting her because of how tight my hold was.

Couldn't help it, though. My body was instinctually fighting to keep her near, when deep down I knew I was minutes away from sending her running.

I tried to bring her deeper into the apartment.

She pulled back, refusing to budge.

Confused, I turned back to her. "Demi?

Her gorgeous, sad eyes stared up at me. "You said you wanted to talk. So what's going on?"

Fucking hell. That expression on her face sliced my insides wide open. She was bracing herself for me to break it off with her. It made me that much more determined to not lose her. Moments ago, I was prepared for the fact that I might.

Now, all I cared about was doing whatever I had to do to keep her. "Demi, come into the living room."

My stubborn woman's jaw hardened. "I'd rather talk here."

Why? So she could have a clear path to the door?

Fuck. That.

"Demitra, come in and sit down. This isn't something we should talk about standing here."

When she closed her eyes, the space between her brow furrowed, the rage I had toward Monica morphed into something much, much worse. At the rate I was going, I would end up killing the bitch for making an already delicate situation even more stressful.

Sighing, I tried to soften my tone. "Demi, please just—"

"Dorian," she mumbled, eyes still closed. "Just tell me what you have to say and I'll leave."

I'd known it, but hearing her declare it still came as a shock. "Leave? Demi, what"—My mind spun faster, and the fear I was trying so hard to contain burst out of me—"you fucking think that—Jesus. Baby, just come and sit with me." I grabbed her hand and rushed toward one of the couches.

The same one I'd fucked her on God knew how many times now.

I couldn't even bring myself to look at the coffee table. Not with all the scenarios rushing through my mind. She was going to try to leave me once I confessed everything, and I had no idea how to stop her.

Pausing in front of the couch, I motioned with my hand toward it. Demitra sat down. My initial thought was to join her on the couch, but there was no way I could remain still with these emotions coursing through me.

Pacing in front of her, I took a deep breath and finally let the truth out. "There's no easy way to say this, so I'm going to just say it outright. I'm being threatened."

"What?"

I stomped right back to my old position in front of the windows and stared out into the city once more. Crossing my arms, I gritted my teeth.

"Dorian, what are you talking about?"

"Monica," I ground out, hating the sound of that name more and more.

Demi's gasp behind me was like getting kicked right in the gut. "Why is she threatening you?"

Groaning, I spun around and walked back toward her. Sitting on the coffee table, I rubbed my face with my hands. "Fucking shit."

"Dorian . . . it's about us, isn't it?"

chapter two

Of course she would figure it out that quickly. My girl was nothing if not astute. Lowering my hands, I locked eyes with her, knowing she could see the turmoil in my stare. Unable to bear the distance between us, I reached for her hand. "Demi."

She jerked away from me. "Just tell me already. Please."

Her need for space shattered me. I doubted she even knew how much. There was no shaking the feeling that this was just the beginning. Soon, her need for distance would become something more tragic. "She found out about us."

"Obviously."

Her voice was so small, so demoralized, that I wanted to hunt Monica down and torture her. Make her suffer until the day she died.

"She's going to tell everyone"—about me and Demi. About the things I'd done with her before Demitra and I were together—"or so she says." But first she would make us pay for loving each other. Of that I had no doubt.

"What does she want in return for her silence?"

She wouldn't meet my stare.

A pained sound left me and I lurched forward to grab her hands.

"Look at me."

Her watery eyes finally rose to meet mine.

"I'm trying to prepare you. That's why I'm telling you this." And because she deserved it. I was a selfish, stupid bastard for keeping it from her this long. For making her wonder. "She's throwing a damn fit. She found out you're the reason I'm no longer interested in her. I don't fucking understand where she's coming from. She made it clear that I was 'replaceable' and it was supposed to be just sex—"

"She wanted you for herself." When Demi closed her eyes again and the space between her brows furrowed, I wanted to rage like an out-of-control beast. Destroy everything in this city on my way to obliterating Monica. "What woman wouldn't?" my girl whispered under her breath.

My heart throbbed violently and all I could think was, *I love you. I fucking love you. I've never been this obsessed with any woman before. Don't you dare fucking leave me for this.* "Damn it, Demi. Open your eyes and look at me."

She didn't move.

I cupped her jaw. She actually attempted to pull away from my touch *yet again*. Fury rising, I tightened my hold on both her jaw and hand, and my legs caged hers from the outside.

She wasn't going anywhere.

Demitra didn't understand. There was no out for her. I didn't give a fuck what I had to do, but she wasn't allowed to leave me.

She would be mine forever. No matter the cost to us both.

"Demitra—"

"We have to end it, don't we?"

Her question was like getting slapped by a motherfucking brick. For a few seconds, I couldn't voice my opinion past my rocketing blood pressure. Then, my voice finally burst out of me with every ounce of desperation I felt. "Stop thinking like that!"

Ignoring her shocked expression, I grabbed her arms and forced her to stand with me. "Do you want to leave me?" The thought made me murderous. Psychotic. In the back of my mind, I was aware that I was actually shaking her, but I couldn't stop myself. The last thing I wanted to do was hurt her, but she was fucking *killing* me with her obvious desire to end our relationship. I jerked her into me. "Answer me, Demi."

She gasped my name.

"Do you, Demi? Do you *want* us to end?" *Go ahead*, I silently dared her. *Try it. We'll see how far you actually get.*

Those beautiful light blue eyes searched mine, full of so much fucking emotion. When her hands fisted around my shirt, securing me in place, I felt the beast calm somewhat. "No, Dorian. *No.*"

A momentary second of relief.

It was gone as fast as it came. Because she still didn't know the whole truth. Because I was absolutely sure that once she did, she might end up changing her mind about being with me, when she really didn't have a choice.

I couldn't give her one.

The love I felt for her imprisoned me. It was beyond comprehension.

"Good." I released her arms to hug her against me, effectively trapping her even more. "I'm not letting you go. Do you understand what that means?"

Her eyes searched mine again. I saw the instant she realized something more was at work here. Of course she did. My woman was too smart, too analytical to just take this entire scenario at face value.

"Dorian, what aren't you telling me?"

That was my chance. My chance to finally come clean.

But first, I needed her to understand why, no matter how bad things were about to get, she wasn't allowed to leave me. "Demi, you do know what that means, don't you?"

"I—"

Cupping her face, I stopped her before she could continue. "How could you not know?" I sounded as unhinged and out of my mind as I felt. "It's obvious, isn't it? I'm a fucking mess because of *you*."

She attempted to extricate herself from my hold.

Again.

"Dor—"

"I love you, Demitra."

Fuck.

Fuck.

The words just flew out of me without my consent. Out of my control.

Too late now.

Just as her eyes began widening, I locked gazes with her and repeated my all-consuming truth. "Damn me but *I love you*."

No response from her.

Silence.

And that shell-shocked expression, as if me telling her this was the very last thing in the world she ever expected to hear.

It was.

Why?

Because a man like me wasn't supposed to be able to love. A man like me was only good for fun and games. The reputation I'd carelessly let go to shit solidified the world's view of me.

How many women had tried to tie me down, all with their eyes set on the prize, although they'd known I would never love them?

Too many.

But this girl—this young, honest girl with no ulterior motives— had slid past whatever fucked up wall had been around my heart. She'd dug deep, and slid into my blood against my will.

Her, the same woman I loved.

The woman who continued to stare at me, unblinking.

God-fucking-damn-it. The first time in my almost thirty-two years of life I'd told a woman I loved her, and she still hadn't responded.

My hands shot into her long, brown hair that I loved so much and fisted.

She whimpered at the pain.

I knew I should have eased my hold, but the emotions were more than I could bear. Yanking her into me, our noses bumping, I growled out, "*I fucking LOVE you.*"

"*Dorian.*"

I didn't let her finish. The fear clouded my mind. That voice inside me that whispered that she didn't feel the same way. That she was about to end it with me.

A rough sound left me, and I slammed my lips against hers, bending her over backward and taking control of her body in the only way I knew how.

Maybe I couldn't control her emotions.

Maybe I couldn't have her heart.

But her body was fucking *mine* and I was about to prove it.

chapter three

Eyes closed, lips fused with hers, I lifted her into my arms and stumbled my way through the apartment. I couldn't see shit, but there was no way I would tear my lips away.

Demi clawed at my hair. Her legs tightened around me in an almost-painful hold.

No more words had been said between us. They weren't needed. I would have sold my soul to hear her say she loved me back, but the desperate emotions echoing from her to me were more than enough for now.

Our tongues dueled in a vicious power-play, both of us desperate to consume the other. When she fisted my hair in that ruthless way of hers, I stumbled blindly into the wall.

Her back slammed against it.

I was so far gone that I couldn't even bring myself to feel concerned.

Pressing my body into hers, caging her against the wall, I bruised her lips with another rough kiss.

A sexy, feminine groan echoed in her chest.

A sound I'd heard maybe a thousand times by now.

It would never be enough.

My skin on fire, I pulled away long enough to rip my shirt over my head. Her shirt practically disappeared off her body; that's how fast I divested her of it. Then it was just her skin and mine, and the million electric pinpricks she set off in me every time we touched.

Fusing my lips with hers again, I licked and sucked at her, my hands reaching beneath the flowing, silk skirt she was wearing and tearing at her panties. "I want you so bad it hurts."

She choked on my name.

Using the wall and my body to keep her in place, I squeezed my hands between us to tear at the button of my jeans. "I need to be inside you, Demi. It hurts so fucking much."

Her lips parted.

I fisted my cock and slammed straight into her.

She was wet.

Swollen.

Eager.

Fuck, I needed that.

I set an instant, vicious rhythm, pounding her into the wall. Her wide, glazed eyes locked on mine. On my next thrust, her glasses fell off. Neither one of us gave a damn.

Pressing my forehead to hers, I held her stare and rotated my hips with my cock deep inside her.

"*Oh God*," she whimpered, nails sinking into my shoulders.

"Feel that?" I rasped, eyes momentarily falling to her lips. "Feel how fucking hard you make me?"

She nodded breathlessly, throat bobbing.

Struggling for breath.

The sight of her like this was beyond necessary for me. I could never live without it.

Reaching for her wrists, I forced her arms above her head and held them against the wall. "Who does this pussy belong to, Demi?"

Another forceful thrust drove my point home.

Despite her sexy, breathless gasps, she refused to answer me, and that spark of defiance came back into her eyes.

Why? Damn it. Why was she denying me ownership of her?

Why was she denying me her love?

I paused, cock throbbing wildly in her wet cunt.

As always, Demi writhed in my grip, hips churning to take my dick regardless of my will.

"See that?" Breathless, I tightened my hold on her wrists. "See how mindless you get to have it?"

"Damn you," she gasped, fucking me with every thrust of her hips. "Keep moving."

"No."

She hissed at that, and bared her teeth. "Why?"

"Tell me what I need to hear."

"You're always doing this to me!" Her cry echoed through the penthouse. "You don't get to decide what I do and don't tell you!"

Fury rose at that. I didn't? Was she out of her fucking mind? I was as close to her as I could get, but I pressed my weight against her even more. "Just because we're having problems, that doesn't mean you get to quit."

Above her head, her hands curled into fists. "What the fuck are you talking about?"

Her walls rippled along my length. My eyes rolled back momentarily and I had to talk myself down from fucking her into a hole in the wall. "You still want to leave me."

"I didn't say that!"

"I just fucking told you I fucking love you, and you don't even have a response for it!"

Her lips snapped shut.

I gave it another few seconds, looking into her eyes, praying. Hoping.

Going mad from her refusal to answer me.

A strange sort of darkness began coursing through my veins. A violent, nearly psychotic thrumming that put my possessiveness of her to shame. "I'll make you," I growled, pulling my hips back to slam into her.

"*Fuck!*" Her eyes slid closed.

I released her wrists to fist the hair at the back of her head. "Look at me."

She didn't want to be a slave to my demands, but we both knew she had no choice. Neither one of us did. We owned each other on a sick, utterly dependent level.

When her eyes locked with mine again, I kissed her roughly. "I'll make you love me, Demitra. Even if it's the last fucking thing I do."

"Oh Dorian," she whispered, tears leaking from her eyes.

I froze momentarily in shock, the look on her face searing me.

There was no denying it.

It was *right fucking there*.

"You do love me," I mumbled, my mind a confused mess.

More tears, but still the words wouldn't come.

Why wouldn't she tell me? I could see it clear as fucking day in her expression!

Growling like the beast she'd turned me into, I lifted her off the wall. Hands on her ass, I held her still as I began pounding into her again. She tucked her head into my neck and caught my earlobe between her teeth.

I groaned, feeling my balls drawing up tight.

Every. God. Damn. Time.

Before her, I could go for fucking hours straight without coming.

With her, she took my cum from me before I was ready. It didn't matter how many times we fucked, I was nowhere near being desensitized to her.

Her teeth sunk into my neck, biting harder than she ever had. She'd always been careful of where she marked me, but there was no denying it.

This time, she meant for the whole world to see.

Yanking her off my neck, I cupped the back of her neck and laid her back against my forearm. I didn't care about the strain of keeping her in that position. Didn't care about anything but having her at my mercy.

Holding her at that angle, I fucked her with every bit of strength in my body, feeling that explosive release crawling its way up my dick. "I love you. Fucking love you. And *you* love *me*. Everything about you is mine, and it's only a matter of time before I force you to admit it, Demitra."

Her expression was intense. Possessive. The light in her eyes was slightly unhinged. Her constant moans grew shorter and shorter, her body tightening in that way I'd come to know so well.

"That's it, baby. That's it." I pressed my cock deep again and rocked my hips, letting my groin graze her clit. "Give it to me. Drench my cock."

"Dorian!" She came in a wild rush, her legs shaking around me, her eyes rolling back.

Letting my head fall back, I growled up toward the ceiling as my cum erupted inside her. The magnetic pull between us coupled with that insane love sliced through my awareness. In the darkness of my closed lids, all I could sense was her.

All I could feel was this connection.

I pumped shallowly into her, feeding her the last drops. Her pussy throbbed rhythmically, as hungry for it as I was to give it to her.

An entire lifetime of crazy, out-of-control, no-holds-barred sex, and none of them—absolutely none of them—ever felt like this.

chapter four

The last rush receded and the numbness that settled over my legs was instant. Walking backward, I blindly searched out the wall behind me and pressed my back to it. Sliding down to the floor with her legs still around me, I cradled her on my lap, feeling our hearts racing against each other.

Nuzzling her cheek, I struggled to catch my breath. "Tell me you love me."

Another small whimper left her and she tucked her face against my neck. When she shook her head *no*, I almost lost my goddamned mind.

"What the fuck, Demi?"

She reared back, eyes narrowed. "Don't fucking take that tone with me."

Her own tone left me blinking in confusion for a few moments. Striving to calm my voice, I tried again. "Why won't you just admit what we both feel?"

Just like that, all the tranquility and affection leaked out of her. In a matter of mere seconds, she was off my lap and searching for her shirt. "How in denial can one man be?" she snapped, snatching it off the floor.

"Now wait a goddamned minute." I forced my legs to lift me off the floor. Buttoning my jeans, I followed her as she stomped back into the living room while shoving her shirt on. "What is this all about?"

It wasn't until she whirled on me, her hair flying in every direction and her eyes wide with indignant disbelief that I realized how badly I'd just fucked up.

"Are you freaking serious right now?" she cried. "You've been hiding shit from me for weeks—"

"To protect you from all this!"

"Bullshit!"

The sheer hysterical volume of that scream stopped me in my tracks.

Fuck my life, her eyes were tearing up again.

"This isn't about protecting me. This is about protecting yourself!" Her eyes squinted as she tried desperately to find her glasses.

Glasses that had fallen off in the hallway by the wall.

Something I was in no hurry to tell her, especially now that she was gearing up to run from me once more. "Listen to me. I did it for you. I wanted to handle this without—"

Demitra whirled on me once more. "What is she holding over your head?"

My heart dropped. "Excuse me?"

"You heard me. What. Is. She. Holding. Against. You?" That last sentence was pushed out through her gritted teeth.

Astute. Supremely analytical.

For the first time ever, I realized just how dangerous of a business woman my girl would one day be. A mind like hers only came along once in a while and there was no fooling it.

My jaw twitched as I tried to force the words out. *Be honest with her! Tell her everything!*

I can't! I'll fucking lose her!

Demi's head reared back slowly at my silence.

Then, with a nod, she stepped away from me.

I took a step toward her as if pulled.

She held up her hand and shook her head. Looking behind her, she found where her purse had fallen by the coffee table.

Still no glasses.

Something that apparently wasn't going to stop her. "Listen to me very clearly, Dorian. This isn't going to work if you aren't completely honest with me."

"Why can't you just trust me to handle this and do the right thing?" It burned. Maybe I had no right to feel that way, but her lack of trust in me cut me up inside.

"Don't you get it?" Suddenly, she looked exhausted. As beat up as I felt. "I did trust you. The last few weeks, I *knew* something was off and I let it rock. I let you handle it. And that entire time, you never bothered to open up to me. To tell me the truth."

"I'm telling it to you now."

"Not all of it!" Something about that last shout seemed to drain all the fight out of her. In its place was nothing but a resigned sadness. "You're right. You own me. You're right about how I feel about you—"

I moved closer. "Then say it," I begged, needing those words more than she would ever know. "Please."

Her chest heaved with her next breath. "No. What I can promise you is that I'll be waiting for you."

"Waiting for me? What the fuck does that mean?"

"It means I'm leaving—"

"The hell you are!"

"*Dorian.* I can't be here right now. I'm going home to try and calm the hell down. When you're ready to be open and honest with me, fully open and honest, come find me. But"—she slipped her purse over her shoulder and began walking toward the door—"don't you dare come near me if it isn't with the full truth. I deserve as much."

"Demi—"

She was gone, the door closing behind her.

Cursing, I ran out of my penthouse.

Just as the elevator door slid closed.

Fuck! It must have never gone back down after she came. That's why it was conveniently there, waiting to take my woman from me.

Disregarding the fact that I was shirtless, I spun to take the stairs—

"Well, well. I'll admit I never looked too closely at her, since she seems unremarkable at first, but after hearing the way she moans, I have to admit she's fucking sexy."

I slammed to a halt, my mind screaming at the sight of Monica leaning against the doorframe at the entrance to the stairwell.

Arms crossed, she smiled at me, the gloating glint in her eye triggering that darkness in me again. "She sounded so upset about your lies to her. Apparently, she's holding out some false hope that you're different than you really are. If only she knew how many dark secrets you're hiding—like the time we had that massive orgy and it was just you fucking five of us. We all took turns loving that dick the entire night. Till this day, I don't know how you managed to give all of us such equal attent—"

I snapped, the murderous rage taking control of my body.

Within the blink of an eye, I was in front of her.

Another blink, and I finally had my hand wrapped around her neck, squeezing down tight.

She now knew about Demitra. Had seen her running from me. Had heard her moans and was lusting after my girl.

She now had a name to go after Demi if she so wanted.

My vision bled red, my mind sending orders to my limbs without my consent. Tightening my fingers and bringing me one step closer to ridding myself of this problem.

One step closer to ending this woman's life.

Even as her face turned red, Monica smiled up at me, mouthing, "*So much fun.*"

Disgusted, I shoved her away from me, uncaring of how she bounced off the closed door behind her. "This is the last time I'm warning you, Monica. Back the fuck off. Or I'll bring you down with me. So help me God, I *will* ruin you."

Laughing, Monica straightened her hair. "Don't you get it, Dorian? It's too late. Even if I wanted to back off now—which I don't—it's only a matter of time before she truly leaves you. Either you'll have to come clean or she'll go searching for answers on her own. And if you think I'm the only ex-lover from your past willing to enlighten her . . . well, honey, they say love makes a man foolish. Guess you're proving just how right that is. Aren't you?"

She left before I could respond.

Disappeared into the stairwell before I could snap and finish what I started.

But she left here one step closer to achieving her ultimate goal.

With Demi's identity no longer a secret, that woman now held the power to wreck my life on multiple levels.

Thank God I held the power to wreck hers, as well.

It was time to play hardball.

And while I was at it, time to start preparing for the fallout I was about to have with Stephen.

Dating his much younger daughter was one thing—sullying her with the scandal of my past transgressions was another.

It didn't matter that we lived in modern times.

For our social circles, there were things that could never be forgiven.

Especially when it came to coveted daughters.

This was heading toward cluster-fuck status whether I wanted it or not.

chapter five

"*M*y *best advice is to wait and see if she'll go as far as exposing you. Per the terms of each contract, neither party can act in a way that interferes with the other party's performance. There's also laws against revenge porn now. This would definitely qualify." -Howell.*

I scowled at my phone. The advice my attorney, Joey Howell, was giving me wasn't enough. Nowhere near it.

Even if Demitra wasn't a factor in my life, I didn't like the fact that he was telling me my best option was to remain a sitting duck, waiting for an attack that was certain to come.

"Our design for the new plaza on Fifth and East 27th will help us take the lead at the design festival. I have no doubt about that," Stephen announced on the video call we were having with the other CEOs on the project.

Five architecture firms, including my own and Agathen Designs, Calum's company.

He was on the call, too.

I should've been tuning in, participating, instead of focusing on my phone, but this couldn't wait.

'I still think we should meet in person to discuss this." -Howell.

I didn't appreciate feeling trapped. It was something I'd never had to deal with in my life, and I sure as hell wasn't going to put up with it now. Darting a glance at the screen, I made sure everyone was too engrossed in what Stephen had to say to pay attention to me, and pounded out another furious text.

'I don't understand why I'm paying you, if you can't offer me a more proactive solution now that I need it the most.' -D.

'I can't advise you to break these contracts. The losses in compensation owed would total in the hundreds of millions. Most likely more. And it would do nothing to stop her from divulging personal information, or leaking the videos she has of you two.' -Howell.

Of us "two".

That was the problem. It wasn't just us.

Why did I ever let her record us? Because I used to rewatch the videos and get off on them in the past.

God fucking help me.

No. God help Demi. It was as she once admitted to me: she wasn't experienced.

And, sometimes, even the most experienced women caved in the face of such sordid scandal.

It would be the biggest test of her feelings for me, and it was happening too fucking soon. Four in a half months, close to five. I hadn't even made it official with her, yet.

I wasn't an expert on relationships, had never truly had one in my life, but the writing was pretty clear on the wall.

This thing between Demi and I was hanging by a thread.

The way we left things yesterday was proof of that.

She ran out on me.

I told her I loved her, and she fucking *fled*.

"Dorian?"

Hearing my name made my head rear back. My phone, which I was holding on my lap beneath my desk, almost fell out of my hand.

Four pairs of eyes were focused on me, awaiting my response.

The problem was that I had no idea what I was being asked.

And I didn't like the way Stephen's gaze, in particular, was narrowed in my direction.

"I'm sorry. I received an urgent message," I said, opting for some partial honesty to cover up my lack of attention. "What was the question?"

Calum was quick to jump in and save my ass—which didn't surprise me, and I was more grateful to him than he could imagine. "The city council wants a say on which contractors we bring on board."

I barely bit back the comment: well, the city council could kiss our collective asses. Grinding my teeth, my frustration tolerance lower than it'd ever been, I responded, "We already picked the best ones in the city to suggest for the project. I'll handle the city council."

Stephen nodded. "Good. Good." He went on to address the meeting members, but my attention was gone again.

Howell had sent me another text and I hurried to open the thread.

'She knows the consequences for breach of contract as much as you do. Leaking damaging, personal information about you that can be traced back to her would ruin her company.' -Howell.

But what if she found a way to make it untraceable? And Howell remained under the impression that I was only concerned with the public scandal.

And I was, but not more than my sick fear that Monica would reveal my skeletons to Demitra personally.

Then she wouldn't be engaging in breach of contract, and I wasn't sure if it fell under the legal definition of "revenge porn".

Howell needed to know about Demitra. Perhaps with the full picture, he could give me a more aggressive attack plan. *'There's more you don't know. Are you free in the next few hours?'-D.*

"Alright, gentlemen. I believe we're ready to take control of the design festival. My office booked the conference room for the meeting before the event. We'll reconvene then," Stephen announced, at the top of his game as usual.

Even as his personal life began to fall apart.

A reflection of his true feelings for his wife, I guessed. Because his daughter's lack of communication with me was clearly tearing me apart and affecting my work ethic.

That failure must've not been lost on him. "Dorian?"

My head came up again. "Huh?"

The space between his eyebrows furrowed, but that was the only sign of his confusion at my actions. "Remain on the call. I have something else to discuss with you."

My heart sped up a bit; considering it'd been full speed ahead due to stress lately, the difference barely registered. "Alright." What did he want to discuss? My general lack of concentration?

The fact I looked like I felt? Utter shit ground into the sidewalk.

Or had Demitra told him something?

That final one might've been an option if their relationship had remained as it once was. Now, Demi couldn't get far enough from him. Physically, emotionally . . .

It's where I was heading with her, wasn't it?

In her book, I must've started approaching the dark realm her father was now in. It began the night she found out about Stephen cheating with Lucia, and it's been getting worse ever since.

My stomach turned as I imagined Stephen sleeping with one of the women I had. It's true. He had been more than a friend—he'd been almost a surrogate father to me since my own died.

And he'd slept with a woman I had once been with, as well.

Calum's expression and the way he glanced over in my direction before logging off wasn't lost on me.

I placed my phone face down on my desk to avoid the temptation of checking my messages. Taking a deep breath to center myself, I steepled my fingers and met Stephen's gaze head-on. "What is it that you wish to discuss?"

Any effort at calming myself was in vain, however, because he wasted no time on going straight to the point.

A very dangerous, very nerve-wracking point.

After checking to make sure everyone was truly logged off the call, he ran his fingers through his brown and gray hair, and let his facade of control collapse. "Dorian," he said, expression taut. Ragged. A man approaching the end of his line. "I need to speak with you about my daughter."

chapter six

There was no helping it—I stared at Stephen, mute, my brain scrambling to come up with a response.

He knew.

Demi did tell him.

But why? What did it mean?

I was more preoccupied with that then whatever explanation I was about to give him.

But I had to say something; it was the right thing to do.

An apology. That would've been a good starting point. I wasn't sorry I had fallen in love with his daughter, nothing could make me regret that, yet as a father he deserved to hear it, at least.

I let out the breath I hadn't realized I'd been holding, and opened my mouth to give it to him—

Stephen beat me to it. "I shouldn't be involving you in my family drama, but I haven't spoken to anyone else about this. No one else knows and I'm trying to keep it all under wraps. My family's personal business isn't for tabloid consumption."

What the hell was he . . . Was this about Demitra and I? Or about him cheating on his wife, and the fact that he was cruel enough to cut his daughter off financially?

All because he knew she was romantically involved with someone, even though he didn't seem to know who it was.

The reminder cooled a good portion of my regret. There was a simmering rage in me, one I hadn't acknowledged yet, and it was all aimed toward that man.

Same man I viewed as a father once.

Perhaps I was a hypocrite for judging him, but I was starting to look at him in a very different light. "I'm sorry, Stephen, but I don't understand."

"Demitra has stopped responding to any of my calls. And Antonia already announced her intention to file for divorce."

It would've been easy—so easy—to believe that the strain on his face was due to a man who was losing both his wife and his daughter.

Just a few months ago, that would've been my automatic assumption.

But Antonia held all the power in the family.

By the time Stephen married her, the Davis line had been financially crippled. On the verge of losing all standing. He came from a long line of financial irresponsibility.

Antonia's side, the Kastellanos, were rich the world over.

So rich that the Greek financial crisis hadn't even caused a chink in their networth.

As such, and as was the standard back in the days, Antonia's parents would've made sure there was an iron-clad prenup in place to protect their daughter's wealth.

She could've taken everything from Stephen. Including SD Interiors, the company. The SD might've been his initials, but there was no way she didn't have some legal standing.

Best case scenario, she swept it out from under his feet in the divorce.

Worst case? She obliterated it entirely.

A possible issue for my company, and others, due to the ongoing projects and contracts between us, but it was barely a blip.

I just couldn't bring myself to care as much as I should've.

"I'm sorry that you're losing them both at the same time," I said, choosing my words carefully. "You told me that you cut Demitra off—"

His chin jutted stubbornly. "She chose that option when she refused to tell me which boy she's become involved with. She preferred to strike off on her own then simply be honest about it. And whoever he is, he clearly has no respect for her. I walked in and found her with a disgusting bite mark on her neck. Who does that?"

Me.

That's who.

Jaw twitching, I fought to control my sudden desire to confess, take responsibility, and tell him exactly what I thought of his treatment of her. "Stephen, I'm not a father, but it is the twenty-first century. Most girls Demitra's age are doing worse and, since they're legal, their parents can't stop it." Translation: he needed to get the fuck out of his legal-aged daughter's business and remember that he was her father, not her owner.

"If she's grown enough to make such choices, then she's grown enough to take responsibility for all consequences. Including her life."

I stared at the screen, at the man on the video, wondering just who I was looking at. Was he the same person I'd always known? How come I never noticed what an asshole he could be?

Perhaps because he was like my father, and I was like his son.

A male.

Whereas Demi was female.

Which brought me to my next point.

I bit back the urge to tell him the same opinion could be leveled at him—if he wanted to cheat on his wife, he could be man enough to face the consequences of that—and struggled to calm my tone. "You almost raised me after my father died, and I've done much worse in my life."

Stephen tsked impatiently and wove my comment away. "It's different for us men, and you know it."

Misogyny.

It shouldn't have surprised me. It wasn't rare. And, perhaps, I could've been accused of indulging in it throughout my life, but I doubted it had ever been this bad.

Again, I wasn't a father.

I did possess some common sense, however, and I didn't think any daughter could easily overlook that kind of double standard.

Soon, I would have to confess to that man who I really was—namely: the man responsible for that bite mark.

The man his daughter had been hiding from him.

The man that was lost for her and would raze an entire city to the ground just to keep her.

Therefore, I needed to end that conversation as carefully as possible.

And it had to end now.

I wasn't in the mindframe to discuss this.

Not when his daughter ran out of my condo yesterday, after I confessed I loved her, and hadn't agreed to see me today.

"Stephen, I wish I could be of more help. With both Demitra and Antonia. I have no idea how to get a wife to forgive infidelity, and obviously I'm not a parent, as you said. I just hope it all turns out for the best." For all of us.

He nodded, expression pensive. "You're right. God knows when you'll finally cave in and get married, but I need to go see how to fix this mess."

When his daughter agreed, that's when.

My heart slammed into my rib cage at the thought.

Shoving it to the back of my mind, I wished him good luck and ended the video call. My phone had vibrated with notifications during the entire conversation. I ignored it only because of my distraction during the meeting, and the danger of Stephen catching onto the truth, but I rushed to check them now.

One was from Howell agreeing to meet at my office tomorrow afternoon.

The second text had me sitting up straight in my seat.

'Are you free?'-Dem.

I dialed her number so fast that I didn't remember doing it. All I knew was the urgency thrumming through my veins, and the fact that my phone was suddenly at my ear.

She picked up on the second ring.

I didn't even wait for her to greet me. "Demi."

"Yes, Dorian." No question mark, just her tired, resigned tone.

"You've been ignoring me the entire day." Spinning my chair around, I stared out the wall of windows at the New York skyline.

"To be fair, I wasn't. Work was extremely hectic, and I didn't have the emotional space to focus on our problems until late in the day."

"You didn't have the emotional space for me, you mean."

"Don't be cruel," she snapped above the sounds of the city—she was outside, but where?

Had she arrived home yet? Or was she heading somewhere else?

"Did you want me losing it at work?" Demi continued, clearly angry with me.

I rubbed my forehead and softened my tone. "God damn it, no. I've just missed you."

"I've missed you, too," she mumbled softly.

Cracked my chest right open with that one. She really did. "Let me see you tonight."

"Fine. Meet me at the Thai spot across the street."

For the second time, I straightened in my seat. "From your place?"

"Yeah. I'm on the way."

"Demitra, I'd rather we go straight to your apartment."

"Dorian, I'd rather we talk. And we can't do that in private. I know you."

"As I know you." And I knew it was a fact that as hard and needy as my dick currently was, her pussy was dripping for me just as much.

"You're ex is threatening you, and apparently, what she has over you is so bad that you're fucking afraid of her. If you want me in your life, you're going to talk, nothing more, and you're going to be fucking honest about what it is that she has over you," Demi warned in a tone I'd never heard from her before.

"She isn't my ex," was the only lame response I could give her, as my mind flashed to that confession.

To what I would have to do.

Practically lay it all out on the table, tell her that Monica had videos of us engaged in threesomes, foursomes . . . and there were never other men.

Ever.

Not in the videos, at least.

It was always me and the women.

All of them consented to being recorded.

I planned to ask Howell to track them down and see if they'd consent to those videos being made public in any way.

Because if they didn't, then I had more power to make Monica pay. More power to threaten her into submission.

Although, I knew that the real danger lay with one person—Monica would probably reveal those videos to Demitra long before she showed them to the world.

She was more interested in ruining what I had with Demi, then in ruining our companies.

After all, we made so much money together.

"Are you going to meet me to talk or what?"

No denying the warning in her voice that time, either.

Full honesty, or I could forget about this thing between us.

She was exhibiting a level of strength and resolve for her age that I couldn't help but admire—even as it threatened to drive me insane.

"Okay . . . Okay. I'm on my way." I stood from my seat.

"I mean it, Dorian. Full honesty. Or don't bother coming. I deserve that much if you want me to continue this with you."

"I know, baby," I said softly. "I know." Even though I couldn't help but feel like I was going to lose her anyway.

It was only a matter of time.

chapter seven

Demi was already seated at a table when I walked into the restaurant. I spotted her right away.

Not like it was hard. That table was positioned to be viewed from the entrance.

The hostess at the stand shot me a brilliant smile. Dark eyes trailed me, appreciating the view and assessing her chances. "How can I help you?"

I ignored that grin and pointed at Demi's table. "My girl is already seated." With that, I walked past her, headed for the one woman that hadn't noticed my entrance, yet.

"Oh. Okay. Enjoy your dinner," the hostess said, just loud enough for me to catch.

Not that I paid her attention.

Demitra was busy munching on her appetizer with small, precise bites. Her eyes were downcast, focused on her meal.

She didn't wait for me.

To sit or to start eating.

A calculated move? No doubt. But was it conscious or subconscious?

Either way, the message was received.

I grabbed the back of the chair and slid it away from the table. Finally, her eyes came up to meet mine.

All I wanted was to drape her across the surface, head hanging off the edge, and throat-fuck her into oblivion.

Her gaze flashed. The glaze of hunger was familiar—fucking relieving—and it took all my self-restraint to sit in the chair calmly.

Versus reaching for her and giving the people here a show.

"Demi."

She swallowed her latest bite, throat bobbing heavily. "Dorian."

This wasn't the time to beat around the bush, as much as I wanted to. I shrugged off my blazer, watching her expression as I did so.

My Demi was a violent lioness, even at her tender age. An apex predator that had no problem pouncing and taking what she wanted.

And each time that other side took over, the change in her was dangerous and obvious.

Like now.

She was angry with me.

Disappointed.

And ready to milk me for all I was worth.

My cock was always hard for her, always aching like I hadn't ever had her, even if it was a mere hours between the last time.

It was yesterday morning. Almost forty-eight hours. Didn't matter. I was throbbing and needy in my slacks, desperate as if at the end of a drought.

How the hell did I ever make it four weeks without her on my last trip?

It would never happen again. Ever.

At least that time I wasn't on the verge of losing her. A fact my body was clearly aware of.

Her eyebrow arched. "Well?"

I took her chopsticks from her hand. Ignoring her gasp, I picked up a coconut shrimp and popped it in my mouth. "This isn't going to be easy," I confessed once I was done swallowing.

"Coming clean, you mean?" Twisting in her seat, she waved the waitress over.

I placed the chopsticks back on the plate. "Putting those images in your head."

"They're already there," she mumbled angrily, avoiding my gaze.

"No. They aren't. Not yet." There was no hiding the misery in my tone.

Demitra's pale blue eyes snapped my way.

Too late. The waitress was already there, smiling down at us. "Are you ready to order your main dish? Or would you like your own appetizer?" That last one was directed at me.

"I'm okay for now—"

"Sabai Sabai, please," Demitra cut in. She held out the menus for the waitress to take.

It was my turn to raise an eyebrow.

The glare she gave me spoke loud and clear: *try and stop me.*

She wasn't legal, yet.

Didn't stop me from filling her with my dick, so it was hypocritical of me to interfere with this.

And the waitress didn't bother asking for ID.

My girl looked young, but her air of maturity made her seem legal, at least.

Or was it just the exhaustion and bitterness that kept encroaching on her face?

"You know what? Make it two," I said, knowing I'd need it. Bad.

When this conversation was over, they'd probably need to drag me out from the amount of alcohol it'd take to get me through it.

The waitress walked away to put in our drink order, and I didn't waste any time. I'd already wasted enough and Demi wasn't in the mood to indulge me much longer.

Leaning forward, arms on the table, I went to reach for her hand but thought better of it. The next words out of my mouth would dictate if she ever reached out for me again.

Or not.

"It . . . it wasn't just me and Monica."

Stillness.

An eerie, unpredictable stillness.

That was Demi's reaction.

And the comprehension that hardened her stare even more.

Hardened another part of the innocence I'd been chipping away at since the moment I decided to taste her.

I opened my mouth to continue—

Demitra held up a finger, composure admirably controlled. "I think I'd rather wait for those drinks before you go on."

So we did. An awkward, strained silence consumed us, and we sat there, the coconut shrimp forgotten.

It seemed to take forever, with me drowning in the sight of her, and Demi studiously ignoring me, head turned.

The vein on the side of her neck pulsed violently—I wanted to reach inside her and somehow calm her raging heart.

Mine wasn't much better, but it was my fault she was going through this.

Reckless.

Selfish.

Arrogant.

I was that and more.

And like a ricocheting bullet, the consequences were coming back around and hurting the most innocent bystander of all.

The waitress finally returned and placed our drinks on the table.

"Keep them coming," Demi ordered, reaching for hers.

The waitress eyed us both, before hightailing it out of there.

I'm sure she could see what anyone else that looked at us could: a couple being torn apart by distance. Even though it was only a table standing between us, the magnitude of my mistakes stretched much, much further.

"Demi." I picked up my own drink and brought it to my mouth. "I'm sorry. I can't even begin to tell you how much."

"It's fine," she mumbled behind her drink. "It's my fault. That's what I get for falling in love with one of the craziest bachelor's in the city."

I choked on my swallow.

Not the first time she did that to me, and I doubted it would be the last. "So you're finally admitting it?" I asked, wiping my mouth with a napkin. "You're finally admitting you love me?"

She poured every ounce of her anger into chugging that drink, and it was gone with a speed that concerned me. "You know damn well I do!" She slammed the glass on the table.

On the one hand, I didn't want her drinking like that.

On the other, my confession had barely begun, and I happened to have a knack for angering my woman like few ever could.

That waitress needed to run over here with her next drink.

"You ran away instead of saying it back," I explained in as calm a tone as possible. "Can you blame a man for doubting?" I reached for my glass.

Gone.

In Demi's hand faster than I could blink.

"How the fuck would you feel if it were me in this seat, confessing to having threesomes with other men? And one of them happened to be a crazy ex stalking me and threatening me?" she hissed, the venom of her attack hitting its aim with perfect precision.

Anddddd my drink was gone.

This was the part where I needed to shut my damned mouth up, but I'd promised her honesty, and I loved her too much not to live up to that promise. "I'd be going insane—"

"Exactly."

"And the images in my head would be haunting me day and night—"

Ice blue irises flashed with flames unholier than any fire hell could ever house. "*Exactly.*"

"I'd want to kill any stupid motherfucker you ever touched—"

Her next interruption was an "*Mhm*" and a jerky nod.

That one almost ripped a smile out of me.

I was smart enough to somehow hold it back. "Baby, I'd rain hell upon this city. But one thing I wouldn't do is let you go." I snatched her hand in mine. "I wouldn't be able to."

She jerked it back. Staring to the side, she blinked back tears, and her pulse pounded twice as hard in her neck. "Don't do that."

"Do what? *Touch* you?" She had to be fucking kidding me with that.

"Don't use my inability to deal with this as some screwed up barometer to judge my love for you." She brought her face around, that pleading gaze slicing up parts of me I hadn't even known existed. "Don't you dare somehow assume that you love me more than I love you just because I don't know how to handle the pain I'm going through—or the extra pain we both know is coming."

To think: hearing this young girl admit she loved me almost derailed me entirely. The chair helped keep me somewhat steady, but my hands were shaking as I rubbed my face. "Jesus, fuck. You almost killed me waiting for that." When I lowered my hands, Demi was glaring at me.

"This isn't a joke."

"You're damn right it isn't." I placed my hand palm up on the table, offering it to her.

It took her way too long for my liking, but eventually her smaller hand slid into mine.

I tightened my grip immediately. "Say it again. Please."

She clenched her jaw, and I could see her struggle to control her emotions. "You know I love you."

I closed my eyes for a moment.

What would I have done if she didn't feel the same way as I did? Fought for it, that's what.

Which would've been a million times harder now that the bomb of my past was ticking away beneath our feet.

"But that doesn't mean everything is miraculously fixed between us."

"I know that, baby. But people in love work to fix the problems. Don't they?"

Her answer was interrupted by the arrival of the waitress with another round of our drinks.

Demi wasted no time picking up hers. "You were out there having threesomes with Monica and she's going to come regale me with all the amazing details . . . after she lets the entire world know that I seduced my older ex-boss."

"You mean that your older ex-boss seduced you." Her hand was clammy in mine, and I swore to ruin Monica all over again. Forever.

Irrevocably.

There'd be nothing left of her if she dared cause my Demi that kind of heartbreak.

She lowered her almost empty glass to the table. "That's debatable. Trust me."

With those words, she confirmed a suspicion I had from the beginning.

The outfits were purposely chosen with one goal in mind.

Not that they were necessary. I damn well almost fell out of my seat the first time she walked into my office, all grown up.

I rubbed my thumb along the back of her hand. "I've never wanted anyone the way I want you, and I think you know that deep down. Our chemistry is irrefutable."

"It's something new for you—"

"Almost *five* months in?" I asked, incredulous that she would think that.

"Eventually you'll crave your old life again. You'll see."

Speechless.

Utterly fucking speechless.

That woman clearly had no clue as to the irrationality of my thoughts when it came to her.

The insane, possibly out of place desires.

The dreams in the back of my head that I hadn't begun to let myself analyze yet.

I was keeping her. That much I couldn't deny. But the totality of what that meant . . . to feel that way so suddenly, so violently, in such a short amount of time . . .

After never even having a relationship.

Like a skyscraper brought down.

That's how hard I'd fallen.

"You know that's a fucking lie," I forced out carefully. "And even if you don't, I swear I'm going to show it to you."

I saw the moment her walls began to crumble.

It was in the trembling of her lower lip.

The sad, shuddering breath she struggled to take.

Lashes fanning rapidly in front of her pretty eyes.

"I love you." I lowered my head and stared up at her from under my brows. "I've never felt that—much less said that—to anyone."

"Does it change where we stand, though?" she asked me sadly. "You're entitled to your past. But your lover wants to destroy what we have by airing those details to me. To everyone. She clearly doesn't care if I, or anyone, knows you were out there having threesome—"

"Sometimes more than that." Her hand tensed in mine. "And . . ."

"And *what*, Dorian?"

I braced for the impact my next words were going to have. "There are some . . . videos."

"Are you fucking kidding?" Her words were an exhaled whisper, more air than actual sounds. As if she were punched in the solar plexus.

I was pretty sure that was exactly what it felt like for her. It was what it would be like for me if the tables were turned.

She slid her hand from mine and just sat there, staring at the table, lost in the reality of our situation. No. *My* situation. The one I was bringing to her door, when it was the least she deserved.

Expression contemplative, she finished her third drink.

Silent, I did the same, and wished that the beginnings of the buzz I was feeling would actually numb my anxiety.

The fourth round came. Demi never looked up and I took the opportunity to signal the waitress for the check. Didn't like that look on my girl's face. I was going to have to get her out of there soon.

If she didn't run from me, that was.

She took longer to drink the fourth round, which gave me some hope, but eventually the quiet between us became too much.

"Talk to me, Demi. Say something."

"What do you want me to say?" she asked the alcohol in her glass, refusing to stare at me.

"That you love me."

"You already know that."

"That we'll find a way through this."

"It's one thing to be told about it. Another to imagine it . . . now you're telling me there's a chance I'll have to *see* it?"

"I'll use everything at my disposal to make sure it doesn't happen," I hurried to add. "I've already begun setting a plan in motion." That meeting with Howell couldn't happen fast enough.

"I—I've never even been in a relationship before."

"Me neither."

"How do you expect me to handle this? How . . ."

The desperate agony oozing off her gutted another part of my soul. I didn't think I'd ever empathized with someone's pain to this extent, but I experienced every bit of what she was going through on a visceral level. "Can you just take it one day at a time with me? One step at a time?" *Just don't run. Not like this*, I pleaded mentally.

In the time it took her to answer, her own buzz must've started kicking in. Her cheeks turned pink and her eyes glazed over in a way

I remembered well.

Too well.

Especially when those same eyes moved over my body, and her expression melted as she got lost in a memory.

Which one? I didn't know. But I could guess what it entailed.

Every inch of my body did.

"This would be so much easier if you weren't so fucking irresistible," she complained in a petulant tone.

My hand snapped around her knee under the table; my leg bounced from my impatient arousal. There was one way to prove to this woman who I belonged to, and I was revved and ready to go. "You can hate-fuck me until it's out of your system. I'm okay with that."

"Dorian . . ." Resigned, sad eyes met mine. "This is going to destroy me. I don't need to be an expert at this relationship thing to know that what's coming will probably stay with me forever."

"I'll do everything in my power to protect you. And, if that somehow fails, I'll love you through every second of it. I'll love you until it's all you can feel and then nothing will touch you."

She leaned over and cupped my cheek—the first touch she'd initiated tonight. "How is it that you're being the naive one right now?"

I placed my hand over hers. It didn't matter to me if the people in the restaurant could tell we were having a private moment while in public. Fuck them if they assumed correctly that we were having problems.

There was only one person in that place whose opinion mattered to me and I was looking straight at her.

"Not naive, baby. Hopeful. Determined. When it gets tough, you need to remember me right now. How much I love you and how far I'm willing to go not to lose you. Because it's all that's gonna matter."

She trailed her fingers down my cheek, across my mouth, as if committing it to memory. "Okay, you crazy man. You win. I'm taking you home with me tonight."

"And every other night." I was giving away too much, possibly being too intense, but fuck it. We were almost half-a-year in. If I wanted to take it to the next level, I would, and the entire world could kiss my ass if they didn't like it.

Including her father.

But that was a conversation I would save for the morning.

"Fine." She exhaled that shaky breath again, the one that hit a soft spot in my chest, and nodded. "And every other night."

"That's my girl," I mumbled against her fingertips, smiling.

chapter nine

The next morning, I was right where I wanted to be.

On Demi's couch, with my girl curled up next to me, and our puppy playing on the carpet at our feet.

I rubbed her shoulder and stared at the rapidly growing pup that was busy tearing at his chew toy. "I gotta admit. This right here?" I drank my coffee, savoring the taste, the moment, the unexpected flood of tranquility. "This is the life."

Demitra shifted next to me, but she didn't raise her head off my shoulder. "Really?" The question was punctuated by a barely restrained giggle.

Normally, I adored that sound. But considering the context, I couldn't help but wonder what prompted it. Scowling, I stared at the top of her head. "What's so funny?"

"I'm just surprised you're content with something so . . ."

"So?"

"Oh, I don't know." She placed her hand on my stomach over my t-shirt. "Something so domesticated, I guess."

That's what it was.

The perfect word for this moment.

One I never even contemplated having before her.

It had finally happened, hadn't it? I could run from it, refuse to acknowledge, and it still didn't change the facts. I had entered that stage in my life where I was ready to leave the craziness of my past behind.

Ready to settle down.

Was it age?

I knew the answer to that. It had nothing to do with being thirty-one, and everything to do with the girl pressed to my side.

A sudden image overcame me—Demitra in her mid-twenties, or whenever she decided she was ready, belly swollen with our child.

Fuck.

"Dorian?"

I'd be almost forty when I had my first child, but that didn't matter to me at all. As long as it was with her.

As long as she was the mother.

Sonofabitch. There was no denying it anymore. I wanted her to marr—

"Dorian!" She sat up and fisted my shirt. "Are you okay?"

"Huh? Oh. Yeah . . . yeah." Staring into her light eyes, I waited for a sense of panic to hit.

Perhaps even a little bit of worry.

Well, that was there, but it had nothing to do with my desire to eventually put a ring on her finger.

I couldn't lose her.

I *really* couldn't now.

That brief glimpse of our possible future that I saw? I had to make that a reality.

There was no other acceptable outcome for me.

"You don't look okay," Demi said dubiously.

"Come with me to Chicago," I blurted out, a request I hadn't even considered making, yet.

But an inevitable one nonetheless.

It'd only last a week. Less than that if I flew back right after the main night of the design conference.

I promised myself on my last trip that it wouldn't happen again—we wouldn't be separated like that. Which meant Demi had to be there with me.

She was still blinking at me, flustered.

I grabbed her hand. "Please."

"You want me there?"

"I want you everywhere." On all counts.

I got a happy, loving smile for that, and it was hard not to drag her onto my lap. "Okay," she said.

"I know we're going to have to tell your father on a video call, or something. We can't spring it on him right before the conference."

Demitra's eyes clouded at the mention of her father. Beck ran up to her and placed his paws on her lap. Rising up on his hind legs, he offered her his chew toy.

Brow furrowed, Demi took it from him and flicked it across the living room.

Panting happily, he ran to pick it up and brought it to me next.

She watched as I took my turn playing fetch with the pup. "I really don't care how he finds out anymore. But, even so, a video call might not be right, either. I don't know."

"Demi . . . I know he fucked up—bad—but he's still your father."

"Don't do that." She rose from the couch and headed to her kitchen. Through the serving hatch, I saw her open the fridge and reach inside. "There are sides to that man that I'm just starting to see, and the last thing I need is you standing up for him because of any sense of solidarity."

Solidarity.

Not loyalty.

I knew what she was implying with that. Mulling over my best response, I watched her unscrew a bottle of water and make her way back to me. "Baby, I understand how you feel. There are sides to him I didn't anticipate, either."

Beck curled around my feet, finally out of stamina it seemed, and huffed as he got comfortable.

Demi bent down to give him a quick scratch behind the ears, then resumed her seat next to me. "I always assumed you two were so close that you'd know almost everything about my father."

"We were close, but not like that. If anyone knew what your father was up to behind everyone's back, it was my father. Not me. Your dad took me under his wing when Dad passed away. That's it." And, although my own father had a careless streak and a reputation a mile long, it was more common to be discreet back in the days.

Especially when an iron-clad pre-nup like Antonia's was in place.

Stephen had been careful. He hid his wrongdoings so well that there was never even a whisper.

Even if he didn't step out at first, I doubted this was his first transgression.

"I'm just not ready to let him into any private part of my life right now. I understand if you care about how this will effect your relationship with him if he finds out another way—"

"It's fine." Normally, it wouldn't have been. The circumstances had changed on every level, though, and I couldn't blame Demitra for how she felt.

First, Stephen all but disowned her over a hickey. An unsightly thing—although I loved covering her body in my marks—and something every father would take offense to, but his reaction had been cruel and extreme.

Then, Demitra found out he'd cheated on her mother . . . with a woman he'd known I'd slept with in the past.

If Stephen viewed me as I had viewed him, as almost a son, the logic behind that, if there was any, was disturbing and profound.

"Fine. We'll do things your way, baby. But there's a chance he'll find out if our relationship is leaked." If Monica unleashed whatever attack she was planning before I could find a way to restrain her from doing so.

She gave a mirthless laugh. "And? It's not like your reputation isn't known. Sure, I never guessed there'd be videos—"

I reached for her hand on impulse; her expression and tone sparked that anxiety again. The thought that she might pull away.

Demitra curled her fingers around mine before continuing. "But he's going to be furious regardless of how he finds out. I just don't feel like I owe him an explanation about the things I do anymore."

"You're right," I acknowledged. He technically pushed her out and forced her into a fully independent life. One she had embraced admirably, considering she was raised with all the advantages money could buy.

I suspected her mother was helping her financially, but I hadn't asked.

And it didn't matter. Demitra asserted her independence the moment Stephen threatened to take it from her.

She didn't owe him explanations anymore.

"Okay. We'll do this your way. But you're coming to that conference with me. It's non-negotiable. Right?" I raised my eyebrow in mock sternness.

Giggling one more time, she threw a couch pillow at my chest. "I already said yes, Neanderthal. Don't push it."

Laughing with her, I lunged, tackling her to the couch.

Where we ended up staying for the rest of the morning, clothes strewn all over her living room floor.

A perfect day, in my opinion.

And one of the last ones we'd have for a while. A memory that would haunt me in the weeks to come.

10

Those contracts needed to be terminated. I didn't give a fuck about the consequences anymore.

It was my last board meeting before the design conference, and she was here, sitting at the end of the table. I'd refused to look at her for more than a second when I greeted her upon entering.

There were no words to describe the experience of sitting in the same room as your blackmailer—borderline stalker—and feeling their stare boring into you.

Monica was being indiscreet.

Unhinged.

I wasn't sure if anyone else had picked up on it, but for me there was no escaping it.

I tried to keep my prior meeting with Howell and the advice he gave me in mind.

No breaking the contracts without massive financial losses.

Not unless she screws up first.

Get evidence against her by any means necessary.

To that aim, I'd had hidden cameras installed throughout the boardroom. It'd been a mission to get the tech team in here on time. Thank God for today's wireless technology. No wires needed throughout the walls.

The small, imperceptible devices were placed in strategic places throughout the boardroom.

An inappropriate, all-consuming thought arose.

Demi, on the boardroom table again, as I devoured every inch of her while the cameras recorded from different angles.

I was the only one with access to the feeds.

It was certainly doable.

And suddenly necessary.

Nevermind my current situation and the fact that recording myself having sex is what got me there in the first place.

I didn't give a damn about the women I fucked before—I just wanted Demitra, and I wanted to see us taking each other from all angles.

The image washed over me, and I mentally cursed as my dick hardened on a rush.

Most disturbing? This was happening while a psychopath had me in her sights. I couldn't give anything away. Every piece of me, every reaction, was being analyzed on a pathological level.

Every detail being cataloged to be used against me.

I was now playing the most dangerous game of my life; push Monica far enough to slip and expose herself in a way I could legally use against her . . . while waiting on pins and needles for the attack she was sure to unleash against me and my girl.

All because I decided to no longer be her fuck toy.

Jesus. How the fuck did I get to this point?

"There is no other team that's set to dominate this year like we are," Stephen announced over the video call, sounding more like the coach of a sports' team than the CEO of a design firm.

Admirable self-control, considering Antonia pulled the trigger this morning.

She had her lawyer begin filing for divorce.

She'd take everything that he hadn't secured—she'd take everything that was still hers.

A sense of unease slithered down my spine.

Antonia was Demitra's mother, and I had already seen a glimpse of that iron resolve in her young daughter.

A genetically handed down infusion of strength that was just starting to blossom.

If I wasn't careful, I'd find myself in a similar situation as Stephen without even committing the same crime.

Discarded.

Shut out.

My life flipped upside down.

Soon, Stephen's situation would hit the news.

The likelihood of it becoming known that Lucia was the other woman was extremely high.

How long before that association came back to haunt me as well?

How long before my name got dragged into his scandal? A double-edged mess that would hit Demi from both angles.

Most importantly: how long until my new nemesis used this information against me?

For the first time since the meeting, my eyes moved toward her—

Fixated on me.

As she had been the entire meeting.

Slowly, her lips curled into a knowing smile.

As if she knew my thoughts.

I didn't doubt it. Although the news hadn't gone fully public yet, the whispers had already begun spreading in our circles.

Everyone knew that the Davis' marriage was ending and why.

Because of *whom*.

I ripped my gaze from her and spent the rest of the meeting trapped in my own head.

If I wasn't with Demitra, I probably would've released my own copies of the videos I had with Monica to the public.

Not the ones that featured the other women, just the ones of me and her.

I didn't enjoy the idea of dragging my family's name through the mud, but I wish I could attack first. Ask questions later.

Instead of cowering in fear waiting for her to launch the first volley.

My phone buzzed in my pocket, bringing with it a much needed distraction. I pulled it out and read the text under the board table.

'I found a solution to the conference.' - Dem.

'Oh yeah? What's that?' - D.

I pretended to pay attention to what was being said after that.

Calum was halfway down the table, and it seemed that he was also typing away. His hazel eyes were fixated on the phone, brow furrowed, and I wondered what had gripped his attention so tightly.

My phone buzzed. As much as I hated reading that text with Monica's attention on me, ignoring Demi was impossible at this point.

I needed at least a small connection to her to remind myself why I must stay focused. Why I needed to win this silent war against that psychotic bitch.

'I'll tell my parents I'm going with Livana and staying in her room. But I'll stay with you as planned.' - Dem.

I knew she was best friends with Livana Payne, but why was Livana attending the conference?

'She agreed to do this favor for you?' - D.

'Not exactly. She's already attending with Calum and it'll help if I'm her alibi.' - Dem.

My head reared back—

Calum was already staring at me, eyebrow raised, as if awaiting my confirmation.

If I was correct in my assumption, then it was also safe to assume Ms. Livana Payne had just text him at the same time Demi was texting me.

One of my best friends had also gotten involved with Demitra's best friend?

I met him a few weeks ago to confess about Demitra. He told me at the time he was dating a young woman, around the same age as Demi, but we got so caught up discussing my own shit that we never got around to his own.

Livana Payne. That's who it was.

I had to be assuming wrong because of my own situation. Right?

I was so caught up in my shock that the danger in the room slipped my mind. There was a villain watching my every move, awaiting for any excuse to destroy my woman.

A fact I would be reminded of shortly.

The last meeting ended, Stephen signed off, and I stood at the head of the table, shaking hands with everyone before they left.

When it came to be Monica's turn, I burned with a hatred I had never felt before. The thought of having to shake hands with her and pretend everything was alright galled me in ways I could never explain.

But she didn't come up to me to shake my hand.

Hips swinging in her pin-stripped, gray skirt, Monica took her sweet time walking past me. When she smiled, her teeth were bright white against her tanned skin. Her hazel eyes all but sparkled. "See you in Chicago, Dorian."

Shots. Fucking. Fired.

Even if I wanted to refuse that fact, I couldn't.

As she walked out of the boardroom, her long black hair swinging against her lower back, I stood rooted to the spot. Adrenaline was a brutal mistress, the kind that abused every cell.

Whatever she was planning, she was going to do it at the conference.

It was as clear as the stars in the fucking sky.

My sudden urge to get to Demitra was all-consuming and brutal. As if having her near would be enough to forestall the incoming wave.

Calum came up beside me. "Do I need to know what that was about?"

I swallowed heavily. "Yeah. Yeah, you do. Both you and Luke. I think I'm going to need all the help I can get. That bitch is trying to

chapter eleven

11

The thing about brainstorming with your friends?

When you happened to be me, one of them was a lifelong bachelor with no relationship experience—as I once was—and the other was knee-deep in his own relationship problems.

Which meant that I was shit out of luck in the "help" department.

Sure, Calum and Luke were trying their best to think of a way to help me out of this, but it always came down to the same thing.

The same thing my lawyer had told me:

If I struck first, the legal fall out would be catastrophic to my company.

The end result would be the same.

She'd follow that up with her own counterattack, and I'd still be right where I would've ended up anyway; my relationship with Demitra would be put through its hardest test, without a guarantee it'd come through on the other side, and everyone we both knew would drag us through the mud regardless.

It was bad enough Demitra would be judged for dating a man eleven years her senior at her age . . . when I thought about the stain of my own reputation touching her, the self-loathing grew by leaps and bounds.

It was already unquantifiable. I was choking on it on a daily basis.

Let her go. Do the right thing. Set her free before this touches home. Before anyone finds out. If I wasn't a selfish bastard.

If I wasn't so in love with her I couldn't see straight half the time.

If my sweet girl didn't love me back.

"Almost there, Mr. Sorenson," my driver Carl said as we turned on to Demitra's block, misjudging the reason for my restlessness in the back.

"Thank you, Carl," I replied by rote, my mind split in too many directions to give him my direct attention.

I'd text Demitra to meet me at the entrance to her building before we headed to the airport to board my private jet. It was risky, someone we knew could happen to see her getting into one of my cars with her suitcases, yet I didn't care.

We already had so much going on. I wasn't going to add forced distance to the list. It was torturous enough that we had to pretend not to be together at that conference, sneaking stolen moments in my hotel suite when no one was watching.

But at least she'd be with me. Her nights mine . . . her body mine . . .

I shifted in my seat, dick already half-hard for her. As I imagined her spread out on my suite's bed, those big tits bared for my mouth, my cock, it got even harder, and I bit back a curse at this insatiable lust.

It was delicious.

It was mind-wrecking.

At times it was the most inconvenient thing of all.

We crawled through the slow traffic closer to her building—

Demitra was already there, as I had asked her to be.

But she wasn't alone.

A young boy I recognized was standing in front of her, a little too fucking close for my liking, and my face flared hot at the sight of them.

Perhaps it was innocent.

Perhaps he was just saying hi.

But I remembered how he watched her that night at the gala nearly five months ago.

The first night I made her mine.

"Carl, meet us at the corner instead of in front." I pushed open the door and took off in Demitra and Keith-fucking-Bennett's direction.

He wanted her.

Who the fuck wouldn't?

Was that the only reason for this urgency pushing me forward? Was I being toxic and irrational?

Sadly, gut instincts exist for a reason, as I was about to find out.

Demitra seemed impatient and uncomfortable.

Was I walking fast before? Funny. That was nothing compared to how fast I was walking then.

Snippets of their conversation began to drift to me the closer I got, above the murmurs of the population around us, and sounds of the city in movement.

"At least explain it to me. Can you at least do that? Tell me where we went wrong?" Keith asked Demitra, and the tone of his voice rubbed me wrong in so many different ways.

"I just don't understand," Demi responded softly—*sadly*. "It was just something that happened."

Keith laughed, but it was one of those mirthless sounds full of disbelief. "This is kind of hilarious. It was a first for you, yet it ended up meaning more to me."

What in the fuck was this boy talking about?

I knew.

Maybe I wasn't ready to admit it to myself, but I knew.

I got within feet of them before Demitra's head jerked in my direction.

That pale skin.

Her expression . . .

Yeah, I knew now who that boy was to her—*what* he was—and if I wasn't careful, news of our relationship was going to blow up in our social circle before we even got on the plane to Chicago.

Demi's lips moved silently, and I had no trouble deciphering what she was mouthing.

My name.

Schooling my facial features, I stopped next to them.

Keith didn't look too happy to find me interrupting them again.

Well, fuck him. I wasn't having the time of my life, either.

"Ms. Davis," I commented, as if greeting an acquaintance and nothing more. "How are you?"

The emotions that played out across her own features solidified my assumption. First, it was the fear of discovery, of an omission being brought to the light. It didn't last long, however.

Why should it?

I had hidden my own dirt, which was threatening to barrel into our lives with the force of a putrid tsunami.

A fact that registered in her mind. I saw the moment the change came over her. The very second her anxiety morphed into a silent dare for me to take it there.

I wouldn't, but this was definitely a discussion that we would have once I got her alone.

"Hello, Mr. Sorenson. I'm well, thank you. It's nice to see you again. Passing by?"

"Yup. Passing by. But I see you two are in the middle of something. So I'll take my leave." I nodded at Keith, hands in my pockets to hide the fact that I had fisted them. "Bennett."

"Sorenson," the fucker had the nerve to mimic.

Jaw twitching, I nodded at them both one last time, then continued on my way down the block, knowing that Demi would eventually follow.

Or, at least I hoped.

Carl had pulled up next to a fire hydrant, which meant we only had a few minutes, if lucky, before we were asked to move.

It took everything in me not to slam the door once inside the vehicle. More time passed, my leg bouncing, until eventually Carl turned in the driver's seat to look outside.

"I see her approaching the vehicle, Mr. Sorenson. I shall help her."

Fuck it if someone saw us, I would be the one to greet her out there. "I got it, Carl. Just pop the trunk."

Demi was standing at the corner, cheeks flushed, her suitcase and carry-on next to her. "Dorian."

Silent, I made quick work of getting both of them into the trunk, next to my own luggage.

"Dorian."

"Inside, Demi." Turning, I put my hand on her back and led her around to the other side of the car. I got her situated within, closed the door, and made my way back to my end.

Carl wasted no time driving away from the curb. He also raised the privacy screen, and I suspected he could sense every bit of the tension in the car.

"Dorian, you can't be mad right now."

Staring out the window, I tried to organize my irrational, chaotic thoughts. "You slept with him."

"Once. Months before you."

"He was your first." And while I was not a saint and sure as hell didn't expect any woman to be, the fact that she remained friends with the guy who took her virginity was hard to swallow.

Especially when it still meant something to Keith.

"You're really going there. You're mad." She scoffed. "I can't fucking believe this—"

I reached for her hand and intertwined our fingers. "Tell me you love me."

"Even when you're being fucking irrational, yes I do."

Okay. I couldn't deny it. That one made me smirk. And when I finally gazed in her direction, her frustrated pout was eighteen different kinds of cute. "I think he's in love with you."

"He isn't. He's being stupid. And it doesn't change that I love you."

Tugging her hand, I brought her closer, until her heat and scent were right where I needed them to be. "I can't do this anymore, this pretending you aren't mine while the entire world tries to get in our way. As soon as we're back from the conference, we're going fully official. If you want your dad to find out through the grapevine, I don't care anymore. I just know I'm not hiding you or what we have after that." I would have loved to say "consequences be damned", but the specter of that psychopath Monica loomed large.

"Fine. I agree. But once we're back, you're going to involve me in whatever plan you have to control your crazy ex." She cuddled into my side, which softened some of the harshness in her tone.

"She isn't my ex."

"And Keith isn't mine."

I tilted her chin up and pressed my lips to hers. "Good. Now that that's settled . . . tell me you packed that sexy little lingerie you sent me a picture of last night."

She giggled against my lips. "And other things."

I groaned. "I'm violating you every chance I get."

"I like it when we stay on the same page."

Laughing, I pushed back my jealousy over Keith and let myself be optimistic about our future once more.

A ship fast approaching the end of the flat world, oblivious to the fate looming up ahead.

chapter twelve

Checking into the hotel turned out to be another test of my tolerance.

An unnecessary one.

First, I had to allow Demitra to leave the airport in a separate vehicle. God forbid she stepped out of my rental in the hotel's parking lot and our acquaintances saw her.

My bitterness only grew as I arrived at the hotel and made my way to the main desk.

Demitra was already there, alongside her friend Livana and—

I recognized the brunette with them and cursed under my breath.

Calum was going to be pissed.

I couldn't blame him.

Although, it was hypocritical to feel that way. At least on my part.

But seeing Angelina here didn't make my sense of unease any better. While neither Calum nor I could truly prohibit his brother Lucas from going after her—and the fact we were dating her friends left us with no leg to stand on—I couldn't help but feel like we were heading toward the worst social scandal our circle had seen in a long,

long time.

Livana's father was related to Calum's by marriage. To be more exact: Livana's father was married to a second cousin of Calum's.

As for Angelina? Our parents were united at the hip growing up. There was no need to imagine what the world would think of all three of us once this got out.

We were horny perverts running around seducing the younger daughters of our friends.

Page Six was going to love this. And social media? I should've just started shutting my accounts down now, before the storm hit.

I entered the suite I'd rented for the conference with the bellhop following in my wake. My luggage was deposited near the door and I handed the young man a two-hundred dollar tip.

He thanked me enthusiastically and closed the black, wooden door behind me, leaving me in the vacant room.

Empty.

Like I felt most of the time lately.

The only thing—person—that helped alleviate the feeling was nowhere to be found.

I stood there, in this presidential suite, by myself, wondering what was happening out there.

Was Demitra on her way to me? I gave her the suite number. What I couldn't give her before now was the card key, but I had a spare one in my pocket waiting for her.

Like I was.

Monica would be staying here, as well. No way she wouldn't. Most of the companies participating in the conference had booked rooms here.

Would she intercept Demitra? Launch whatever emotional attack she had planned then?

She could chose to fucking do it during the conference itself, in front of everyone we knew and associated with, and there would be nothing I could do to stop her. Which made my bringing Demi here even more reckless. But what was the alternative? Leave her at home, separated from me once again, so the distance and the doubts could wedge between us even more?

Exhaling, I ran my hand through my curly, blond hair and turned away from the door. To my left, a kitchen that would never be used awaited, done up in shades of white, silver, and black. To my right, the equally-as-modern dining table. Straight ahead, there was a sitting area with a flat screen.

Beneath it, a welcoming fire was lit in the chimney, the flames dancing behind the golden grate.

Next to the seating area was the hallway leading deeper into the suite.

I should head that way, begin settling in . . . fuck that. Where the hell was Demi?

I checked my phone for any messages from her; saw none. Just as I began calling her, a soft tap sounded at the door. I rushed over and opened it.

Demi was on the other side, chewing on her lip nervously, her luggage next to her.

"There you are." Ignoring the luggage, I brought her to me and dipped my head to take her mouth. I lost myself in her lips immediately, relief and hunger palpating through my veins.

But even that wasn't enough to stop me from noticing how tense she was.

I pressed my forehead to hers, breaths panting. "What happened out there?"

Demi smoothed her hands along my shoulders and exhaled a slow breath. "I just don't like this. The anxiety of sneaking up here and hoping I was unseen . . . the fact that I have to do it every night until this is over."

God damn it. More proof that I'd fucked up by convincing her to come here. "I'm sorry." I pressed my hands to her lower back and brought her even closer. "I'm torn between two alternatives. Did I come without you? What would that have done? You already don't trust me, and Monica is going to be here—"

Demitra moved out of my arms. "Yeah." She placed her hands on her hips and looked around the suite, eyes landing blankly on the stainless steel stove in the kitchenette. "Like I said, I really hate this."

Everything was so wrong between us, even when I tried to make it right.

I stared at her, at a loss for words, hands itching to have her back within reach.

Sadness leaked from every inch on her body, but she shoved it all down with a sigh. When she faced me again, there was resolve in her gaze.

And the last thing I expected to see: compassion.

"I'm sorry, too," she mumbled, smiling sadly. "I can see how hard this is for you, and I shouldn't be bitter about it. I decided to stay with you and try to work things out, right?"

"It's more than I deserve," I admitted, reaching for her suitcase and carry-on. "Come. I'll show you the rest of the suite."

"Okay." Her small tone wasn't lost on me, but I let things lie for the moment.

Leaving my own suitcase by the entry, I led her past the small sitting area and into the hallway. To the left, there was another door that led to a bigger, all-black living room, with an obscenely large flat screen. At the very end, the last doorway opened to the bedroom.

Our steps were muffled by the plush, beige carpet as we stepped inside. I deposited her bags by the wall and turned to face her.

Demi stood by the entry, arms crossed, eyeing the California King that dominated the room. Under normal circumstances, I would've already had her flat on that bright white duvet, her clothes halfway across the room, the leather headboard banging against the wall.

I was dying to have her in my mouth now.

But I knew her, and I could tell when she was working up to something. So I kept my distance, even though it was the last thing I wanted to do.

It was unhealthy how often I needed to touch her, yet it was what it was. I'd accepted it.

She licked her lips, unaware of the flare of heat that move sent through me, and faced me head on. "You haven't told me what the exact plan is here. And . . . I think . . . that I deserve to know before we head out there and face whatever is coming. Am I wrong?"

I shook my head. "No. You're not." Sitting on the bed, I ignored the sensation that my world was shifting beneath my feet. What was coming wasn't going to be pretty, ugly scandals tended to play out that way, and Demitra deserved for me to stay as steady as I could.

One of us had to be.

And it wasn't fair to expect her to be the one.

13

chapter thirteen

The tension was oppressive between us, a gap she didn't know how to cross, and one I didn't know how to approach. Did I bring her into my arms as usual, refusing to give her space?

Or did I leave her there, so many goddamned feet away from me, stewing in whatever turmoil she was struggling with?

"I've had a lawyer advising me," I opted to say instead. "I wanted to go on the offensive, but the mutual contracts make that an impossibility. If I want to keep my company legally and financially afloat, that is." The company was worth an insane amount of money; the sheer amount of contracts between mine and Monica's firms were worth the same amount.

Perhaps more.

"Which means what? Exactly."

"I can't throw the first offensive. I can't be the one that leaks anything derogatory against Monica. There's no telling if it could lead back to me, or not. All the dirt I have relates to me, therefore I can't divulge what I know. I can only wait for the investigator to bring me new material."

"New material." Demitra laughed without humor and stepped

fully into the room. "You mean dirt that doesn't include you fucking her and other women at the same time."

"Something like that. Yes," I answered solemnly.

"And you just leave yourself open to whatever she decides to do."

"Yes. And hope that she isn't insane enough to not value her own company. She's an obsessed daddy's girl. That's another point in our favor. She won't want to do anything that enrages her father or ruins his company."

"Me."

I frowned in confusion at Demitra's comment. "What?"

"She isn't going to blow you up to the world. She won't risk her company." Running her hands down her dark jeans, Demi stepped further into the room, but it wasn't to head my way. If anything, she put more distance between us by walking toward the bathroom and turning to look inside. "I'm the target. She's going to find a way to make sure I see those videos."

It was the wrong thing to say, I'm the one that put her in this situation with my past actions, but the words left my mouth regardless. "It'll only get between us if you allow it."

The silence in the room was deafening.

I regretted the words as soon as I said them. How could I not? Yes, they were true, but they were also inadequate when it came to describing what I was asking of her.

I stood with the intention of reaching out to her and apologizing—

Demitra turned and her expression stopped me dead in my tracks.

Or lack of expression, if I was being honest.

"You're right. I'll wait to see if she finds a way to get to me while you work on getting to her first. I'll just have to avoid her and everyone else here that doesn't know about us." She looked away from me and reached for her suitcase.

I held a hand out to stop her. "There's still a chance she actually might not—"

"She will." Demi grabbed the handle of her suitcase and dragged it toward her.

My hand dropped to my side and I mumbled her name under my breath.

She paused and finally met my gaze once more. "Look, Dorian. It's just a lot to deal with. Especially while my own family is imploding and my relationship with my father is in the trash. But you need to focus on doing what you need to and I'll focus on what I need to do. Okay?"

"I can't stand this. The distance feels like it's getting worse, not better. I don't know what else to do to convince you that I'm fucking in love with you and I can't lose you—"

"I'm here, aren't I?" she whispered. "Just . . . can I take a shower? Settle in?"

"I'm going in there with you," I insisted.

She almost giggled at that, which was partially my intention. Yet another part of me was dead serious. I needed that closeness with her again, the reassurance that she was still mine.

"Later. I promise."

"Alright. I'll wait for you."

Another sad smile and she was gone, dragging her unpacked suitcase into the bathroom with her.

The door closed with a finality that I couldn't stand.

I needed to accept it, nonetheless. She was right about so many things, including how stressful this was while her family was already going through shit, and if Monica did make this public, it was about to get worse.

Which meant I had to get my head out of my ass and back in the game. I had a psychopath to take down and, in that vein, an investigator to touch base with.

Monica's impulses would be her downfall. One way or another, I'd catch her and back her into a corner until she learned to fucking behave herself.

I didn't care how far I had to go at this point.

As long as it didn't cost me Demi.

LATER TURNED OUT TO BE MUCH, *MUCH* LATER.

Too late for my fucking liking.

Demitra took a long time in the shower, something I knew was by design.

The perfect excuse to maintain distance from me.

I couldn't blame her.

The sick part? I kind of wanted to.

I wanted her to do what I'd do in her shoes—fight harder. Want me more. Put her foot down and refuse to let my crazy ex-lover come between us.

Selfish and ignorant. I knew that. Not only was I not the one in her shoes, I couldn't guarantee how I'd handle it.

Then again, when I remembered who Keith was to her, what he still wanted from her . . .

Damn it, where was she?

Not like we could be close in this setting.

Conversation continued to flow around me—right over my head, if I was honest—and I hated this even more with every minute that passed.

Across the hotel's lounge, her father was holding court among some of the other heavy hitters attending this conference. He was all smiles and perfect charm.

I loved that man my entire life. Even more so when my Dad died a decade ago. I never thought badly of him, never figured him to be fake. Deceitful.

Yet, that's what I saw now. As if the mask had fallen off.

Was it my connection with his daughter?

Undoubtedly. Not only did he treat her like shit for exercising her freedom and sexuality, but he did much worse to Demi's mom.

Maybe I was a hypocrite for judging his infidelity, but I'd never forgive him for what he was putting Demitra through.

At the same time you're putting her through shit, too.

Yes. Couldn't forget that important tidbit. Thank you, Conscience.

Angsty, I darted another glance through the area, ignoring the conversation taking place around me. Where was she?

No, seriously. Where the fuck was she?

Starving for a glimpse of her. Dying for a taste. Desperate not to lose this in my life.

She'd ruined me.

And I couldn't even bring myself to care.

I slid my hand into my pocket and palmed my phone. If she didn't appear soon, I was going to sneak away and track her down—

There.

Flanked by Livana and Angelina, she walked into the lounge area, and I swore my fucking jaw hit the floor at the sight of her.

Sadly, I knew it wasn't just mine. I could almost sense every asshole that stopped in his tracks to look her way.

That silver, glittery dress was just shy of being indecent, and it was more of a clubbing outfit than something one would wear to this gathering. It took me a few seconds to realize the other girls were dressed similarly.

Took me even longer to notice that they weren't walking in the direction of this lounge.

No. They were walking toward the hotel's entrance.

Just as instinct engaged and I was about to start following her,

Calum appeared at my side.

He wasn't the only one. Lucas was with him and he seemed ready to kill someone.

Or something.

"Easy," Calum mumbled, nodding at a man who waved at him. "They're heading out together and it was better than them sticking around here and causing suspicion."

Of course he'd think that. He wasn't the one on the verge of losing his relationship. Livana wasn't slipping through his fingers faster than he could grasp her.

At least, it didn't seem that way.

"You're both fucking stupid. If I were you, I wouldn't let either of them out of my sight. Especially dressed like that."

Before Calum and I could fully digest that that comment came from his brother of all people, Luke was off, storming in the direction of the bar.

Jenson Fleming, one of the architects that worked for Stephen's firm, whistled under his breath and turned away with a shake of his head. "I'm telling you, man," he said to another guy next to him. "Gotta remind myself how young those girls are. Their fathers would killllll me. Would be almost worth it, though." And the fucking asshole had the nerve to laugh.

Glaring at an annoyed Calum, I followed in Luke's wake, needing a drink ASAP.

Demitra leaving to go to some club, or wherever they were heading, without letting me know first was something that was going to be addressed.

As soon as I got my hands on her, I was going to remind her of a few things she seemed desperate to forget.

Namely? Who she fucking belonged to.

14

I wouldn't be *that* guy—the possessive, psychotic boyfriend that didn't allow his girl to have her own life. I had no interest in stepping into that role, nor did I want that for Demi.

My actual identity at the moment was bad enough, thank you very much.

I stood in the suite's kitchen, eyes glued to my phone. The text thread between her and I had been open for ten minutes, and I couldn't stop myself from going over the last few lines of our conversation.

'I can't believe you're mad at me for going out. Again.' - Dem.

She was referring to the night she came home from partying with her friends, only to find me in her apartment pissed off. Horny.

Worried.

She'd disappeared from me that night, too, refusing to answer my texts, and it'd sent my mind spiraling.

Maybe she was right. Maybe this wasn't so different from then.

'I'm not angry. But you have a habit of running from me when things get hard and not communicating about your plans.' - D.

'Oh really? That's why I'm on my way back to the hotel now.' - Dem.

It was only 9:22pm, so seeing that message was a huge relief. I couldn't deny it. Last time, a few weeks ago now, she wasn't home until nearly 2:00am, and as I said, I wasn't in the right state of mind when she did get there.

Not that I was doing so much better tonight.

Room service delivered a bottle at my request, and I let the burning liquid slide down my throat as I waited for another message to come through.

Or for the woman herself to walk through that door.

Although, another thing I had to admit was how convenient her absence turned out to be. It gave me time to set up the device in the room and make sure it was well hidden.

God, I prayed it didn't come to that, prayed with every fiber of my sick being, but if it did, that was my final card left to play.

My stomach turned at the thought of what it would mean if it did come to that, but as my lawyer warned me, I had to be prepared from all angles. Monica would pay if she hurt Demitra in any way. Especially if she did what we both suspected she was planning to do.

As a matter of fact, I'd hidden devices all through the suite, at various angles, in case it didn't happen in the bedroom.

If I could've gotten into Demitra's phone and computer, that would've been the best option. Then I could've found a way to install some kind of software, something that would stop Monica from delivering that file to my girl.

Yet, I didn't have the passcodes, and it wasn't right for me to ask.

So the devices were my only option, and that was only if I failed to stop Monica through some other means.

My mind was fixated on the wrongness of this entire situation, distracted by the details of this twisted game, when I heard the lock disengage behind me.

My head jerked to the side.

And there she was, a fucking vision in that silver dress, the recessed lights in the hall setting off all that sparkle.

She had her contacts in, no glasses, and her lined eyes instantly found my own.

That look . . .

An inferno seemed to blast from her to me, ramming into every nerve ending, and in an instant every bit of icy distance between us seemed to vanish.

Now it was just fire. Pure heat.

And something that felt suspiciously like hate.

Expression intent, Demi pushed the door the rest of the way open and eyed me like I was nothing more than an object to be used.

The quintessential piece of meat to be devoured.

There was no affection or love in her gaze, only raw hunger, and one would think it'd bother me.

Nope. My cock was already full and throbbing, tip wetting my boxers, and I could only grip the counter and mumble her name as my brain spun.

"God damn you." Demi stepped inside and slammed the door shut, making me glad that we were the only ones on this side of the hallway. "Even when I don't want to fucking want you . . . Even in a club with all those other guys hitting on me . . ."

I slammed the glass in my hand on the counter, nearly breaking it. "What the fuck did you just say?" I was already facing her, ready to . . . What? Make her pay for being so fucking beautiful that every man that saw her wanted her?

Yes.

I was a screwed up asshole from every angle for even thinking it, but that was exactly what was on my mind.

She ignored my deadly question, eyes on my dick, and flung her clutch across the room. "Get fucking naked. Now."

Like setting off a nuke.

Instead of obeying her command, I stormed toward her like an animal intent on taking her down.

She met me halfway, brimming with the same fury, and our mouths collided on a painful glide.

Her tongue dipped inside, tasting me, owning me, and I let her, my hands dropping to the hem of her dress.

I'd ripped God knew how many articles of clothing off her body.

I attempted to do the same now.

But the damned material wouldn't give way, and she was sucking on my lower lip like it was the tip of my aching dick.

I was achingly aware of the soft skin of her thighs—of the addicting cunt that lay between.

With a growl, I swept her off the floor and made a beeline for the dining table by the door.

Demi groaned my name, clearly frustrated that I was taking the control she wanted to wield, but after the events of tonight, I just couldn't bring myself to care.

I had her on the dark, wood surface in seconds. As she glared up at me with those baby blue eyes narrowed, I reached under her dress and ripped the only thing I could—a small strip of white cloth that was too small to be considered a thong.

"Who did you wear this for?" I demanded in a low, tense voice.

She pressed her lips together in defiance.

On the same breath, she bent her knees, resting her feet on the table, and let her thighs fall open languidly.

Alright, then. If that was how she wanted to play, I'd play.

I spun her around on the table, her head facing me and her pussy in the other direction. Ignoring the flash of confusion on her face, I dragged her until her head was all but hanging off the edge.

Then, I slid two fingers into her dripping cunt while working at my belt with my free hand.

Demi gasped, hips jerking, already seeking an orgasm I had no intention of giving her any time soon.

"Get my dick out, Demi." I released my belt to circle one hand around her throat, caressing the column languidly. "I'm fucking this mouth and throat until you remember who you belong to."

She tightened around my fingers, getting even wetter.

"Now, Demi. You're swallowing every bit of it."

Her shaking hands came up to finish what I started with the belt.

I almost came in my slacks with each brush of her hands against my throbbing erection.

I was so far gone that I forgot all about the dangers. I forgot to be on guard, to keep my eye on the ball.

Another thing that would come back to haunt me later.

But for now, I planned to face-fuck Demitra into oblivion, and nothing was going to stop me.

chapter fifteen

Demitra pushed my jeans down past my hips. Her warm hands circled my hard length, and I hissed out a breath as she blew softly over it. Leaning over her, elbows on the table, I rasped, "In your mouth, baby. I want to be in you before I lick this pretty pussy."

With a soft moan, she let her lush lips part along the tip of my dick, and my eyes almost rolled back at the sensation.

Didn't matter how many times I fucked her, it was fucking perfect each time.

Groaning deep in my throat, I flexed my hips in shallow thrusts, working my way further into her. Using my fingers, I parted her smooth lips, exposing her swollen clit.

Adorable. The perfect shade. Pulsing eagerly for me.

I started out with a soft kiss that made her hips jerk and her mouth tighten around me. "Ah, ah, baby," I admonished, rubbing my lips against her clit. "Loosen up. I'm not fully in yet."

She whimpered and her hips rotated, begging me to eat her, but she did as I asked and tried to relax her mouth.

As a reward, I tongued her little clit with the tip of my tongue, loving how it responded to the lightest touch.

Her reaction was as hungry and instant as always, proof that a single touch from me could make her go mindless.

Which was more than alright. Because as I felt my tip breach the back of her throat, I lost every ounce of common sense I had left.

I thrust against her beautiful face and the sound of her gagging around me spurred me on. Making out with her pussy, I licked her in that soft way I knew drove her crazy. The taste of her drugged me each time, an addiction I would never overcome.

Her pussy was pulsing for me, drenched, just like her mouth as her saliva gushed around me with each thrust.

Crying out against her pussy, I sucked on her slick flesh. My hips worked against her mouth, merciless, and I could already feel the explosion building at the base of my spine.

Demi reached around me, nails sinking into my ass, urging me on, and I was helpless to not give it to her. Her own hips rocked frantically against my face, her pussy primed to go over the edge with me.

I pulled her clit between my lips and tongued it. At the same time, I scissored my fingers inside her, stretching her quivering walls.

Demitra convulsed with a hoarse cry I felt all over my dick as she came.

I let her ride every wave until the very end, loving the wet sounds her pussy made as I thrust my fingers in and out of her.

As soon as the last shiver broke through her, I raised up and braced against the table with one of my hands. The other wrapped around her throat—

Then I let her have every inch of me. No thought. No mercy. Just the need to pump my cum down her throat.

She gagged around me, but did her best to open her throat, and I felt it flex with each thrust. Ragged sounds left me, rough praises, but I couldn't decipher a word I said to her. Mindless, I fucked her mouth, hard enough to rock her body on the table.

A convulsive shudder ripped through me. Sweat trickled down my back. My cock jerked, once, twice, and the first spurt of cum that left me nearly made me scream for her.

I growled her name on repeat as I came into her mouth, head falling back in euphoria.

Sadly for her, it wasn't enough.

I was nowhere near done.

The last spurt had barely left me and I was already jerking my erection free from her lips. Demitra swallowed what must've been a heavy load and gasped in surprise.

I manhandled her across the table, lifting and flipping her, and once she was on her knees before me, I yanked her hips backward to meet my own.

Demi's hands fumbled across the table's surface as she struggled to steady herself. "Dorian?"

My answer to her questioning tone was to palm her ass cheeks open and force her onto my cock.

I didn't even know what I was doing anymore, just knew I needed more. Coming in her mouth was the sexiest thing ever, but I never felt fulfilled unless I gave it to her like this, as well.

Fisting her long curtain of dark brown hair, I pulled until her back arched and set a brutal rhythm that left the table pounding into the floor.

The smell of hard sex roared through the air around us. Demitra lost her own ability to speak, breathless cries leaving her lips. Insane with the need to keep her, to anchor her to me, I brought my other hand down hard across her ass. "You'll never belong to any of the other men that want you. Only me." Another slap, her pale skin blooming with color at the impact.

"Oh, God, Dorian. You know I love you."

I spanked her a third time. "Again."

She moaned it for me repeatedly, like a chant. Her hips rotated as I fucked her.

It was the sight of that that did me in. Her ass bounced with each thrust, red with my marks . . . "Fuck, Demi. You make me come so fucking hard."

Shaking like a leaf, she fell apart around me, her second orgasm pulling another painful one from me.

My nerves could barely handle the feeling, yet the pleasure was too addicting to shy away from. We strained against each other, coming for what felt like eons, our moans and groans bouncing off the suite's walls.

I fell against her, mind blank, heart shattered, and struggled to catch my breath. It wasn't the first time she somehow blasted through my recovery time and dragged two orgasms out of me back to back, but holy shit, I couldn't feel my legs. With my forehead against her back, I tightened the arm around her waist and kept her as close to me as I could.

Demi sagged over the table, still twitching. Her ass was bright red from the spanking I gave her, back slick with sweat, and her cheeks framed my dick.

Which was still partly inside her.

The mess we'd made together continued to leak out of her and onto the table.

As always, I couldn't bring myself to be disgusted. What we did to each other was too primal for me to regret.

The wild urge to fuck her *yet again* teased my senses, and I was surprised that it almost took over.

Alas, I was only human, and I'd need more time before we could go for round three.

I shifted and placed a small kiss against her shoulder blade. "No more fighting." My voice sounded like shit, as if I'd been shouting for hours. "Enough. I know everything is crap, but not this. This thing between us is the one thing that's worth focusing on. Holding onto."

My girl melted for me even more. "Oh, Dorian."

I hated that sad tone. The reason it was there.

Sliding out of her, I nearly smiled as another gush left her and she yelped at the sensation. "I promise I'll clean it up so housekeeping doesn't have to."

"But—"

I lifted her off the table and carried her down the hall.

Exhausted, she was nearly limp in my arms, and when her head rolled heavily onto my shoulder, I couldn't help but squeeze her tighter. "Where are you taking me, you brute?" Her voice was just as raspy as mine was.

Maybe our screams really were that loud.

A flush of heavy satisfaction coursed through me. This was the first time since we got here that things felt normal between us. That I felt fully connected to her.

"Shower, baby. It's been a while since we shared one of those." A few days, actually. But I was on a mission to keep reminding her what we loved about each other, and that included all the little things we shared together.

She was wobbly on her feet when I placed her down next to the recessed tub. I worked quickly to get it running, and as the tub began to fill, I focused on getting her dress the rest of the way off.

She was naked underneath, except for two nipple pasties. Those didn't last long, either. Once they were somewhere across the bathroom, I cupped her face and brought her close. "Tell me you love me again," I said against her lips.

Her baby blues were heavy with drowsiness, but they locked on my stare. "I didn't say it enough while you were fucking me?"

"It's never enough. And I want to hear it when we aren't, as well." I kissed her softly.

Her hands came up to wrap around my wrists, and her chest

shuddered with a breath. "What I feel for you might be too complicated to be just love. It's too big. It's everywhere. And . . . Sometimes it hurts too much."

"Good. We feel the same way about each other. Now say it."

She burst into sweet laughter against my mouth. "You obtuse man. I just did."

Smiling again, I kissed her and led her to the bathtub. "Nope. You know what I want," I sang playfully, helping her inside.

It wasn't until I got naked and joined her, leaning against the tub to bring her against my chest, that she finally whispered it to me.

I wrapped my arms around her, whispering it back against her temple. My eyes slid closed. My chest expanded with my first content breath in days.

No one was going to take this away from me—away from *us*. No one.

I wouldn't let them.

chapter sixteen

16

Y ou could tell yourself something over and over, that didn't mean it would end up being true. Intentions could sometimes turn out to be eerily prophetic—or they could be a harbinger of utter failure.

How many people set out with determination only to end up crashing and burning in the end?

I could tell myself I'd find a way to keep my girlfriend all I wanted, that still remained to be seen.

Expecting her to deal with one psychotic ex-lover? That was one thing.

Expecting her to deal with multiple? That's where shit would get way too complicated.

And it was coming for us. I just didn't know it until it was too late.

Demitra never brought up the supermarket incident weeks ago, where one of them cornered me in an aisle to question me about the rumors going around about me. The same ones that were indeed true.

Was I taken? Beyond a doubt.

How did the wagging tongues find out? Easy. I stopped fucking all the women I used to fuck on a constant basis.

God, what a toxic world we lived in.

"Look at him," Luke said next to me, nodding toward Demitra's laughing, at-ease father across the room. "Acting like his wife isn't about to take everything from him in the divorce."

Stephen and his behavior were the last thing I wanted to focus on; I was still busy trying to catch sight of his daughter.

Who couldn't attend this gala with me, and had to arrive separately from me.

Fucking idiot. I should've just outed us here. Convinced her to walk in on my arm. "That's exactly why he's acting like everything is okay." I spotted a brunette at one of the many entrances, but knew almost instantly it wasn't her. "He's trying to solidify his connections for the rebuilding phase."

Lucas scoffed, that sardonic smirk he was known for etched on his face—to anyone on the outside, he looked like his usual, contemptuous self. The man that only graced these events because he had to, not because he gave a damn about anyone present.

Sadly for him, I knew him. I knew him way too well. And the few times I did glance over at him, it wasn't lost on me how his hazel gaze bounced over the people in attendance.

Another hunter searching desperately for his prey.

Prey that I'd given up warning him away from.

I was exhausted with my own problems.

If he couldn't keep his hands off Angelina, there was nothing I could do. Let Calum fight that battle. I had to focus on my own.

"There'll be no rebuilding phase for him. At least no time soon. It's not the cheating, you know? Fucking common. But that pre-nup . . . Hell, even I'd be faithful if I didn't have shit to my name and my fiancé made me sign a savage, iron-clad pre-nup like that. I'm telling you, by the time we get back, this is going to be all over the gossip columns. Demitra's mother is ruthless when needed. That's a stubborn, dead-man walking right there, unless he has a 'Come to Jesus' moment and signs that divorce."

Did not need the reminder of Antonia's ruthlessness, when I was convinced her daughter could be capable of the same.

Definitely didn't need to entertain the idea of Stephen's scandal becoming news . . . Followed by Demi and I going public with our relationship.

The scrutiny Demi would be under was unfair. The pressure. The scathing opinions of people that shouldn't matter one fucking bit, but that held prominent positions in our social circles simply because of who they were.

Or who they were married to.

How many of those wives had I fucked on the side, before they got married to their husbands?

How many of them did I do with Monica during our wild bullshit?

A cold shudder almost ripped down my spine as I tried to count— as I imagined Demitra having to swallow that poisonous knowledge.

"Oh, and this might make you feel better. My brother's ex has decided she made a horrendous mistake and that she lost the best thing that ever happened to her. So you aren't the only one dealing with a clingy ex."

I almost choked on my saliva. "What the fuck?"

"That's what I said." Luke shrugged. "And he told Livana on their way here. As if that's going to somehow work out alright."

"Trust me on this, I'm learning that full disclosure is sometimes the only way to go in relationships. Hiding shit only leads to worse trouble."

"You're both walking poster boys for why it's better to not be in one."

I nailed him with a look. "Newsflash: keep chasing Angelina, and you're going to end up in one, too."

The expression on his face flashed from shock, to something that almost resembled fury. He smoothed it over as fast as he could, but still leaned into me to whisper aggressively, "Since when does sex automatically equal commitment? You're both freaking lost."

I laughed at that. Couldn't help it. It was my first genuine bit of amusement in days. "Second newsflash: *you're* lost. Gone for the girl. Obsessed. Out of control. She has the reins, holds every bit of control in this situation. The fact she's dragging you along and making you wait for it has left you the weakest you've ever been. *If* she were to ever give in and actually let you have a taste of her, you'll end up rearranging your life to keep her faster than Calum and I did."

He blinked, stunned. "Was that really necessary?"

I laughed again at his flabbergasted expression. "Yes. I'm preparing you. Start accepting reality so you can stop fucking it up. If you're really hellbent on going there, you don't need the scandal that comes with it to be another negative added to the list."

"Speaking from experience, are you?"

"Hell, yes."

Those words had just left my mouth when my girl finally walked into the massive ballroom. One look at her and I lost my ability to speak.

Lucas, damn him, did not, and I heard him barely smother his mumble under his breath. "*Poor motherfucker.*"

Demitra's thick, dark brown hair fell over her shoulders, framing her gorgeous face. The white, floor-length dress fit every curve perfectly, and it would've been considered decent if her body wasn't so fucking sexy. Thick shoulder straps led up to a glittering, thick choker around her throat. The effect did nothing but call attention to her chest, and I knew for a fact my cock wasn't the only one that took notice.

Even from this distance, that white dress and diamond choker brought out the shade of her light blue eyes, and the dark pink lipstick on her pouty lips brought memories to mind.

Memories of my dick pushing in and out of her mouth.

I wanted her.

I wanted her like I'd never had her before.

All thoughts except one left my head. I forgot about everything, including the fact that no one knew about us and we were another scandal waiting to be unleashed.

Like a mindless zombie, I began walking to her, ignoring Lucas when he called out my name.

I didn't get far.

A strike of red cut across my vision. I barely stopped myself from barreling into whoever it was.

"Dorian!"

That red-encased body came up against me, and a pair of arms wrapped around my neck.

I didn't even realize I was being hugged until my shocked stare met Demi's across the room.

Yet I didn't linger.

Fuck, no.

I extricated myself from that hug as fast as I could, and stepped back to see who had just invaded my personal space.

Similar in coloring to Monica, the woman in front of me was one I knew well.

Unfortunately.

Viola smiled up at me happily, as if I hadn't just jerked away from her. "I was planning on passing by to say hi now that I'm back in the states, but then I heard you were here."

I knew from who she heard that, too.

It was the first hint I got that tonight was the night—Monica had planned to fuck everything up for me during the design festival's gala.

Those tapes that Monica and I made together? Many of them

featured this woman.

This tanned, dark-haired, dark-eyed Italian that resembled Monica in many ways.

Including her vicious nature when denied.

Maybe Monica hadn't told her about Demi, yet, but I had no doubt she sent Viola to intercept me, knowing Demitra would be watching.

Red, hot anger coursed through my veins, yet I could do nothing but stand there, and analyze what this meant.

Where this was heading.

And what the fuck I was going to do to stop it.

17

I didn't remember what else was said between Viola and I.

An egregious loss of control. When one was engaged in a war—any type of war—one had to keep their wits about them. Information was tantamount to success; caution was imperative if you planned to ward off future attacks.

Viola was just as crazy as Monica. I would've loved to believe she wouldn't join in Monica's insane game, but I knew better.

If Monica hadn't conscripted Viola to her sadistic cause yet, it was a matter of time. Maybe months ago this wouldn't have been a thought in my mind, but it definitely was one now.

Who would've thought that Monica, my "I can take it or leave it because I have options" fuck buddy would go mad at the thought of another woman owning me? Of her losing access to my body because of it?

Yet, it'd happened.

Now, I didn't leave anything to chance.

Except Viola and what my desperate exit from our conversation would look like to her, or anyone else watching.

But I'd lost sight of Demitra. She was nowhere to be found.

Had I been thinking clearly, I would've headed straight for our suite. Could've found her there before it was too late.

Instead, I made circles around the crowd in the massive, thousand-square foot ballroom. At one point, I saw Calum and Livana out of the corner of my eye, but I barely paid them attention.

When I shot past Luke and Angelina huddled in a corner, stances tense, same thing.

Finally, I exited into a less crowded hallway and yanked out my phone. No calls from Demi. No texts.

As if I needed a hint to tell me she was angry at me again.

She probably thought Viola was Monica from behind. Even if she didn't, I'm sure she figured out I'd fucked Viola in the past as well.

These women had no concept of personal space or respect. Having sex with me afforded them some kind of perverse ownership over me. Of course the women I slept with came up to me in public in the past. Of course they would hug me at times, touch me a little too familiarly . . .

I was single as fuck back then. It never mattered.

Needless to say, it mattered now.

I dialed her number. No surprise, she didn't answer.

At least it didn't go straight to voicemail.

I didn't bother leaving a voice message. She'd ignore it until the end of time if she wanted to. She'd probably ignore a text, as well, but I decided to at least try that.

'Can we please just talk about this? You know I'm sorry and I would've stopped it if I could.' - D.

Pausing to calm my thoughts, I tried to imagine where Demitra would storm off to in her anger.

Our room?

It seemed unlikely. She knew I could find her there. But what other option did I have?

Return to the gathering and prepare for the presentation of our design while my head was all fucked up?

The power she had over me was more than inconvenient; at times, this feeling was downright frightening. Yet fighting it never got me anywhere, and I was smart enough to not try now.

I was already one step from ruining my reputation in the architecture world. It was still a better option than losing Demitra.

With one last look at my phone, I headed to the elevators. As I passed by the entry to the ballroom, multiple people in the crowd turned to watch me pass.

Thankfully, no one called my name.

Not until I reached the elevators, at least.

The elevator bay was oddly empty as I approached. I pressed the button to go up, praying that one of them would arrive—

"Dorian."

That deep voice froze me in place as my mind scrambled to place its identity. By the time I turned around, I knew it was him.

And the moment I took in his expression, I knew exactly what had happened.

Who was responsible.

How much worse things were about to get.

An elevator still hadn't arrived, which is the only reason I didn't leave him behind to deal with him later. "Stephen."

His jaw was clenched hard enough to warp his entire face. I'd never seen him look so monstrous before.

So angry.

In two strides, he was in front of me. When he wrapped his hand around my arm tight enough to almost hurt, I had to remind myself not to react. Anyone else would've gotten punched in the face.

"What I just heard better not be true, Dorian."

Menace.

I should've expected no less, yet I'd been holding back my own rage at his treatment of Demitra lately. There was a split second urge to play dumb, yet the icy fury in his eyes could only be about one thing. "Let me guess who you heard it from," I replied calmly.

Perhaps too calmly.

His fingers locked like vices around my arm, a silent threat if there ever was one. "Tell me you didn't have the fucking nerve to sleep with my teenaged daughter. Tell me you wouldn't betray me like that."

Betray *him*? I guessed I could see how he'd see this as a slight against him, but it had nothing to do with him and everything to do with her. I was *gone* for his daughter. Lost.

I yanked my arm out of his hold. "She's twenty," I had the nerve to say, although Demitra was definitely nineteen when it all started. "And considering how you've been treating her the last few months, I'd reconsider the tone."

I expected his fist to come at my face.

I expected blind rage.

His stunned silence is what I got instead.

Guilt flared, followed by a lifetime of memories. His friendship. His guidance. His support as I took over my father's company at such a young age.

My chest tightened at the realization of what I was losing here—what I always knew I'd lose—but there was one thing I dreaded losing more.

His daughter.

An elevator finally opened behind me and I was reminded of my quest for her.

Throat tight, I faced her father one more time. "I'm sorry, Stephen, I am. But it was unstoppable. I fucking love her more than anything in my life, and you're welcome to try to kill me for it later." Right now, I had to find her first.

I rushed into the elevator, leaving him standing there, and

pressed the button for my floor.

The doors had just started to slide closed when he slammed his hand between them, causing them to slide back open, and stormed into the elevator with me.

There was the expected fury.

His injured need for vengeance.

The doors closed and the elevator smoothly slid into motion, trapping me inside with him.

"Stephen," I warned as calmly as I could. "Don't do this. Nothing you do is going to change the fact that she's mine. I love her."

"You fucking bastard!" With a speed belying his age, he flew at me.

His hands wrapped around my lapels.

My back slammed into the wall, followed by my head.

"How could you fucking do this to me? How could you screw around with my daughter like she's one of your whores?"

18

Deep breaths.

That was the only thing that kept my temper in check as I reached up to remove Stephen's hands off me yet again.

"Don't ever insinuate Demi is a whore again, Stephen. We both know she's far from that, and I already told you: I'm in love with her."

The play of emotions across his face should've meant something to me.

Then again, it wasn't sadness I saw there. The betrayal was tinged by a dark rage, and perhaps it was covering the pain he should've been feeling underneath, but I doubted it.

"It's one thing to lie to the women you seduce, Dorian, but how dare you try that line with me? *I know you.*"

Ooof. Some comments were best left untouched.

As much as I tried not to go there, though, a lifetime of history with this man replayed in the back of my mind.

My pseudo-father had just claimed I was incapable of love.

Only good for fucking. Using women.

Yeah, sure, my own actions led to that reputation, but considering his own dirt had come back to haunt him—dirt I would've never thought him capable of—it was a waste of time to argue about his hypocrisy.

"I love her. I'd tell you to accept it, but considering you already tried cutting her off from family money that isn't truly yours, it doesn't matter either way. We're together. That's it." I stepped around him as the elevator door opened on my floor.

It was too much to hope that he wouldn't follow me out, but I would've been lying if I said I wasn't hoping for it.

His steps were silent on the muffled carpet; I felt his presence through the sheer force of his anger close to my back.

"Listen to me, you ingrate. Everything you have is because of me."

Excuse me?

I faced him, incredulous, and on the verge of giving into my own anger. "It was my father's company. He built it from the ground up."

"And the board would've never accepted you so easily without my help. How do you repay me? With hypocrisy. A man with your reputation judging me for what I do on my free time—"

"I'm not *married*." Not yet, at least. My plans for my future were crystal-fucking-clear in my mind. "And you're picking up my scraps without hesitation."

Stephen scoffed. "Please, Dorian. All those sluts pass themselves around. It's what they're good for. I can almost guarantee that you've picked up some of my 'scraps', as you call them, throughout the years without even realizing it. What the hell does it matter?"

I stared into those familiar, light blue eyes, the exact shade of Demitra's, and saw nothing but a stranger. Maybe I was a hypocrite for how I viewed him, but even I hadn't callously crossed the lines he didn't seem to care about. "You know what? Fuck all of that. But let's discuss your double standards, shall we? You tried fucking cutting Demitra off and leaving her without any financial support simply because she was seeing someone."

He stepped toward me, his fury returning full force. "You're the bastard that left that disgusting mark on my daughter's body! Mauling her like a fucking animal!"

"I am going to repeat this one last time: Demi is an adult. What she does with her body isn't your business. Just like she's supposed to mind her business when it comes to your betrayal of her mother."

"You are not going to ruin my daughter's future prospects for a husband—"

"You're out of your mind if you think you're going to choose that for her. You're even more insane if you think you're going to stand between me and that title."

Something flickered across his expression.

Perhaps a part of me was still clinging to our history. To what he once meant to me. Maybe that was why it took a few seconds too long for me to admit what I was seeing in his gaze.

Greed.

Pure, unmitigated greed.

"Are you saying you're planning on marrying my daughter? If so, that might change things. I'm sure an agreement can be worked out."

There were no amount of deep breaths that could control me that time.

He was talking about a transaction.

Business.

What he needed most: *Money*.

No, he wouldn't sell me his daughter. The law in this country wouldn't allow it. But he could try to make sure that she wouldn't enter a marriage under the same circumstances he did—locked into an unbreakable pre-nup.

Marry his daughter into my fortune, and then what?

Make up with her?

Make up with me?

Somehow use us to gain access to the funds he'd need to rebuild after Antonia was done demolishing him?

Of course I wouldn't ask Demi to sign one when the time came, as foolish as some people would consider me for that. That didn't make Stephen's machinations any less revolting.

"You know what? I'm done with this conversation."

"The hell you are!" He shouted at my back.

This was all being recorded by the hotel's security feeds. In case this situation wasn't fucked to begin with.

Stephen clearly was too far gone to care.

So was I.

He wasn't going to keep me from finding his daughter. Fuck him.

"You see? All you do is use women, which I don't give a damn about, but I had a perfect match set up for her. Now I know why she backed off. Dorian, you will not keep getting between her and Bennett's kid. He'll marry her at the drop of a hat."

I couldn't say I was ever into prayer before, yet I guessed there was a first time for everything because I was suddenly praying now.

Please stop me from losing my shit with this man. Please. I'd never envisioned a situation where I'd be itching to lay hands on him of all people.

Again, first time for everything.

I rushed down the hall as fast as I could without actually running. Didn't know how much time I lost having that pointless argument with him, I just hoped she was in our room when I got there.

Once I was in front of the dark wood door, I wasted no time swiping the card key and heading inside.

The lights were off, except for a faint glow coming from the direction of the bedroom.

Heart thudding, I went down the hall and entered the room.

Almost immediately, I knew she was gone.

The large closet door was open and both her suitcase and her carry on were missing from within. The only thing remaining was her laptop on the bed.

It was open.

A video was playing across the screen, sound muted.

I knew what it was before I even walked closer.

Knew what it meant.

Monica had done it.

She'd won.

She'd forced Demitra to watch something she should've never had to see, and now Demi was gone.

Nearly numb, I got close enough to see just how sickening the blow was.

It was a video of Monica and me . . .

And Viola.

The same woman Demitra had just seen throwing herself at me downstairs.

We were at my place. On my bed.

The bed I shared so often with Demitra.

I remembered this video. Of course I did. The reason we recorded the videos was for the same reason anyone would.

Homemade porn to look back on when the mood struck.

Did it matter that I hadn't accessed my porn collection in half a year? That I didn't need to now that Demi was in my life? All I ever watched now were the videos of me and her that I'd managed to capture.

Even worse, the only reason you could tell it was me? You either had to be someone that knew me intimately enough to recognize my naked body . . .

Or you could tell by my curly blond hair.

My face couldn't be seen.

It was lost between Monica's thighs as she rode my face and made out with Viola.

Viola was busy riding my cock.

My stomach churned in a way I'd never felt before. Rushing to the laptop, I slammed it shut, cutting off the visual.

Yes, back when I fucked them like that, I'd loved it. Had lusted for more. I'd jerked off to that video many times in the past.

All before Demi.

All before she came back into my life like a destiny-altering hurricane.

All before I fell madly, irrevocably in love with her.

And she was gone.

She'd seen this fucking bullshit and had run from me.

Just like I always knew she would.

In a blind panic, I ran back down the hallway toward the door. Like a mindless creature, I was compelled by only one instinct.

Find her.

Get to her before it was truly too late.

Stop her and convince her to not let Monica win. To not take this from us.

Whatever I had to do, whatever I had to give, I'd make this up to her. I just had to make her see that giving up on us wasn't an option.

It never would be.

19

I made it to the elevators, only to run into a human barricade.

"Listen to me! She made it clear she needs space, and after what she just saw, you're better off giving it to her."

"Lucas, move the fuck out of my way or I'll make you."

The interaction was so unexpected, so out of character, that for a moment I forgot my own problems.

"Can you just think clearly for one second? Just one?"

"I'm going after her!" Calum pushed his brother.

His brother shoved him back. "She just saw you kissing your ex, dumbass. Even I know that's unforgivable. She asked you to leave her alone and you're going to have to give her space for now."

Calum snapped. I'd never seen his eyes go dead like that, nor the icy fury that emanated from him. Grabbing his brother by the lapels, he slammed him into the wall next to the elevator. "Like hell I'm leaving her alone."

Luke's infamous, well-known temper roared to life and he reached for his brother—

Both their heads turned in my direction on a slow swivel.

They caught sight of me.

I was still confused as fuck about what I'd witnessed. "You kissed your ex?" I asked Calum, dumbfounded. "*You*?" He was the most straight-laced and honorable one among us.

"That's what I said!" Luke cried.

Calum shoved off him with a disgruntled growl. "I didn't engage. I didn't kiss her. I just didn't move away when she kissed me."

And Livana, his girlfriend, saw this. "To be clear, this is Diane we're talking about?"

He didn't answer, jaw tense.

"Your ex-fiancé." Yes, Luke had already stated this fact, but it bared repeating.

His brother threw his hands up in the air. "Again, that's what I said!"

"I'm going to go find her." Calum pressed the elevator button.

Lucas shook his head but didn't try to stop him this time. "We have no idea where she went off to."

"She either got her own room, or she's with one of her frien—" Calum didn't finish, gaze swinging my way. "Wait a minute. Isn't Demitra staying with you? That means Liv can only be with either Mikael or Angelina."

Yeah, his comment reminded me, too. "Demitra is gone. And she might be with one of them, as well." God, those fucking words burned.

Luke leaned around his brother's form, hazel eyes wide. "Jesus. What the fuck did *you* do?"

"I didn't do anything. Monica showed her one of the fucking videos," I snapped.

The elevator door opened.

As we stepped inside, he exhaled a breath and shook his head up at the sky. "I'm really better off single. Seriously."

I didn't even have it in me to correct him about that. He was borderline obsessing about Angelina. Unless he managed to kill the attraction, or perhaps move out of the country for a few years, he was in too deep.

He hadn't admitted that to himself, yet, but Calum and I knew it.

Once in the elevator, I resumed my desperate attempts to reach Demitra on her cell. Next to me, Calum was engaged in the same endeavor as he tried to get a hold of Livana. Neither of us got through. We were idiots for thinking we would, but could we be blamed for trying?

Fuck this entire event. The design festival had officially devolved into a sick clusterfuck.

We arrived at the lobby and tried to get Angelina's room number from the front desk.

Obviously, that didn't pan out. Neither one of us owned the place; we were just high-paying, well-connected guests, and they weren't going to bend the rules for either one of us.

"Listen." Luke pulled us both aside, stare darting from person to person. He'd been our lookout, more concerned about us being spotted by people we knew than we were. "The main event is about to start in an hour."

"I honestly do not give a fuck."

This time, it was Lucas and I whose heads turned slowly toward Calum.

Again, he was the most responsible one of the three. Lucas had often accused his brother of having a stick up his ass.

Yet here we were.

"I have to admit: I agree. With the way my head is right now, I can't get through that bullshit. And I think I'll kill Monica if I see her in person any time soon."

"Well, what the fuck are we supposed to do, then? Our companies need a face present—" Luke went quiet at the look we were giving him. "Oh, no. No. No."

"You're the only back-up plan. Our companies teamed up on

this."

His nostrils flared with an exasperated breath. "Fucking, fine. *Fine*. Just don't get thrown into jail for stalking while I'm gone." He reached into his pocket and flicked a card key at his brother. "Wait in my room. Both of you. I mean it. You're acting like strung out junkies. You don't need to be in your rooms and be reminded of those girls."

For someone with no experience when it came to love, the fucker was really astute.

And that's how Calum and I ended up locked in Lucas' room for the next few hours. We ransacked the mini-bar in the suite; which, thanks to Luke's proclivities, was well stocked with hard liquor.

We drank.

We paced.

We kept trying those damned phones although the calls kept going to voicemail.

Eventually, Calum collapsed on the couch in the sitting area.

I was a miserable wreck on the coffee table.

He nursed his drink and tugged at his bow-tie with his free hand. Hazel gaze flickering to me, he finished off that drink and leaned back against the cushions. "It's a video. It's awful, but it's part of your past. I'm sure you'll find a way to get her back. Especially if she's smarter than I am."

"I don't know, man. Those kinds of images aren't easy for some people to get over." I yanked at my hair, eyes fixated on the screen of my phone. As if I could mentally will her to reach out.

To love me enough to bridge this gap.

"At least you didn't cheat."

That comment brought my head back up. "Does Livana know you didn't actually kiss Diane back?"

Calum flung his bow-tie across the room in his frustration. "I don't think so, and it doesn't matter. I cheated. I cheated the moment

I let Diane fucking kiss me and I didn't pull away."

"Why?" I asked. Even with my own issues eating me alive—this angsty, restless desperation that was vibrating through every cell in my body as I envisioned a future without Demi in it—I couldn't stop myself from wondering what the fuck possessed him to do it. "I thought you didn't have any lingering feelings for her."

"I don't. I really don't. But . . . Livana can be difficult. Distant. I've been falling like a fool for her since I met her, and I knew she felt the same. But she tried so hard to hide it sometimes. To keep distance. I didn't know why until we got here." He paused, as if he sensed that his next words might bother me. "She was still messed up from an ex of hers years ago. I found out about him here. He's after her, still wants her. I lost my shit about it. Like a fucking scumbag, I just . . ." His shoulders jerked in a bitter shrug.

I ran a hand down the side of my face. "I'm so screwed." This had nothing to do with age, maturity. It all boiled down to raw emotions. If Calum, a man in his mid-thirties, could fall so insanely in love that merely meeting Liv's ex sent him spiraling like that, what would those images do to Demi? "Monica stroke first," I growled, consumed by pure hellfire and bloodlust. "I'm going to legally decimate everything she is. Her father. Her family. I don't give a fuck. I'm going to ruin her."

That's how I spent the next hour. In between calling Demi and texting her, I also text my lawyer to bring him up to date. I still had Demitra's laptop in my possession, which was the best proof I could ever ask for.

It wasn't until 3AM, long after Luke returned to the room, that my girl finally—*finally*—picked up one of my calls. "Demi," I groaned, shooting to my feet and distancing myself from the other inhabitants in the room. "Please. I know you're hurting. Just please listen to me."

"I just need some time to deal with this, Dorian."

That numb tone sliced something open within me. I couldn't deal with the resignation I sensed there. "Okay. We'll handle it together."

"No. I can't do that with you. All I can see is . . . and looking at you isn't going to make it easier. Please, understand."

I locked myself in the bathroom and leaned against the door, eyes closed. My heart hammered violently throughout my body. "Tell me you're not leaving me. I'll do my best to give you time, just tell me you're still mine."

"I can't promise you anything, Dorian. You don't know how it felt to see that. How it still feels."

"I fucking love you! I'm bleeding along with you here. We need to figure this out together. I wouldn't leave you if the roles were reversed."

"Well, I'm not as strong as you are. Or maybe not as experienced. I can't deal with it right now." She hung up the call before I could get another word in edgewise.

I almost crushed my cell in my grip.

That only lasted about a minute. Then, I was storming out of the bathroom in search of the other men. It was time to pack our shit and get out of here. My girl was heading back to New York. I felt it in my gut. And I was going to make damned sure I caught her there.

She needed some space? Fine. I'd give it to her. For a few days at most. But she was out of her mind if she thought this was the end of us.

There'd never be an end. Not as long as I held a piece of her heart. I wouldn't let her run from me.

chapter twenty 20

I was empty. My life had everything—Money. Power. Achievement.

And yet, it didn't have the most important thing, someone I'd come to fucking breathe for.

A woman I'd only owned for half a year.

Fuck that. That woman was mine. Every bit of her. I didn't care that we were separated, she still belonged to me. Demitra thought that she could leave me. That simply removing herself from the relationship would end what we had.

She thought wrong. There was no ending it.

I loved her. My entire life, every meaning of it, had dwindled down to her.

An ice block had taken up residence in my chest. As I stormed down the street, pulling my collar up to ward off the freezing, drizzling rain around me, despair choked me.

It was the coldest October in years. Almost as if Mother Nature herself could commiserate with the frost that enveloped my life.

Stephen was on a rampage. I refused to speak to him. It killed me not knowing what was happening on Demi's end, if he was making her life a living hell as well.

Hopefully it didn't last long, as had happened with me. The first week back from Chicago, he tried cornering me in my office to attack me again for loving his daughter. It was clear to me that they weren't speaking yet, since he didn't seem to know that Demitra had left me.

I refused to think back on that argument. How he'd thrown that demand at me a second time: leaving his daughter alone or step up and marry her.

Of course I wanted to marry her. I just wouldn't be doing it to appease him.

Luckily, the news of his divorce and infidelity hit the media, and he was dragged into the PR disaster that came with it. Especially since he had no plans of submitting to the terms of the prenuptial agreement he signed peacefully.

Fucking idiot.

As for Monica? Holding her accountable meant going public with what she did. I could try to keep the lawsuit quiet, her breach of contract by engaging in revenge porn against me, but that meant divulging who she sent the video to.

Demitra would be dragged into it.

Was it worth putting her through that if she was trying to rid herself of this situation? *Rid herself of me.*

A desolate, inhospitable limbo that I couldn't escape no matter what I did.

Couldn't attack my enemy.

Couldn't put Stephen in his place.

Couldn't reach my girl no matter what I tried. She would only respond to my messages in short spurts. Didn't answer her calls. When I went to her apartment, the front desk informed me she was away and they didn't know when she'd return.

Couldn't even tell if I was being lied to or not. Away? Where the fuck would she have gone?

Her social media was dead. Silent.

Three weeks. That's how long it'd been since Demi left me. Three weeks of chasing her down, only to have the door closed in my face every single time.

The irony wasn't lost on me; the possibility of Karma, either.

I got why Demi left me. Everytime I imagined my baby sitting behind the laptop, watching that disgusting fucking video Monica sent her, rage twisted in my gut.

Back in the day, having a girl ride me while I ate out another girl hadn't been disgusting to me. Fucking sexy, delicious, a perfect way to spend the time? Hell yes.

But I understood how gross it was now. Why? Because imagining myself being the one in Demitra's place—sitting back and watching a man pound into her while another asshole slid his cock in and out of her mouth—fucked my insides up. Twisted everything until all that remained was the violent need to throw up.

If I could've gone back in time and changed what I did, I would have. I would give anything to spare Demi the pain I'd caused her.

Anything to have her back with me, where she fucking belonged.

She had reason to leave me, and maybe, *maybe*, I could've accepted it. If at least she would've been happy. If the decision had somehow eased her pain. Instead, her walking away from me only served to slice both of us apart. Neither of us were okay. We were both miserable. God damn shells of ourselves. Her brief text responses gave her heartache away.

How in the fuck was I supposed to let her go when we both needed each other so badly?

Impotence raged. I hadn't felt this helpless since before I'd given into my feelings for Demi. Head throbbing, I slipped my hands into my pockets and continued wandering aimlessly down the street.

When I left my house, I knew where I would go. The only two places I knew for sure to look in.

Demi's apartment, and the campus of her school.

I didn't find her in either place.

Not that it would stop me. She could ignore all my calls, texts, every single attempt I made to communicate with her. I would still keep trying.

Out of the corner of my eye, a flash of brown hair caught my attention. I almost ignored it.

Then I recognized the man sitting across the brunette inside the restaurant.

Keith Bennett.

I slowed to a stop, disbelieving.

No. That had to be another brunette with long, straight hair identical to my girl's. Had to be.

A waitress approached the table. The brunette turned to speak to her, and the sight of her profile punched me through the chest.

Demi.

She was there. In that restaurant. With him. With *Keith*.

I didn't stop to think, to try and analyze why she would be there. All I knew was that I'd just spent days trying to find her again, my insides rotting away with the need to see her, and she was sitting there, in a restaurant with Keith-fucking-Bennett.

The man she hid from me. The only man to have touched her, fucked her, before me. Her first.

Pure instinct engaged, dragging me full-speed into that restaurant. The hostess at the front tried to stop me. Several people watched me with wide eyes as I passed. The waitress at their table saw me approaching and she took a step back as I got closer.

Demi turned to see what the waitress was staring at.

Keith had already seen me. He scooted his chair back, shocked at whatever he saw in my expression.

Demitra jumped out of her seat, stepping in front of me and slapping her hands against my chest. "Dorian."

"What are you doing here with him?" I growled under my breath.

She pushed into me, trying to use her little body to back me away from Keith. "Dorian, just stop."

"*Demi.*"

Pausing at the tone of my voice, she stared up at me, her lower lip trembling. Her light-blue eyes searched mine and I could see the sheen of her contacts covering her irises.

So close. I hadn't seen her or had her this near since the day Monica showed her that video.

My sanity snapped.

I cupped her nape, trying my best to control myself and knowing it was a losing battle. "Answer me . . . please."

"Outside," she whispered in a tearful voice.

The ache in my soul spread to my gut, pounding away at my hard cock. Reaching up, I circled my other hand around her wrist, caressing the back of it with the tips of my fingers. It took all my self-control not to slide her hand down and make her grab my dick. Play with it. Jerk it until I came all over her sexy little hands.

It'd been aching for her for over three weeks, missing every inch of her—that mouth, those tits, the tightness of her pussy.

Hunger choked me, feeding the madness.

Demi's fingers twitched on my chest. "Outside, Dorian."

Yes. Outside. Where I could find us someplace private. Then we could reconnect. I needed that juicy skin in my mouth, underneath my tongue. Between my teeth.

I needed to remind her who she fucking belonged to.

Reminded of Keith, I let my eyes flicker toward him.

He studied us, eyes clouded.

Jealous. Of what was mine. It was so disgustingly obvious. That motherfucker—I stopped that train of thought before I stormed over and clocked him right in the face.

Demi must've sensed the animosity rising in me. She turned

around in a hurry and grabbed her purse off the table.

Keith's eyes met hers.

I couldn't see her expression, but I clearly heard her apology.

"I'm so sorry, Keith. I'll be right back."

No, she fucking wouldn't. Not if I had anything to say about it. I placed my hand on her back, leading her away from that little dipshit.

I couldn't get the memory out of my head—Stephen's plans to have them eventually get married if I failed to come through.

"This is ridiculous. I can't believe you right now," Demi murmured.

Anger nearly blinded me. She couldn't believe *me*? A fresh wave of pain burned through me.

She was hurt.

Rightly so.

Apparently, she was also determined to hurt me as much as I'd hurt her.

So be it. I still fucking owned her. A fact I was about to drive home.

Running on instinct, I led her through the restaurant, searching for a back exit. Anything that wouldn't lead us out into the busy street.

She let me guide her, but the tension in her body wasn't lost on me.

I really, really hoped she could pick up on how fucking angry and hurt *I* was.

21

chapter twenty-one

P ast the bathrooms, I spotted a door with an exit sign above it. On the door, there was another sign that read: "Employees Only."

I ignored it.

My hand flat on her back, I ushered Demitra out into an alley.

She whirled on me instantly.

I closed the door, taking in the vision she made with her long, brown hair whirling around her. The white trench coat she wore highlighted the darkness of her hair and the light blue of her eyes. Her pale skin was flushed from the cold and her anger.

And from excitement. She tried to pretend otherwise, but I had come to know her. I could read her too well. She could try to deny it, but having me near her reignited that spark. The red-hot connection that arced from her body to mine.

"Why are you here with him?" I didn't even try to hide how much the fact hurt me.

She trembled, yearning leaking off her. Still, she raised her chin in a false show of stubbornness. "That's none of your business Dorian. We're not together."

It would have hurt less if she had reached into my chest to squeeze the pathetic organ that adored her so much. Much less.

"You're still mine. I'm still yours," I growled. "*By definition* it means we're still together, no matter what ridiculous ideas you have in your head."

Her small hands curled into fists. Hands I'd had all over my body. Hands I needed on me once more. *Now.*

She didn't answer my statement, so I repeated the question, enunciating slowly. "Why are you here with him, Demi?"

Her jaw clenched.

"Are you on a date with him?" The thought maddened me. I could barely bear it. "Am I that fucking forgettable to you?"

Tears flooded her eyes and her breath left her on a sob. "No, you fucking asshole. I *wish* I could forget you that easily."

That's all I needed to hear.

I rushed to her.

Her eyes widened. Shaking her head, she stepped back.

Too late.

Grabbing her arms, I hauled her up against me. The moment her body collided with mine, sheer hunger exploded in my veins.

A shaky breath left her and she melted into me, staring at my lips with a need as intense as the one I felt.

Damn her.

I laid my forehead on hers and wrapped my arms around her. "Then why are you here with him?"

She turned her face away from me. "It's business related. His father might need me to help out part-time—"

"No." I could never begin to explain how much I didn't want her near him. In any capacity. Didn't want him as her friend. Definitely didn't want her fucking working with him.

Demitra squirmed in my hold. "You don't have a say in that. Now let me go."

I refused to do so, tightening my hold on her. "Yes I do."

"We're not together anymore!" she cried.

Did she have any clue how badly I ached every time she said that? "Look at me."

She ducked her head.

I shook her lightly, unable to stop myself. "Look. At. Me."

Tear-filled baby blue eyes met mine.

My breath hitched and a vibration went through my body—lust in its basic form. I wanted to ease her sadness in the most primal way possible. Give her every inch of me. Fuck the pain right out of her.

"I love you. You're everything to me. Stop pushing me away." I was begging her at that point, and I couldn't bring myself to give a damn.

I'd get on my knees, give her anything. *Do* anything. But letting her go wasn't an option for me. I'd known that the day she disappeared in Chicago. The day she left me.

The last three weeks without her had done nothing but drive that point home. I needed her to live.

"I can't be with you," she whispered, running her hands across my shoulders, up toward my neck. "Not after what I've seen."

"Bullshit." I hugged her close and rocked my hard cock into her. "I know it hurts. That nothing I do will make you forget what you saw, baby. But no one's ever owned me the way you do. You have to know that."

"Oh, please." Scoffing, she pushed at my chest. "Not only does your reputation speak for itself, but I've officially seen that you're a sex god with anyone you sleep with. A great multitasker, too. So don't fucking pretend sex with me is special."

My fist slammed into the brick wall next to her head.

Demi jumped, falling silent.

I didn't care that I'd scraped my knuckles wide open.

Her doubts were understandable. I'd have them too in her place.

Just seeing her *sitting* across from Keith, the first man to ever have her, fucked with my head.

Had I seen her sleeping with him and actually enjoying it, I would've been ruined, too.

And I told her that.

"So please understand," she begged me, pushing against my chest.

"But—" I grabbed her hands and kept them pressed to me. "I fucking adore you, baby, and I would've never left you. No matter how much seeing something like that wrecked me. I would've stayed. I can't live without you."

The fight leaked out of her and her body slumped against mine. She looked defeated. Hopeless.

She'd given up on us.

Cupping her face, I pleaded with her. "Don't do this, Demi. We love each other."

Her fingers wrapped around my wrists, but she didn't try to pull my hands away. "I can't forget what I saw. It eats at me."

I kissed her forehead. "I know. Just like seeing you with Keith ate at me."

She tensed. "It's not the same thing and you know it."

"I do," I agreed in a low voice. "What you saw is a thousand times worse. But I can make it better. Nothing could hurt more than us being apart."

"Seeing you fucking two women at the same time hurts more than you can ever imagine."

Until I met Demi, I had never regretted anything I'd done in the past. Hell, I hadn't thought about my past while with her, and therefore couldn't entertain the idea of regretting anything.

That is, until Monica decided to get territorial. The bitch didn't care if she had to share me, as long as she was free to have some part of me.

Correction: as long as *I* was free.

I was consumed by Demitra. Not once since sleeping with her had it crossed my mind to be with someone else.

She owned me.

I fucking loved being owned by her.

And that's what Monica couldn't stand.

"I'd change my past if I could," I said.

"But you can't. And it's my fault. I'm hurt—"

"It's my fault. And Monica's."

"Yet, I knew your reputation and I was still stupid enough to fall in love with you."

She was pulling away from me again, erecting the necessary shields to hold her pain at bay. I saw it in her eyes.

A delirious sort of panic slammed into me.

After three weeks of no contact, I finally had her there, where I needed her.

And she was about to leave me once more. She would be by herself with nothing but the ache my presence caused her, and the bitterness of that stupid video.

I couldn't let her.

Had to remind her why we were so good together.

Why we needed to be with each other.

chapter twenty-two

My hand shot into her hair, fisting tight. I laid my other hand over her throat, a light but unmistakable hold.

Her eyes widened, pupils enlarging with shock.

And, then, it wasn't shock. No. It was lust that I saw on her face now, that greedy, demanding pull that drew her to me. Made her attack me with all that raw wildness inside her.

"I'm not letting you go." My rough comment was met by a small gasp.

I remembered that sound. I lived for that sound. Loved hearing it while her cunt milked every drop from me.

A growl broke out of me. Leading her backward, I forced her up against the brick wall.

She shook her head at me—even as her body arched toward mine. "Dorian, don't."

"Don't what?" I nudged her legs apart with my knee, crowding her with my much larger body. My hand shot between her legs, cupping her pussy through her pants. "Don't remind you who this belongs to? How much this pretty little cunt needs me?"

Her hips rocked into my hand. A small moan left her, echoing in the alley.

Inhaling through the pounding lust, I nipped at her chin, licking my way toward her mouth. "I love you. Breathe for you. The moment my cock slid into that pussy, I forgot every damn woman that came before you."

She tried to shake her head again, her entire body trembling.

I nipped her bottom lip hard, her taste spearing through me.

Then I took her mouth, every inch, rubbing my lips along hers, sucking, sliding my tongue in and owning it.

"Mine," I panted between kisses. "My mouth. My tongue. My woman."

Her hands slid into my hair.

For a second, I was convinced she was going to try to pull me away.

I groaned, rubbing her tongue harder with my own. My body tensed as I prepared for her rejection. She'd denied me her mouth for three weeks, even knowing I'd come to live for the feel of her. She *owed* me that.

Instead of pushing me away, she yanked me closer, her hips writhing on my hand. Tilting her head, she whimpered into our kiss, making me jerk against her.

My dick throbbed, aching. So hard that I could barely handle the sensation of her clothed body rubbing on it. "Need you, Demi. Holy fuck." Nearly blind with hunger, I grabbed her hand and wrapped it around my dick.

She arched on contact. Groaned. Squeezed down on me. Eyes gone cloudy with lust, she bit her lip and moaned my name.

I almost fucking came. Bracing one arm on the wall, I rocked into her, moving my hand between her legs in time to each thrust of my hips.

Demi lifted her head off the wall and tried to kiss me.

My body on fire, I moved my head back, purposely avoiding

her lips.

Demi tugged on my neck.

I refused to move. "Tell me that's my mouth. I want to hear it from you."

She huffed, eyes flashing, cheeks pink from arousal and the cold.

So beautiful.

So fuckable.

I wanted to bite her.

Her tongue darted out to wet her lips. "You always want to hear it from me."

"Damn right. I want to know that you understand who owns that. Whose cock gets to fuck that mouth and come inside it."

She exhaled softly, cursing.

Demi loved when I got rough with her, and I knew it.

Circling her mound with my fingers, I leaned down to lick her ear. "You miss me pumping my hot cum in here, filling you with it."

"Oh, God. Oh, God."

Her soft, wild cries left me shaking.

"You have me all fucked up inside. I barely recognize myself, and it doesn't matter. I'm still dying to coat every bit of your pussy with my cum."

Head thrashing on the wall, she jerked my cock over my jeans. "I hate you."

Leaning down, I brushed my lips with hers, giving her a mere taste. "I fucking hate you, too. As much as I love you."

"Dorian, I—" Her breath caught on a sob. "I need—"

"*Me*," I finished for her, ready to fuck her straight into oblivion if I had to. Anything to get her to see reason.

Seconds passed. I waited for her to try to deny it. To come up with yet another bullshit excuse why we couldn't be together.

None came.

Her hand wrapped around the back of my neck, nails digging in.

Securing what she wanted.

As if I was going anywhere.

I opened my mouth to tell her that we were heading back to my place. Where I could rip off every piece of fabric keeping her skin from mine.

Her fingers shifted, popping the button of my jeans.

I went still.

My cock had hardened to full-length, the tip pushing its way past the elastic band of my briefs.

Demi's fingers ghosted across the wet head.

Chest heaving wildly, I moved back to see her small fingers wrapping around my cock. It pulsed in her hand.

My hips jerked.

A bead of precum leaked out the tip.

Demi smeared it with her thumb, moaning hungrily.

"Fuck," I gasped. "Fuck." My clumsy fingers worked on her pants, sliding inside, searching her heat. Her eyes met mine; I bared my teeth at her, fighting not to come. "I'm going to make you fucking scream, baby. Right here. Where anyone can hear you."

Her teeth dragged along her bottom lip, and she pulled on my dick.

I slipped my fingers into her, my palm hitting her clit. The sopping wet sound of my skin slapping her sex reached my ears.

Fuck, she was drenched.

Demi gasped breathlessly, her pussy shaking around my fingers. I wasn't even moving my hand and she was already on the verge of coming.

Mine.

I had to mark her. Bruise her skin with my teeth.

Growling under my breath, I did just that, biting down into the tender skin of her neck.

"Yes, please. Please," she cried out, riding my hand faster.

I pulled her to me, licking at her mouth. Her perfect tongue lapped out to meet mine, our groans mingling. I swirled my fingers in her tight, soaked cunt, my cock hungry to be inside her.

"Holy shit, baby girl. I can smell how horny you are . . . it's so strong. Need this, Demi."

Her walls rippled around me. She sucked on my lip in that same lazy way she liked to suck on my dick.

My cock wept more precum at the reminder.

"Dorian." Her tongue circled mine slowly. "Make me come."

I thrust my fingers, shallow slides that I knew were nothing more than a tease. "Whose pussy is this?"

Her head fell back against the wall, exposing that beautiful throat and the dark purple mark forming on the side.

My mark.

"It's still fucking yours, you asshole," she gritted out.

I loved the sound of that.

Grinning, I gave her one hard thrust of my fingers.

She locked up, gushing on my hand. I knew that look. *Beautiful.* Fuck, she was almost there.

I tangled my hand in her hair and angled her face toward me so I could take her mouth.

Our lips met, her moan sliding into me.

I growled, letting her lick my tongue however she fucking wanted, imagining that juicy tongue swirling around my cock. Her body locked up, shaking.

Not yet. I couldn't let her yet.

Too late. I couldn't stop her from coming.

Fuck. Forget that. I didn't want to. I needed to feel her cunt throbbing for me once more.

Kissing her harder, I screwed my fingers into her, giving her what she needed.

Her cries. My groans. The wet sounds of our mouths. It all

seemed to echo up and down the alley. The people walking on the sidewalk could probably hear us.

I'd once sworn no one would ever hear my baby girl's cries but me. Yet I couldn't bring myself to care right then. Her pussy sucked on my fingers, each throb making my balls tighten more. She kept jerking me as she came, seemingly determined to bring me over the edge with her.

Demi ripped her mouth away from mine. "Come for me, Dorian. Give me this. I need to fucking see it."

She had me right there. Aching, shaking, and on the verge of exploding all over her hand.

The thought of my cum shooting onto her, even while she was clothed, wrecked my control. I fought desperately to hold on just a little longer. Just wanted to make her come one more time . . .

Demi squeezed my shaft to the point of pain. Against my lips, she whispered, "Give me what's mine, baby."

Moaning through clenched teeth, I devoured her mouth, thrusting into her fist like a madman.

Her pussy contracted around my fingers.

My head tilted toward the sky and my back arched. The scream that was ripped out of me bounced off the brick walls.

She didn't care, sucking on my neck as she jerked me—adding another layer of sensation to the pleasure pounding through me.

I leaned into her, my dick spurting uncontrollably and my body shuddering.

Demi cradled the back of my head with one hand, breathing as hard as I was.

Pressing my cheek against hers, I tried to catch my breath; a losing battle. I could barely stand, let alone breathe.

Holy shit, three weeks without her, and her hand alone had the power to undo me like that. "I fucking missed you, Demi. Don't ever leave me waiting that long for you again."

23

In a matter of seconds, her body froze up, the tension returning with a snap.

Fuck no. I couldn't let that happen.

Easing back, I stared into her eyes. "Baby—"

"Get away from me. Please." There were tears in her eyes.

"Demi, listen to me."

She cut me off once more, mumbling to herself. "I can't believe I did that. My God, what the fuck is wrong with me?"

"Stop!" I snapped.

She jumped and fell silent, but wouldn't look at me.

"We love each other. Stop acting like what we did is wrong."

She pushed at my chest. "It was wrong. Loving you is wrong."

The cold air hitting my dick finally registered. I ignored it. Refused to move away from her.

"Move out of my way, Dorian."

I pushed my fingers back inside her, cupping her pussy. "No. This is mine."

Her eyes finally met mine, glistening with tears. "She sent me another video."

What the fuck?

I was so shocked by that statement that I didn't protest when Demi squeezed past me. My hand slid out of her pants. Cold air hit my wet fingers next, freezing them.

But it was nowhere near as cold as I felt inside.

Demitra adjusted her pants, head bowed. I couldn't see her face, but I sensed her pain in the air between us.

Voice hoarse, I called out to her, even though I knew she was slipping away. "Baby."

She ignored me, and wiped the cum covering her fingers on her coat since she had nothing else to clean herself with.

"Demi."

Her purse had fallen on the ground. She went over to pick it up.

"What was on the video?" My heart raced at a million miles per hour. If that little bitch showed my girl another group sex recording . . .

Demi laughed bitterly. "Don't worry. It was just you and her this time."

My heart cracked for her.

One video I could've fixed. Maybe.

But another one? Yet another session of Demi seeing me fucking someone else?

Losing her.

I was fucking losing her.

"Demi, wait."

She hesitated, but it looked like it was the very last thing she wanted to do.

"Did she send you the new video via web transfer again?" I hated having to discuss this with her, yet it had to be done. My blood was burning for retribution and I knew of only one way to get it.

I was paying for my actions. Had lost the woman I loved and now had to stand there, seeing the agony in her eyes.

Monica helped put that pain there.

I would fucking make her bleed for what she'd done to my baby girl. No more waiting.

Demitra stared at the brick wall before her. "Yes, she did."

"Her personal account, right?"

A sharp nod from Demi.

"Can I please have my lawyer visit you so they can access the files and trace them back to her?"

Her brow scrunched. "What?" Eyes widening, she finally spun to look at me. "Dorian . . . what are you thinking of doing?"

"What I always planned on doing. She hurt you. Tore us apart. I'm going to fucking *break* her, Demi."

She blinked at me in shock. "You'd do that to her? For me? Even though I broke up with you?"

An unholy growl left me. "God-fucking-damn it, woman! I adore you. What part of that don't you understand? She meant nothing to me!"

"You didn't fuck her like she meant nothing!"

I closed my eyes and breathed deeply. To her, I knew it would seem that way. She was a woman, and a young one at that. I'd always been comfortable with sex, gave it my all, but I couldn't explain that to her. It would do more harm than good.

Without opening my eyes, I simply told her, "I'd fucking rip apart the whole world for you. Anyone. Anywhere. I'd watch them burn and probably fucking laugh about it. No one hurts you. No one." I meant that, and I knew she heard it.

Whether she doubted my sincerity or not was another story.

When I opened my eyes, Demi was still looking at me, eyes wet.

She missed me. As much as I missed her.

But she didn't know how to forgive me for what she'd seen.

I honestly didn't know how to fix this. There was no helping her forget; she never would.

How did I help her get past it?

"Dorian, you don't have to go after her."

"Why can't you love me enough to be with me so we can figure this shit out together?"

Her eyes clouded with pain. "I'm not with you because I love you *too much*. I'm not with you because you just had to be one of the biggest whores on the planet before I came along. I no longer know if that part of your personality can be erased for good."

In other words? She didn't trust me.

God damn, that *burned*.

"It is gone. I'm all yours."

"And that was *my* man I saw on a video fucking two women at the same time! My man I saw pounding into his ex-lover in that other video. I don't give a fuck that it happened in the past. It's still you in those videos, and I still have to deal with that. Not you."

"I *am* dealing with it, Demi. What do you think? That I'm not fucking miserable without you?"

"Oh, Dorian." The sadness and helplessness in her gaze cut me. "I'm not like you. This is all more than I know how to deal with. I have no right to be angry at you for your past, but I can't help it. I just . . . I need more time."

"I'll give you all the fucking time in the world as long as you come back to me in the end." *Don't try to move on.* I was pretty sure I'd hurt any man she tried to do so with. "Please let my lawyers come over and get the proof they need."

She hesitated, shaking her head. "I don't know . . ."

"You don't owe her anything. You don't have to protect her."

"It's not about that."

Was it because she didn't want anyone finding out we'd been together? Didn't want to risk news of us being out there? "Demitra . . . what if she decides to go public with those videos? Do you hate me so much right now that you want that to happen?"

If I'd thought she was angry before, that was nothing compared to what she aimed at me now. "One more stupid comment like that, and I'm walking out of this alley."

I resisted the urge to further explain myself. Demi was on a countdown, waiting for any excuse to escape. "I can legally stop her from doing anything else with that footage, but I need the proof that she's the one sending them to you. I have the first video"—Because I'd kept her laptop—"but this second one would seal the deal."

Her chest rose with a sigh. "Fine. I'll call you when it's a good time for me."

"Tomorrow. Monica is vindictive because I won't go back to fucking her. I have no plans of being with anyone but you."

"Dorian." Demi swallowed heavily, her eyes shimmering. "You can't wait for me forever."

"Watch me," I gritted out, hating that she would even entertain the idea of ending us permanently.

Ridiculous.

She didn't understand. There was no end to us. Never would be. I wouldn't allow it.

Emotions fluttered across Demi's face too fast for me to keep up. "Fine. Tomorrow. I'll let you know tonight what time works."

I jerked my head in a nod.

A final glance, and then she turned, all but running out of the alley.

Away from me.

Lifting my cold fingers up to my mouth, I swiped them across my lips.

Her taste shot straight into the pit of me. My skin felt too tight. Everything did. My chest. My cock. The urge to follow her, hunt her down, coiled inside me, an explosion building.

It was inevitable.

I would hunt her. There was no doubt.

As light rain drifted down all around me, I stood there, plotting every move I'd make.

Everything I'd do to make Monica regret ever fucking with us.

Bringing out my phone, I exited the alley and started dialing.

It was time to finally finish the war Monica started.

I planned to leave nothing of her behind.

DEMITRA

demitra

chapter twenty-four
24

"What a good boy you are," my mom cooed.

Beck barked happily in response.

I closed my eyes, blocking out the view outside my window.

Wishing I could somehow block the memories that came every time I heard my dog.

Played with him.

Said his name—Dorian's middle name.

My mother had just settled into my guest room for the time being and he'd been following her around happily since she arrived. She said something else to him, something I didn't catch, her voice trailing deeper into the apartment. I didn't know where she was heading, and I couldn't bring myself to investigate.

I was stuck there, both physically and mentally. Unable to move. Unable to think clearly. Barely able to function.

"When it gets tough, you need to remember me right now. How much I love you and how far I'm willing to go not to lose you. Because it's all that's gonna matter."

I ran my hand down the side of my face and blinked back a fresh round of tears.

"As soon as we're back from the conference, we're going fully official."

Instead, we ended up separating and it was all my doing.

"You'll never belong to any of the other men that want you. Only me."

Dorian wasn't lying about that, the bastard. The truth of that statement was an unforgivable cage around me, one that grew tighter every second. Instead of loosening his grip on me, the weeks without him made his ownership stronger.

I was approaching critical mass.

Functioning without him wasn't so hard the first week in a half. I was a zombie who barely ate or slept. I showed up to work and school by rote, stuck on autopilot.

But then reality started to set in, one vicious day at a time.

Then he found me in that restaurant yesterday with Keith.

The taste of him after so many weeks without . . .

Relapse is ten times harder than the initial addiction. Another truth I learned since Dorian made me come in that alley yesterday.

"I fucking adore you, baby, and I would've never left you. No matter how much seeing something like that wrecked me. I would've stayed. I can't live without you."

My hand shook as I ran it across my mouth. The same mouth he'd devoured.

The mouth he'd fucked God knew how many times.

The mouth he'd claimed belonged to him solely.

He wasn't lying about that, either.

Oh, God. I was starting to tremble everywhere. The emotions I kept bottling up were bubbling to the surface. The urge to run to my phone and call Dorian grew stronger by the second.

Then I remembered the videos.

What I'd seen.

It's not that I wanted to judge him for his past. When I started falling for him, I didn't even care that he had one. He already had a reputation as a party-boy manwhore. I never thought about it.

It never occurred to me that his past included group sex and sex videos, though.

And had it remained in the past, it could've been ignored. Yet it didn't.

His past had collided with our present, destroying it.

Casting our future into doubt.

I hadn't told him yet, but I was misled when I clicked on the link to download that video. Monica must've somehow gotten into Jocelyn's—Dorian's receptionist—email, because that's where it came from.

Disguised as a memo addressed to me.

I was so fucking messed up by then, that I didn't even realize the attachment I was opening was a video file.

Not until it was too late.

I didn't watch more than a few seconds of it, but it was more than enough.

I'd paused the video, jumped up and escaped. I was in such a hurry I left my laptop behind with the video still open.

The second video? That's where Monica got even sloppier. That one came directly from her.

I still didn't know why the fuck I'd opened it. Maybe my masochism ran deeper than I wanted to acknowledge.

"Demitra."

My mother's voice made me jump.

Turning, I found her standing near the hallway.

The hallway leading to my room.

It was clear by her expression that she had just come from there.

Fuck. I knew what she'd seen.

I came home yesterday in a whirlwind of heartache and anger, and had flung my cellphone at the mirror in my room. I just couldn't stand the reflection staring at me, the lost and broken girl I saw.

Stuck in my head trip, I forgot to clean up the pieces. That's what my mother just stumbled across.

"Thank God I pulled Beck out of there before he could get hurt," she told me somberly.

I let out a sigh. "I know. I'm sorry."

"Sit down."

Oh, oh. I knew that tone. That expression, too. "Mom, I don't—"

"I know about Dorian, Demitra. Your father threw it in my face before I left. Now sit down."

I all but collapsed onto the couch, air whooshing out of me. "He knows? You . . ."

My mother sat in the camel colored loveseat across from me, her movements as controlled as usual.

The only time I ever saw her lose her shit was that night that we all found out about Lucia.

That my dad cheated with her.

One of Dorian's ex-lovers.

"Ho—" I licked my dry lips. "How'd he find out?" Had Dorian told him? I knew immediately he hadn't. He'd never betray my trust like that.

The mere thought was enough to pierce me with brutal longing again.

"That woman . . . What's her name? I remember she's Alessandro Adamo's daughter."

"Fucking Monica?" I gasped. "She went up to Dad and told him?" The loathing I felt for that woman was already monumental. How much larger could it grow? Visions of going after her filled my head, a sea of blood thirst and vengeance.

"Your father is under the impression that you two are sleeping with each other . . . Dorian is the man that gave you that mark your father saw, isn't he?" My mother asked gently.

I nodded. There was no point denying it anymore. Frankly, I was too exhausted to do so. "We weren't just sleeping with each other. We were . . . Together."

Her eyebrows rose over her dark blue eyes, and her voice was soft when she next spoke. "Were?"

There I went again, blinking back another torrent of tears that wanted to break free. "Mom, you have enough problems of your own. We don't need to discuss my failed relationship." Budding relationship. For all the months that Dorian and I were seeing each other, we'd just barely agreed to take it there.

"Honey, your father and I are done. Even though he's in denial because of what he loses when I finish divorcing him."

"You, Mom," I snapped, angry at my father all over again. "He loses *you*." And my mother was ten times more beautiful than Lucia Polidore.

My mother was the best catch he could've ever gotten in his goddamned life, and it still wasn't enough for him.

"My money, Demi," she replied calmly, giving me a small smile.

She'd come to terms with the end of her marriage.

She had the strength to shut down her emotions and see it through.

I was proud of her. So proud.

But I hadn't come to terms with it, yet. The anger I felt toward my father was only eclipsed by my animosity toward Monica.

"Now, I'd rather discuss you, because ever since you came back from Chicago, you've been an empty ghost dragging through life."

Damn, that hurt. It wasn't her intention, but hearing those words was another hammer to the chest. "What is there left to discuss? I've become privy to things I don't know how to stop thinking about. If I stay with him, I'll punish him without meaning to as those images continue to burn in my head."

"So then tell me about it."

Staring off to the side, I focused on the wall next to the TV and confessed to my mother everything.

The relationship.

The love.

Dorian's past.

Monica's insanity.

Keith's inability to let the idea of him and I go.

When I was done, it was a miracle I hadn't broken down into hysterics. My heart was a jagged mess in my ribcage, broken pieces that caused more damage with every beat.

"So he's still chasing after you. And you're convinced he's sincere."

That did it. Every single tear I was holding back flooded out of me as I remembered Dorian's entreaties to me.

"Oh Demi, I wish I could tell you what to do. Of course, I want to tell you to fight for the man you love."

But she wouldn't.

Because that's what she had done with my father.

The gorgeous playboy of his day that came from a financially broken family. He fell for her, hard, passionately, and swore to her he'd change for her.

My mother had demanded that her family allow her to marry him. There'd be no one else for her. She broke off an engagement to the man her father did want her to marry, and threatened to elope with my father if they didn't approve.

It had been one of the greatest love stories I'd ever heard growing up.

Until suddenly it wasn't.

"That's your fear, isn't it? That Dorian will turn out like your father. That you both will turn out like us." She grabbed the tissue box on the end table next to her and leaned forward to offer me one.

I grabbed several. These waterworks were ridiculous at this point. Then again, when losing someone like Dorian, they were probably justified. *You didn't lose him. You let him go.* "I just don't know how a person turns off those desires just like that. Maybe right now he doesn't want that, but eventually he will, and I won't be able to give him that. I love him too much to share him. Mom, people don't just wake up one day and stop wanting the things they're sexually attracted to. It doesn't happen in real life."

"It doesn't happen often, you mean," she corrected. Standing up, she came over and sat next to me. With her arm around my shoulder, she let me lean my head on her own shoulder as I struggled to get my tears under control. "But it does happen sometimes, Demi."

All I could offer her was a nod. I was still fighting to get my tears under control.

"Regardless, Dorian is right. Even if it means everyone finds out that you two had a thing, that woman should legally pay for what she's done. You need to let his lawyers take the evidence you have."

The fact that my mother could advise me of that when our family was already dealing with one brewing scandal was eye-opening.

I knew that what Monica had done was serious. What I hadn't contemplated until now is that she would continue to escalate unless she was stopped.

Or, unless Dorian went back to sleeping with her.

Visions of clawing the bitch's eyes out filled my head once more.

"You're right, Mom. I know."

She nodded at my cracked phone on the coffee table. The same one that I threw into the mirror yesterday. "So text him and set up a time. Don't give her another opportunity to strike."

chapter twenty-five

"**E**asy, boy. Easy."

Beck gave that happy bark of his and jumped up and down in front of the door.

My heart was already messed up from everything that'd happened, and from just being here, but seeing the pup's eagerness to get within the penthouse just made everything worse.

Of course he recognized this place. I'd brought him here often since Dorian gave him to me.

Of course he smelled his second owner from the hallway.

I swear I could, too.

Why'd I bring our dog to this meeting?

That was exactly why. Because although I swore I'd left Dorian, I still thought of Beckham as *ours*.

It was an impulsive move I was sure I'd regret.

I reached up to knock—

As usual, I never got the chance.

Perhaps Dorian heard Beck announcing our arrival—perhaps, like he always did, he sensed me here waiting for him—and the door flung open.

The sight that greeted me knocked the breath right out of my lungs.

He'd clearly just finished taking a shower. His hair was even longer and swiped back from his forehead, the curly strands wet. A drop of water slid slowly down the side of his face.

His facial features were taut. Ragged. It seemed as if he hadn't slept in days, yet he was still the most beautiful man I'd ever seen.

Always would be.

He hadn't shaved today and that five o'clock shadow set off every hormone in my body.

Dorian's eyes flashed, as if he was picking up on my sudden need. His lips parted to say something.

Beck barked manically and flung himself at Dorian, breaking the moment.

I watched our dog frantically pawing at his legs, his tail wagging with sheer ecstasy at the sight of him, and everything shifted inside me.

Around me.

Dorian's expression melted as he bent to greet Beck, and the happiness I saw there, the way the strain disappeared from his face, speared through me.

Any more hits, and I'd bleed out here, in his hallway, for his eyes to see.

I tightened my hand around the strap of my laptop bag and prayed for a strength I knew I didn't possess.

"Yeah, buddy. I know. It's so good to see you." Dorian scratched behind Beck's ears and smiled up at me. "Thank you for bringing him. I've been missing him, too."

It wasn't lost on me what he meant by that. And, no, he wasn't talking about Beck obviously missing him.

I swallowed, throat tight. "Of course. It's not fair to keep him from you because of all of this."

"He was my gift to you. You could, if you so chose."

God, look at us. We were like parents that had separated and still had to work out visitation with our child.

I was going to fucking cry.

Dorian's brow twitched and he shot to his feet. That blue gaze studied me, picking up on my emotions—something he was too good at—and he raised a hand toward me.

"Mr. Sorensen?"

I looked over his shoulder into the penthouse to see who had spoken.

The man standing in the vast living room seemed to be around Dorian's age. His red hair was curly, as well, but he had tighter curls that sat close to his head. Wearing a navy suit and round, horn-rimmed glasses, he was dapper and interesting to look at.

I'd also never met him before or seen him around.

Which made me suspect who he was.

Dorian held up his hand, but he didn't touch me, simply motioned me inside. "Joey, this is Demitra, my—well, yeah. Demi, this is Joey Howell, my attorney. Well, the lead attorney in charge of my legal issues and whatnot."

That pause in his sentence echoed through my body like a rung bell.

He'd been about to call me his girlfriend. It was undeniable.

I was shaking again as I approached Joey and held out my hand.

Joey smiled at me warmly and shook my hand briefly. There was sympathy in his green eyes.

Of course he knew what'd happened. That's why he was there. Not only that, but the ease between Dorian and him told me that they'd known each other a long time.

"I see you brought your new laptop. That's great. We'll need the password for your other one, as well. If you don't mind." Joey was next to motion me forward as we headed to the couches.

The couches Dorian had fucked me on.

And the coffee table.

Oh, God. The fucking coffee table.

I ripped my glance away, and forced myself to move forward.

"Demi." Fingers grazed my hand.

I hissed at the contact, too raw to filter through the pleasure that simple touch incited. When I whirled around, Dorian was standing there, chest heaving beneath that white, v-collared t-shirt. "Just . . . I'll take Beck and get him settled in with some water in the kitchen."

He'd been reaching for the leash when our skin touched.

I wanted to drag him by that white t-shirt into his room and do so much fucking more than that.

I couldn't. Not just because his lawyer was waiting for us, but because I still didn't have my head straight. Dorian would be more than okay with me using his body, but what was the point?

I didn't know a lot about relationships, but I was smart enough to know one thing: if I got back with Dorian, I had to be ready to forget what I saw. I couldn't be with him and punish him for the images in my head, either. It wouldn't be fair to either of us.

Letting him take Beck's leash, I forced myself to turn away from the scrumptious sight he made. Once seated in the living room with Joey, I proceeded to open my bag and bring my laptop out.

Anything to keep myself occupied lest the memories of this place overwhelmed me.

"It hasn't been easy for him, either."

Joey's murmured comment brought my head up.

Tore through another piece of me that I couldn't afford to lose.

He wasn't looking at me. He was busy bringing out my other laptop—the one I left in that suite in Chicago.

Rage blossomed at the sight of it; the memories would never leave me, I knew that, but suddenly they were too fresh. Too vivid. The sounds Dorian made as he fucked both of them would probably haunt me into my next lifetime.

Thank God I only watched like five seconds of that fucking thing.

When Dorian rejoined us in the living room, he paused right before the couch I was on. I didn't look at him, but I knew he was looking at me.

Knew that he was studying the hatred on my face as I fixated on that laptop.

He wanted to say something, I felt it in the air.

I closed my eyes to block whatever it was out.

Dorian must've taken that as the sign it was, because he walked by me and sat on the other end of the couch.

Opening my eyes, I saw Joey holding the laptop toward me.

I shook my head, refusing to touch it, and rattled off the password for him.

Which happened to be the date of the Jackson fundraiser.

The one I attended with Keith the night Dorian carried me away.

The first night we slept together.

His sharp intake of breath wasn't lost on me.

He knew that date as much as I did.

Out of nowhere, his hand shot out for mine. He intertwined our fingers before I could stop him, grip unrelenting. Dorian didn't move closer, but it was clear he wasn't going to let me go. "I'm just holding your hand. Don't fight me."

I focused on Joey with every ounce of strength I possessed, even as my eyes watered again.

Dorian's attorney was kind enough to hold my gaze, giving me the distraction I needed. "I'll be able to have our team trace where she sent the file from now."

Licking my dry lips, I said the one thing I knew would change the course of this entire situation. Legal consequences were coming for Monica and, with my next words, I had the power to unleash that tsunami in her direction. "She sent it from Dorian's assistant's email. Jocelyn Rayford. So either Jocelyn gave Monica the log in, or somehow Monica got someone to hack in for her. I opened the email without thinking, but if I'd known it was from Monica, I would've never opened it in the first place."

26
chapter twenty-six

I had believed that nothing would get Dorian to release my hand.

Until those words left my mouth.

He was out of his seat and on his phone in a flash. Since he paced down the hall toward one of the guest bedrooms, I couldn't fully hear what he was saying.

Yet I had no doubt he was on the phone with the IT department of his company.

The thought registered, but suddenly it wasn't what mattered.

That hallway was.

The last time he took me there.

Right after he confessed he loved me.

Blinking rapidly, I tore my gaze away to find Joey on his own cell, typing away. He threw me a rueful smile. "I'm already in contact with the head of his IT. But, you know. He's impulsive."

Did I ever.

I'd be lying if I said it wasn't one of the many things I loved about him.

Damn it, being in this apartment was nothing more than a study in heartbreak. To make matters worse, Beck came bounding out of the kitchen. Instead of running straight to me, he rushed down the hallway in search of his true master.

I couldn't even fault him for it. For all the heartache and nightmares that tormented me lately—any woman who had seen her love sleeping with someone else could probably tell you how disastrous those dreams could be—here I was.

I told myself it was to help bring Monica down.

It was partially true.

But everyone in the universe would be able to see that wasn't my only reason. His pull was too strong. I was too weak. Giving in would be my only option at this rate.

What kind of relationship would we have moving forward?

Joey put away his phone. Out of the corner of my eye, I saw him study me.

Running on impulse, I asked him, "How does one forget the unforgettable?" Jesus, that applied to every level of our situation, and it didn't occur to me until after I mumbled it.

"I've never been in your situation and it isn't one I envy at all," Joey said carefully. "And it's most likely not my place to tell you this . . . But I've never seen him this crazy over any woman."

"Why isn't it your place? It's not like you're telling her something the whole world doesn't know already."

I almost flew off the couch at the sound of Dorian's voice.

Fucking hell. He was always sneaking up on me. And his words . . .

I refused to look at him. Not because I didn't want him, need him, *adore* him. He wanted a promise from me I didn't know how to keep, and it wasn't just because of Monica.

Perhaps it hadn't occurred to him yet.

I resolved to tell him at the first chance.

Joey stayed a bit longer to go over the plan with us—they were going full blown legal. Sue Monica and the company to begin breaking their contractual agreements.

File the police report to alert the authorities of Monica's crime.

"In New York, revenge porn is a real crime, and this falls under the exact definition of it. Ms. Adamo took an intimate video that was meant to be kept private by herself and Dorian"—I had to close my eyes at that, and he paused to give me time to compose myself—"and unveiled it to you, a third party, with the intent to cause harm to Dorian's emotional welfare. The fine is pathetic, only a thousand dollars, but we're talking up to a year in jail. And, aside from breaking the contracts, and being owed financial restitution for the setbacks Dorian's company will incur on the projects, he can also sue for personal financial compensation."

"Which means I get to financially ruin her and her family for this," Dorian told me solemnly. "And, no, Demi. I don't care if everyone connected to her is innocent. She didn't give a damn that you are."

I could do nothing but nod at him.

At them both.

Joey slipped both my laptops into my bag and took them with him. He promised to have them back to me once his investigators were done tracing the files. Dorian walked him to the door and they paused there for a bit, speaking in hushed tones.

Refusing to be that girl who ease-dropped on their conversation, I went in search of Beckham. If I stayed alone in this apartment with Dorian too long, I knew exactly what I'd end up doing.

Unfortunately, I found Beck on the second floor, in Dorian's room, playing happily with one of his chew toys—we kept toys and supplies for him at both our places—and I stopped short upon entering.

This place should bring me nothing but good memories. Sexy memories. Reminders of everything Dorian and I had shared over the last five months.

Now, when I stared at that huge bed, all I saw were those videos.

Because that bitch made it her mission to send me videos taken *there*. On that bed.

The thought that Dorian once set up a camera to record himself fucking other women in this room soured every good memory I once had of us here. Which is exactly what Monica's goal was.

I wished with all my broken heart that I was strong enough to overcome that. Maybe one day I would be, I just hadn't figured it out, yet.

Going over to Beckham, I picked him up in my arms and headed out of the room. He was getting big fast, which was expected for his breed. He'd end up over two feet tall on all four legs, and could top one-hundred-forty pounds once he reached maturity.

Dorian was in his kitchen when I reached the first floor. Thanks to the open-floor design, I had no problem catching sight of him as I descended the stairs.

And he had a perfect view of me, as well.

Those dark blue eyes stalked me, and I could almost tell what he was thinking by his expression. He knew I'd been in his room. He knew what was going through my own head because of that.

I put Beck down on the floor.

Dorian finished closing his fridge. He placed his glass on the counter and leaned on it with both hands flat on the surface. His cut shoulders strained beneath the short sleeves of his t-shirt.

I wanted him to fuck me on that counter again.

The thought was followed by another: had he done Monica on there, too? Any of the others?

It was petty, it was probably immature, but it was also uncontrollable. My mind was now geared for this, and I didn't know how to turn it off.

"Joey says you should hire someone to handle your P.R.," Dorian finally said. His tone was calm, his facial features anything but.

"My mother is already handling that for me."

He blinked in surprise. "Antonia?"

"She's the reason I came here. She told me to help you go after Monica."

If I thought he looked shocked before, it was nothing compared to now. "She knows about us?"

I went over to where Beck's leash was hanging near the foyer. "She's staying with me for now. My father threw it in her face as she was moving out. Well, leaving. She still has to find a new place and have all her stuff moved. I'm pretty sure she'll get him kicked out of the home in the divorce, but he's being stubborn and refusing to leave immediately. As you can imagine, she doesn't want to see his face at the moment."

When I turned around, it was to find him staring at me with that grave, forlorn expression.

"Yeah. I can imagine."

He knew how to hurt me with just a few well-placed words, and I wondered if it was on purpose. "Am I not standing in front of you?"

"You're not in my arms, Demi. As cliché as that sounds."

I was about to explain yet again why, when the doorbell rang behind me.

"Shit. I forgot. They called to tell me they were on the way up while you were looking for Beck. Give me a second." He walked past me to open the door.

Not sure who I expected to be on the other side, but when I saw a delivery crew, I didn't quite understand what was happening.

That is, until Dorian began giving instructions. "The bedroom is on the second floor. You can leave it down here while you disassemble the old bed and bring it down."

"Sounds good." The guy at the front motioned to the others, and they worked together to begin sliding a massive box through the front door.

Gaping, I moved to the side to give them room to pass.

It wasn't until they were by the living room and the stairs leading to the second floor that Dorian came to a stop next to me. "If I'm honest, I already put this place on the market. It's hard to look for a new one without your input, but I plan to be out of here as soon as possible."

There had to be an end point to a body's ability to produce tears. When would they stop? With a rough exhale, I turned my head away from him while fighting to keep them under control. "Then why did you buy a new bed before moving?"

"Stupidly hopeful, I guess."

That I'd be back with him before he found his new home.

"It was building up for months. It wasn't just the video. I think it started getting bad that day in the supermarket when that woman approached you," I decided to confess, in the hopes that he'd understand. "Everywhere we went there was a reminder, and I was your hidden secret—"

"Not by fucking choice, and you know that. Every time I look back on it, I can't figure out why I didn't just make it official with you immediately and then shouted it at the whole world. We were both worried about the wrong things. Your father—"

"Whether it was just sex between us . . ."

"And we both knew it wasn't. We knew from that first night it fucking wasn't."

A single tear slid out as I stared at him; I wiped at my cheek, not giving him a chance to reach for it. "But it was building, Dorian. The resentment. The jealousy. I lied to myself, shoved it all down."

"You think I didn't know that, baby? Of course I did. From day one I knew I wasn't good enough for you."

"Stop," I whispered, seconds from sliding to the floor and balling my eyes out. *Again.* "Stop putting it like that."

"It's the truth, isn't it?"

"No. It isn't. This has nothing to do with your self-worth, and everything to do with what I can handle. It'll always be like this. Maybe Monica is the worst of it, but there will always be reminders."

"We'll be out in the open this time around. We'll be able to publicly lay claims on each other."

Despite the incoming tears, the way he rasped that sent a lick of heat through my body. Heat that settled in my core, pulsating. "We'll be toxic if I get back with you now. You think I'll be able to easily forget . . . I want to fucking kill both of you every time I think about that video and it doesn't fucking matter that it happened before me."

There. I said it. I got it out. Even if it proved what a psycho he'd turned me into, it was the freaking truth.

Dorian stepped closer to me, body tense. Vibrating. Hands twitching restlessly at his sides. "So let's be toxic together. Punish me. Hurt me. Mark me even more than you already have. But be with me so I can fucking prove to you who I belong to. Don't just shut me out."

"I'm here, aren't I?" I said, repeating a question I'd already asked him during one of our previous arguments. "I'm here to help you destroy her."

Some of his tension leaked away. "That's true. At least you aren't completely shutting me out any more." Running a hand through his drying curls, he gazed at where the men left the pieces of his new bed while they worked to dismantle the other one upstairs. "I'm not giving up, Demi."

"Okay," I all but whimpered, my mind stuck on what that meant. What he'd do to try to break me down. "But I also can't promise to be with you if I'm not sure I can control those memories and the reactions they cause me."

"I admire that, but I told you: I don't care. We'll be toxic and fucked up together. As long as we're *together*, Demi. That's it."

'*I officially pressed charges this morning. And Jocelyn's been suspended. She's claiming innocence, but there's no way to know for sure. Not yet, at least.*' - D.

Possibly not ever. Unless they were legally allowed to search through her phone records, there'd be no way to confirm if she and Monica had been in contact.

If Jocelyn gave her the email password on purpose.

I had only begun reading into the law and didn't fully understand how far authorities could go to investigate. Her email was company property, but not her phone. Only one of them could be looked into without legal approval.

My mother got me in contact with lawyers from her attorney's firm that specialized in that type of thing. We signed the retainer this morning.

While Dorian was busy setting the law after his ex.

Ex-lover.

Right. That distinction was starting to sink in, although I wasn't sure what that meant, yet. I just wish it could do something to erase the images in my mind. How would I begin to heal and forget?

Well, this might've been the beginning.

That, and Livana was my best friend. So that man was going to give me some answers.

I slammed my fist into the door, announcing my arrival with as much aggression as my tiny fist could convey. I meant business and I wanted Calum Alexander to understand that.

Unlike the times I visited Dorian, it took at least a minute for the door to open.

When it did, I was taken aback at the wrecked man on the other side.

I hadn't seen Calum too many times throughout my life. Of course we frequented the same social circles, and I got to see him in Chicago. All those times, he'd been his usual self.

Handsome.

Polished.

Put-together.

An aura of self-containment surrounded him, which matched with his reputation in general.

Lucas, his brother, was the wild one. Calum was exactly what he was groomed to be: the stoic, controlled, responsible head of their family.

That's not who was staring at me now.

In a navy blue, rumpled button-down that was left open at the collar, and a pair of jeans, Calum stared down at me with bloodshot eyes. In his hand was a glass of amber liquid.

It was 11:00am.

The beard gracing his jaw was growing out of control; not that he seemed to care.

As a matter of fact, the man before me carried himself in a way that told me he didn't really give a damn about anything at that point of his life.

"Hello, Demitra. I was shocked when you reached out. Can't

deny it." The glass was lifted to his mouth and its contents finished in a single swallow.

Well, at least his words weren't slurred. "Hello, Calum. Mind if I come in?"

"Sorry." He scoffed, a self-deprecating sound, and moved aside to make room for me to pass. "As you can see, this isn't my finest hour."

I played witness to Livana's breakdown in Chicago, and I didn't expect the way my heart pinched with sympathy for him. "Well, we can't deny that you did it to yourself."

"No. We can't. Can we?"

I heard the door close behind me.

"Is that what you came to remind me, Demitra? Because if so, I assure you, it's with me every second of every day."

Another pinch.

Damn it.

I looked around his living room and scowled at the bolt of familiarity that went through me. "Did you and Dorian hire the same interior designer or something?"

Calum walked around me, chuckling. "He copied me. I assure you." Pausing near the entry to his kitchen, he looked at me over his shoulder. "Drink?"

"I'm okay. Thank you. Mind if we sit?"

"As you wish."

Together, we made our way to his living room. He sat on the loveseat, which I took as my signal to sit on the couch. Once situated, tension settled around me. Calum made no move to initiate conversation.

As a matter of fact, he sat there, deadened, yet expectant at the same time.

He was waiting for me to let him "have it" on behalf of my friend.

Perhaps that had been part of my intention when I reached out to him and requested this audience.

Now that I was in front of him, seeing his own deterioration, I couldn't find it in me.

Instead, I opted to go with my main reason for being here. "Why did you do it? Why'd you do that to her?"

Something akin to agony flashed in his gaze. "I didn't mean to."

"You didn't mean to kiss your ex?" I asked, fighting back a wave of indignation. It was a common excuse used by guys—"I didn't mean for it to happen!"—as if they just slipped, tripped, and fell into cheating.

"My ex kissed me. I didn't react. I . . . also didn't pull away fast enough." His fingers twitched, as if itching for his now empty glass on the coffee table.

Calum had a reputation for being self-contained.

The small cracks I was witnessing were more powerful because of that. This wasn't a man known for, or used to, showing emotion.

"So you did have residual feelings for her. That's why you didn't pull back."

He barked out a harsh laugh, white teeth highlighted by his black beard, his hazel eyes shining for a second in time. "Hell, no."

"Then what?"

"I was fucked in the head because of Livana. I'm assuming she told you what happened right before."

Yes.

Livana spent years messed up after her ex-boyfriend.

Walking in on your boyfriend eating out one of your best friends your freshman year of college is the stuff of nightmares. I was sitting here wrecked by a video from the past. A video that didn't feature women who were my friends. I could only imagine what that experience did to Livana.

And then that ex-boyfriend showed up to beg for another chance at the conference.

Calum happened to walk in on that conversation.

"So it was revenge?" I prayed like hell he didn't say yes.

"No! I just froze. I wasn't even fully present. In my head, I was still thinking about all the times that she would emotionally withdraw from me. All the times she tried to run away from what was happening between us. Next thing I knew, Diane's lips were on mine, and I was too shocked to immediately react."

My mind flashed back to nearly five months ago, to the day I walked in on Monica kissing Dorian. A dangerous place to be now that my hatred for her had ballooned to toxic levels. I was pretty sure I saw Dorian reach up to push Monica back, but by that point it'd been too late.

The tray with his coffee had fallen out of my hands.

My heart along with it.

The pain I'd felt at the time had been terrifying. Eye-opening. I ignored what it meant by sheer force of will. For another few months, that is. Eventually, the truth of what I felt became too powerful to deny. "So . . . you didn't actually kiss her?"

"I let her kiss me. That's bad enough."

The last chunk of iciness I felt toward Calum fell away. "Shit. Did Livana see that?" What was I saying? I knew she hadn't. "Fuck. I think she was too far away to actually see if you were kissing Diane back or not."

"Hence, how fucked I am." Calum waved a hand around weakly. "I'm still confused why you're here, if it isn't to tear me a new one."

"Oh, that was part of the plan. But mostly . . . I needed to understand why you did it," I admitted in a small voice. "For Livana's sake."

"And your own."

My eyes flew up to lock on his. "Excuse me?"

Calum chuckled again, but it was a sound without humor. "You think I don't know what everyone says about me? I'm the last person on Earth who should be fucking up like this, yet I did. What hope is there for a man with Dorian's past instincts then?"

My stomach twisted. My heart raced painfully. I hadn't even thought of it that way, at least not consciously. To hear him say that . . .

I fisted my damp hands.

"That thought isn't fair to Dorian, though. Yes, his past is shit. I was there. I told him and my fucking brother to behave themselves better. But you're completely ignoring how much he loves you. How stressed he's been for months to keep this from you. He would've done anything not to lose you."

God damn that man. Instead of me laying into him, he was laying into me, and he was being vicious. Perhaps his words weren't, but their effect could not be denied.

Against my will, I started crying.

And that was when he melted back into the couch, regretful. "I'm sorry. It's just hard seeing him as he is. He's my friend."

"And you're his friend." I reached into my pocket book for the small packet of tissues in there. Thank God I carried these around.

Calum sighed. "Tell me that this helped his cause a little, at least."

"I don't know. I had already seen a kiss in the past, but now I've seen so much worse. But it certainly helped yours."

"What do you mean?" He blinked those hazel eyes at me, and in that brief period he lost all his hard edges. A broken, boyish man stared at me, and it wasn't hard to imagine why Livana lost her shit over that man.

"I'm going to find a way to help you out, because my friend isn't okay without you, either."

"My friend isn't okay without you."

I glared at him. "I'm aware of that. But something tells me you can imagine how difficult this is for me."

"Dealing with exes, in any form, sucks."

"It does. But it's up to us to work past it. Isn't it?"

He rubbed his beard and gave me his first genuine smile since I got here. "Something tells me you're almost as ready to do that as I am."

"Maybe."

chapter twenty-eight

My mind wouldn't stop churning with realizations.

Information.

Schemes.

Yes, schemes. Things were becoming very clear to me.

If Monica, that bitch, wanted to play games, I was going to have to learn to play them, too. It didn't matter that the law would be going after her, she clearly had the power to set bombs off in my direction.

And Dorian's.

She was now my target.

She'd made us her targets, first.

Admittedly, that viper had a decade of experience on me, but I had something she didn't.

Dorian's heart was mine. Calum was right about that.

It was time I fucking did something about it.

I was tripping over everything I saw, always would be. Yet, I had choices to make.

Whether I kept my man or not.

"Are you listening?" Angelina asked me over the phone.

I unlocked my door, shopping bags in hand, and walked into

my apartment. Almost immediately I could tell it was empty and that my mother wasn't there. "You've only been working there for three weeks, and you've already mastered this whole thing?"

"*Ne sois pas frustrant*," she grumbled in French. Don't be frustrating. "You know very well this is what my mother did for a living. Different times, but public relations remain the same."

Very true. Her mother, Janelle Molyneux, had weathered a few complicated scandals back in her day, before she moved with Ang to France. "And your job is okay with you handling this, although you just started?"

"Of course not. Not the Davis' account. Lord forbid."

I cringed at the way she said that. Walking into my bedroom, I dropped my shopping bags on the bed. "You can't mean . . ."

"Oh yes. Your parents' divorce is already tainting you with the delicious stain of infamy. When I mentioned, in confidence, that you're dating Dorian Sorensen and shit is about to hit the fan, my boss practically threw the phone at me and asked me to call you back."

"Oh Jesus."

"They're assigning a professional to your account, and I'll be 'shadowing', so to speak. We'd like to meet with you to sign the contract tomorrow."

I eyed the Neiman Marcus and Louboutin bags on my bed. "What if I'm planning to unleash a scandal tonight?"

Angelina was quiet for a moment. "Demitra . . . What are you planning?"

"Exactly what I just mentioned." Thanks to my mother, who was surprisingly on board with my plan, I was able to find out that there was a very important event taking place tonight.

An event that a certain executive had no choice but to attend.

The question was which event, and where?

The only reason my mother even found out was because of the whispers going down the grapevine. A lot of the single women in our class kept tabs on where every eligible bachelor went, or at least tried to find it out.

It was such petty, antiquated bullshit, and a stark reminder of what I'd have to deal with while being with Dorian.

I was always going to have to deal with it. Even if I'd never seen those videos.

"You do know the whole point of PR is to avoid crisis situations as much as possible, right?"

"Ang. There is no avoiding crisis situations when it comes to *this* situation. I'm unleashing my own scandal before someone else unleashes one on me, and I need you to promise me that you guys can navigate this ship where I want it to go." I pushed the curled ends of my hair over my shoulder—another change. I'd had the ends permed into big, loose curls this morning. The rest of my hair was still straight, but the new ends gave me a whole different look.

I'd seemed older when I saw my reflection in the salon. Sexier. *Edgier*.

Exactly what I'd been hoping for.

Angelina's squeal of excitement was such a delayed reaction that I jumped at the sound of it. "I'm not going to say I am Team Dorian, but I am so Team *This*!"

"So you're in? You can start tonight?"

"What exactly are you planning, *mademoiselle?*"

Sitting on my bed, I told her. Every detail, what the endgame was.

And that I didn't know where I was ending up tonight, only that wherever it was, I planned to show up dressed to fucking kill.

"This is going to be the funnest period of our lives." Was that a sniff I just heard on her end of the phone? "It's almost worth convincing Liv to forgive Calum. Imagine the shock ripples. There are some stuck-up assholes that really need to see these kinds of things happen."

I wisely kept my mouth shut. She was only excited because it was me and Liv. If it were her in our place with Lucas . . . "I just have to find out where I'm heading."

"I know exactly who you're going to call, and yes, *you* are doing it. No way I'm going to make that call for you."

"Why not?" I teased, although I already knew the answer.

"For what? So he can tell me again how he supposedly spends his nights alone in bed now, fantasizing about me, and fucking his hand? No thank you."

I choked on my own saliva. Coughing, I tried to expel that image out of my head. "He did not say that to you."

"He most certainly did." And there was no mistaking the breathlessness in her tone.

My poor friend was a guitar string one pluck away from snapping.

No wonder she couldn't handle even hearing his voice on the phone.

"Okay . . . Well, TMI Ang."

"Oh. Please. Like you don't have experience with such things."

"Yes. Yes I do." After all, Dorian had that same intensity, and I'd been helpless under the onslaught of it.

"I need your social media passwords. And I have the perfect dress for tonight, haven't worn it before now."

"Wait, you're coming?"

"If you're going to go around triggering scandals, my love, you need someone from your PR team there to take pictures, and manage your social media. Duh? Anyway, let me know where we're meeting up and send me those passwords. I need to start getting ready."

"I need his cell number, Ang." Since he'd been all but stalking her as he tried to seduce her, I knew she had it.

"Ugh. Fine. I'll send it. But don't tell him you got it from me." She hung up the phone on me.

I stared down at my cell, bemused. He was going to know I got it from her. Who else would it have been? When her text with his number came through, I wasted no time dialing it.

It took a few rings, but eventually he answered. "Hello?"

"Hello, Lucas. It's Demi."

His shocked pause was to be expected. "Demitra . . . How . . . Oh."

My lips twitched. Told you he'd know how I got his number.

"I'm assuming Ang gave you my number for a reason. What can I do for you?"

I wasted no time getting to business. "Where's your friend going to be tonight?"

"Uhhhh, Dorian? I . . . You can't ask him yourself? I'm pretty sure he'd be ecstatic to know that you're hunting for his whereabouts, and whatnot."

"Lucas, I need his surprise to be genuine, therefore I need *you* to tell me where he is. And to keep this call between us for now."

"You plotting women scare me."

I giggled. "We should. Ang should scare you most of all."

"Oh, she does. She really, really does. Speaking of her . . . Is she going?"

God, he was like an eager puppy with a bone. His tone made me laugh this time, but I was already determined to help one Alexander brother with his woman. Lucas and Ang were a situation I wasn't ready to touch. "Not sure. But if you know where Dorian is going to be, and you want to help your friend out, tell me which event he's attending."

"Fine. But you're going to owe me a favor and I'll come collecting when it's the right time."

Poor Ang was so, so screwed.

29

The almost billion dollar home my mother's driver pulled up to was exactly as it was originally advertised—a staggering, massive, near perfect replica of a 17th century French château. It was breathtaking on first sight.

Made of white limestone, the two story, over twenty-thousand square foot home screamed affluence and excess like only mini-palaces could.

I knew how much it'd cost because my mother was close friends with Sherri Goff, the wife of billionaire Norman Goff.

As the car slowed to a stop in front of the black wrought-iron and glass door, I had to admit to myself: it was the perfect place for what I was planning.

A better setting could not have been scripted.

The door was opened by one of the uniformed young men awaiting next to the driveway. I exited, careful with the short train of my dress. The man who opened my door stared a little too long at my body, and I knew exactly why.

I chose this dress for a reason.

It was the same color as my skin tone, an effect that made it seem as if I was nude except for the jeweled filigree design spread throughout. A corset-like waist within the dress made my curves stand out even more. One shoulder was bared; a strap rose from the side of the dress, wrapping around my other shoulder, where it fell to the ground to join the short train.

Nude Louboutins and large, diamond chandelier earrings finished off the look.

If I was going to step into a realm filled with vipers, I had to be ready to be just as brash as they could be.

Perhaps more.

Besides, I was here to reclaim what was mine. To seduce the love of my life all over again. No, it wouldn't be rainbows and roses on the other side, but it was better than the emptiness I'd been living in.

The emptiness I'd condemned us both to exist with when I decided to walk away.

Determination settled over me. Head held high, I walked to the door. Another man opened it for me, bowing at the waist, and considering that wasn't a standard greeting in America, regardless of station, I took it as the compliment it was.

Sheer palatial elegance greeted me within the foyer. The floor was white, grey-veined marble, a favorite among our social class. A massive crystal chandelier overhead added its glow to the natural sunlight pouring in from all angles.

The entire home was breathtaking from what I could see, but it didn't hold my attention for long. Standing in front of an archway leading deeper into the home, Angelina called my name and waved me over.

People turned to stare as I passed. Some did a double-take. If they disapproved, I didn't know and didn't care. My generation was known for pushing the boundaries with our revealing clothing, especially at these types of events. I, myself, always dressed as sexy as I wanted.

This just happened to be the first time I was this brazen.

My father was going to have a fucking heartattack if he found out, and I honestly didn't care.

Angelina rushed to meet me halfway in her black heels. That skin tight, dark green gown brought out the shade of her light green eyes, and I wondered in the back of my mind if Lucas would actually show up here to search for her.

Because, if he was, he was going to die at the sight of her.

"Jesus," Ang hissed, eyes glittering with excitement. "You aren't playing around."

"I'm here to reclaim my man. Of course I'm not."

"Speaking of him, I already saw him inside the ballroom. Yes, he's dancing with some of the ladies, but trust me, girl, he's mentally a million miles away."

My heart thumped hard against my chest.

Dorian was mentally with me, she meant.

How did I know? I practically felt it, the pull of his love and desire strong enough to break down my walls. To overpower my resentment.

Weeks without him had torn me down. His obvious agony over losing me would forever be embedded in my soul.

"You were able to log into my accounts with no problem, right?" I asked Ang. The plan was that she'd stay in the background and capture the best images possible.

Images of my reunion with Dorian.

If he'd have me.

A cold sweat threatened, and my throat tightened with anxiety. His messages to me remained the same—loving, caring—but he hadn't mentioned us getting back together again. Hadn't mentioned anything about his search for a new home.

It'd only been three days since my visit to his penthouse to meet

BOOK THREE   201 his attorney. I was being irrational. Needy. A position I found myself in because of my own choice.

A choice born of emotion.

Heartbreak.

I hated to use the word trauma, but sometimes I had flashbacks of those videos so intense, that I could barely function past them.

"Demi? Are you listening?"

I blinked into focus and found Angelina's green stare inches from my own. "Sorry. You were saying?"

"*Mon Dieu*, girl. I said I'm logged in and ready to go. Now go get your man. You're almost as much of a mess as Liv."

My eyes narrowed as I glared at her. "Lucas might be here tonight. Good luck." I left her sputtering angrily behind me.

I'd never been here before, but the main hallway was gigantic, and every ten feet or so, liveried servants in white uniform either offered a refreshment or pointed in the direction of the ballroom.

The event began two hours ago; I planned to arrive once it was in full swing for maximum impact.

Everyone must have been in the ballroom, or roaming around this sumptuous home. I was the only one in this hallway except for the servants—

I saw her before she saw me. The fact that she was facing away from me and I still knew it was her sickened me. I not only loathed that woman, but wished with every fiber of my being that she didn't have such an impact on me.

Maybe she sensed my venomous stare, or somehow felt my intent encroaching into her personal space.

Monica stared over her shoulder, straight black hair sliding along her tanned back. She was wearing a white dress, the color of my gown that night in Chicago when she fucked up my life. I had no doubt she looked spectacular in it.

She always did.

I refused to let it intimidate me, but I couldn't deny the memories of those videos threatened to overwhelm me again.

Turning to face me, she attempted something akin to a sneer, yet her gaze kept bouncing up and down my body.

Even she was impressed, and the bitch would rather be caught dead than admit it.

Good. Exactly the effect I was going for.

"I didn't have to look for you. Perfect. I'm going to say something, and you're going to listen to me," I said.

Ire flashed in her expression. "Excuse me, little girl?"

I held up one nude-tipped nail, silencing her. "Actually, if we're going based on behavior, the only child here is you. I'm pretty sure by now you know my man isn't messing around. Thankfully for you, that ballroom is probably over a thousand-feet. Remember, five-hundred is as close as you can get, or—"

Monica stepped into my personal space, seething. "Are you fucking threatening me?"

I laughed. "I haven't gotten to my threat, yet. I'm reminding you of Dorian's. The restraining order says five-hundred feet. Learn it. Live it. Fucking abide by it."

She opened her mouth to retort once more.

"No," I snapped, talking over her. "I love him, and you've already cost me enough time with him. You won't be doing it anymore. And although you love him, too—"

"*What.*"

It wasn't a question, more of a horrified whisper.

"Yeah, you do, that's why you're losing your shit over him. The problem with you is that you're too emotionally stunted to understand that love, and it doesn't fucking matter. Because he's mine. Mine. And you're going to stay the hell away from him."

Her dark pink lips moved wordlessly.

I dismissed her with a disgusted look and walked around her

toward the ballroom doors. When two servants reached to open them for me, I shook my head at them.

I would be the one opening those doors.

My entrance depended on it.

"You won't win," I heard behind me suddenly. "I don't even care anymore if he comes back to me, but we both know he will. I've been here forever. You're nothing but a child that's managed to confuse him. He'll get bored of you eventually."

The reminder of how long they'd been lovers set off a wave of acid fire in my veins.

I placed my hands on the doors and turned my head to stare at her over my shoulder, as she had done when sensing me coming closer. "Monica, let me put this as simply as possible: come near my man again, and I'm going to break your fucking face."

And I pushed those doors open, shoving her to the back of my mind and focusing on my search for Dorian.

chapter thirty

I didn't expect to find Dorian as soon as I walked into the ballroom. The space was massive, almost as large as the one in our hotel in Chicago. Yet I shouldn't have doubted that I would.

His pull was inexorable.

Undeniable.

No more than ten steps into the room, I lost my breath at the sight of him, a blow that gave me no choice but to pause.

The sea of people that surrounded me faded into the background.

Even the woman he was currently slow-dancing with blurred in my vision. He was the only point of focus. The only point that mattered.

As Ang had mentioned, he was detached from his current situation. Those piercing blue eyes I adored were fixed above the woman's head, staring unseeing into the distance.

Although this was a gala, the eclectic Goffs had decided to eschew the black-tie portion of the event.

Dorian's suit was bright, eye-popping, different from what he'd usually wear.

It was a light-grayish blue with pinstripes, and it'd obviously been tailored specifically for him. The most eye-popping part of that outfit was the light orange tie, an unexpected splash of color that worked too well with his light coloring. Those blond curls were combed back, a single strand falling in front of his slightly darker eyebrows.

Polished black Ferragamo's finished off the look. I knew what type of shoes they were because they were Dorian's favorite dress shoes.

Just one look at him and I was trembling.

Wet.

Needy.

I'd been out of my mind to run from that man, to let him go. I knew that. The universe knew that. Setting him free meant risking that chance that some other woman would have him one day.

I'd kill them both.

Awful. Psychotic. Irrational. And yet it was the truth nonetheless.

That was mine. All mine. He'd said so. He'd *made* it so.

Whoever that woman in his arms was, she needed to go.

Now.

It wasn't lost on me that I had become the center of attention myself. That my lack of movement served to aim that spotlight on me even more.

Good. That part was according to the plan.

So was what came next.

My skin broke out in goosebumps from the reality that I was about to be with him again. That I'd have him in my hands once more.

The whispers and heads turning must've finally registered to Dorian. Right as I took my first step to begin walking toward him again, his head jerked in my direction.

As if he, too, were being pulled.

Shock fluttered across his face. He all but stumbled to a stop, the woman in his arms forgotten. Those gorgeous lips I loved to suck on parted.

Nothing could've stopped me. Nothing.

I knew there was no mistaking the force of each step I took, nor my intent behind them. My entire body vibrated with the need to be close to him once more.

To get rid of whoever that was in his arms.

I powered through the crowd straight to them, giving the people on the dancefloor no choice but to part.

Then, *finally*, I was right there.

Where I needed to be.

Where I always would be from now on.

Dorian was practically glaring at me with the intensity of his confusion and fury, and I had no doubt this dress was pissing him off.

My heart tripped even more. I needed that possessiveness from him. That sign that he was still with me, despite the distance I'd imposed.

"Sorry," I told the woman. "This one is mine. You'll have to find another dance partner." As I'd done with the crowd, I muscled my way between them, giving her no other option but to step back.

I slid my hand over Dorian's shoulder, and grabbed his other hand, resting my fingers in the cradle between his thumb and forefinger, as was standard for the waltz.

His arm snapped around my waist, as if on instinct, and I had to bite back a whimper. "Demi . . . what in the flying fuck are you wearing?"

My hand on his shoulder slid up the back of his neck, into his hair. "Aren't you going to kiss your girlfriend hello?" Not that I gave him a chance. The last thing I saw were those turbulent eyes, that tensed brows, those lips parting on a shaky breath . . . my whimper broke free and I tugged his head down.

Our lips connected in a lush, smooth kiss that started out

innocently enough.

That lasted about a second.

Dorian's groan of agony shot straight into my core. His hold on me became painful, unrelenting.

Against my stomach, even through the inner corset of my gown, I felt his dick harden on a rush.

He tilted his head, his tongue invading me.

The moan that left me was indecent, improper. If I'd been in my right mind, I would've worried about the people around us hearing it.

Instead, I was a raging inferno inside. My entire being burned with lust.

With love for him.

Dorian kissed me with everything he had, almost bowing me back in his hold, and it still wasn't enough.

Lost in the feel of his tongue, his lips, I stopped caring about the massive audience around us. It was just him and I in that moment, trapped in this greedy reunion that should've never been necessary.

I'd done this to us when I ran.

Monica did this to us when she started her war.

And right then, we were reconnecting with everything we had.

Dorian was the first to pull away, lips wet from our kisses. Even though he managed to control his expression, his raging breaths gusted across my mouth. His heart was a tribal beat against my own. "Demi," he groaned under his breath. He began swaying me back and forth to the music, and I knew it was only because it occurred to him that we were in public. "You're fucking naked."

I giggled, delirious with the taste of him. With his scent and heat so close. "I'm not, and you know it. It only looks that way. I promise."

"You're wearing this on fucking purpose and I'm about to come all over you. In front of everyone here." His gaze became unfocused with his desire, and I had to bite my lip to hold back another whimper.

"How about inside me?"

His hand flexed along my lower back. "Oh God, baby. It's been weeks since you gave me that—"

"We made each other come in the alley," I reminded him, although I really didn't want him thinking of me and Keith right then.

He led me in a circle around a group of people. "*Inside* you, Demi." He lowered his head, lips tantalizingly close to mine. "I miss your perfect pussy and you damn well know it."

My heart cracked open and bled for him, even as my body throbbed with a wild hunger that was starting to frighten me. "I'm sorry. I couldn't deal. I shouldn't have run. I love you and I've missed—"

He silenced me with another hard, wet kiss. The entire time, he led me. In the back of my mind, I thought it was for the sake of keeping up the appearance of the dance.

When Dorian pulled back, chest racing, I realized he'd led us right off the dance floor.

In plain view of everyone watching us—and I do mean *everyone* was watching—he spun me around until my back was pressed to his front.

I nearly stumbled in my nude heels at the feel of his hard cock against my ass.

"Walk in front of me, baby, or they're going to see just how close to coming you have me," Dorian demanded, leading me straight through an archway—

And into another hallway.

Where Monica-fucking-Adamo was waiting, her lip curled into a sneer.

chapter thirty-one

Dorian bumped into my back, which only served to bring my attention to his raging erection even more.

"Do you think that putting on that little show will change anything?" Monica asked, and for the first time since meeting her I had to wonder if she was truly mentally ill.

Dorian's hand wrapped around my nape, holding me in place.

Did he think I would run?

Or was my sudden instinct to destroy that woman so obvious?

"If you don't move out of our way, I'm going to make sure we give *you* a show," I warned her, purposely pressing back into my man and basking in the feel of his tense body.

He was practically vibrating with need and I could finally lay a claim on him in front of everybody.

Monica's smile was pure maliciousness. "There's more videos where the first two came from. Let me know if *you'd* like some more shows to watch."

More videos.

Of them.

Together.

With others.

Dorian used his hold on my nape to jerk me to the side and he began leading me around Monica. "Five-hundred feet. It was made fucking clear. I'll make sure to let the authorities know you didn't understand the instructions as they were given to you. And if you threaten Demi again, I'll do much worse to you than I'm planning."

The desperation vibrating through his body was the only salvation I had. My mind was spinning with the reality that they'd recorded more.

Years.

That's how long they were lovers. Fucking *years*.

Just how many videos were we talking about?

"Oh? And I'll be more than happy to inform them of that little girl's threat to break my face," she called out as we left her behind.

"You did what now?" Dorian asked near my ear.

"I fucking meant it, too." He began herding me up a curving staircase that was much smaller than the one in the main foyer. "And right now I kind of want to do the same to you for recording yourself with her so many goddamned times!" I hissed over my shoulder.

Tears threatened.

The agony of those memories mixed with the frenzy of lust that pulsated through my entire being. I needed him like I'd never needed him before.

I'd seen him fucking two women at the same time.

Worse, I saw him fucking just her, and in that video, there was no mistaking the similarities between them, and how he took me each time.

We reached the landing and he wasted no time leading me toward the first door he found. "I had Joey destroy every one of my copies, so there was no risk of me viewing them again. Every single one is gone, Demi. Forever." Without even bothering to knock, he jerked the door open. "And I'm going to make sure every copy she has is also destroyed. I'm going to eradicate her and those videos, so help me God."

I'd never loved him more than I did then.

But my decision to fight for us—to fight for him—didn't mean I'd forgotten the torment of what I saw on those videos.

I was all but pushed inside the room. I caught a glimpse of pale blue walls with Boiserie panels, a white, marble fireplace, and pale blue and gold furniture.

It was a small sitting room.

And Dorian was determined to lock us inside it.

I turned around in time to see him closing the door and flipping the lock. If I'd thought his gaze was turbulent on the dancefloor when he first saw me, it was nothing compared to then. "You're going to stop thinking about those videos and get over here."

We were going to fuck each other senseless in here. That knowledge was inescapable and heavy in the air, suffocating me as much as my heartache was. "I never forget about them. They're always right here." I jammed my finger into my forehead as I said it.

The pained sound he made was worse than getting slapped.

Dorian reared off the door and came at me like a whirlwind. Hands around my face, he brought me close. "It's too late now. You claimed me down there, in front of the whole fucking world. You aren't leaving me again."

My knees went weak from desire. "You are mine, you fucking asshole, and for the rest of my life I'll always know what you look like fucking someone else."

His hands shot into my hair and tugged my head back roughly. "It was nothing like you and me. *Nothing*. And if I didn't prove that to you already, I'm sure as hell going to prove it now." He devoured my mouth without mercy. Even if I'd wanted to deny the crude thrusts of his tongue, it was impossible. He dominated me with his hold, with his brutal kiss, and began leading me again.

Between kisses, he mumbled words against my lips.

Words I barely heard past our panting breaths and my frantic whimpers.

He kissed me until my lips hurt, until I couldn't think straight. Then, he ripped his lips away from me, even though he knew it'd drive me crazy.

Before I could bring him back to me, he spun me around to face one of the settees.

A settee that happened to be positioned in front of an extra large, gold framed mirror.

I was pushed onto my knees on that settee and bent over the back of it in seconds.

Dorian's reflection in the mirror froze me in place.

The deadly intent on his harsh expression was the most gorgeous thing I'd ever seen. I understood the fierce emotions he was battling. Understood his rabid urge to claim me in a way that would ensure I never left again.

I wish I could own him in a way that would erase his past and the impact it was having on us.

An impossible wish, and the fact it could never happen drove me mad.

Dorian yanked the gauze of my skirt up over my ass. His eyes flared at the sight of my intricate, crotchless thong, and his tongue slid out to wet his kiss-swollen lips. "You're lucky I know you wore this for me."

I didn't get a chance to respond.

In his suit, he reared over me from behind. I hadn't felt or noticed him freeing his dick, but suddenly it was right there, nudging against the tight opening of my—

He took me with a ruthless, brutal roll of his hips.

I was soaked down to my thighs.

His invasion seared me with a fiery ache regardless.

It was nothing compared to the pleasure, the all-consuming relief of having him in me again. I'd take any kind of pain just to have that. My eyes rolled upward. My back arched. I trembled against the settee.

Dorian snarled behind him, hips twitching to shove himself even deeper. "God damn, Demi. God damn."

I gasped as his cock somehow got even harder inside me. Forcing myself to open my eyes, I was hit with the vision we made—with that near violent, agonized look on his face.

He fisted my hair, pulling me back as he loved to do, inundating me with a different set of memories.

Him.

Me.

The ways he loved to own my body.

My pussy pulsed around him. "*Dorian.*"

"You know very well that I've never felt this way with anyone else," he murmured in a silky, dangerous voice. His free hand slid up my chest to wrap languidly around my throat. "But in case you forgot, I'm about to show you."

His name left me again.

Desperately.

Brokenly.

He cut off the word with a simple tightening of his hand.

Grinding his teeth, he began pounding me into the settee, hard enough to send it skidding across the floor. I couldn't even cry out at the mind-blowing sensation. Couldn't even warn him that I was already close. Too close. My walls were swollen, throbbing harder, milking him as my body prepared to hurdle over that edge . . .

Dorian leaned down near my ear, holding my gaze in the mirror, and he started fucking *talking*. "I'm addicted to this pussy. To your mouth. I'm going to fuck you in the ass, too, one day. Take you there and make you fucking love it. I'll be the first and the last to do that to you, to make you take my cum in there, and you're going to beg me to do it to you over and over again. And it doesn't matter if I've done that with anyone else. You know why?" He began rotating and slamming his hips against me, screwing me hard enough to bruise me. The sound of my wet pussy taking his cock filled the room, followed by his mindless grunts each time he hit the end of me. "Because I never loved any of them. Damn you, I've never loved anyone until you. Only you, Demi. Only. Fucking. You."

I couldn't breathe, his hold on my throat was too tight.

Didn't matter.

I flew over that edge into the messiest, craziest orgasm of my life.

Dorian chose that moment to ease his hold on my throat.

The horny, nearly inhumane sounds leaving me became the dominant sound in the room.

No doubt we could be heard from outside.

I didn't care. Couldn't care. My core clenched around him and I kept coming so hard, my hips arching back to take more of his dick.

"Fuck. Fuck. You're squirting. Shit, baby." Reaching around me, he found my clit and began rubbing it, giving me no choice but to feel how much wetness I was leaking around him.

I lost my hold on the settee with a breathless cry as a second orgasm came at me out of nowhere.

"Holy fuck, it's all over me. All over my pants, my clothes. You want that. You want everyone to see it on me. To know what we were doing to each other in here." He yanked me back into him, fucking me harder, his face glistening with sweat. "Give me that mouth. Give it to me, Demi, I'm about to—"

I leaned back, our lips colliding.

One feel of my tongue and he froze, his pained growl the most delicious sound I'd ever heard. Tasted.

He shook through each wave, his erection pulsating inside me.

I ground my hips against him, taking all of it, wanting more.

"I love you, Demi," he rasped against my mouth. "Say it. Tell me you still feel it." He pressed his still pulsing dick deeper inside me. "Say it."

"You know I love you, Dorian."

"You're not leaving me ever again," he swore in a hoarse voice. "You're going to stay right by my side and we're going to fix this fucking mess. Together. It's going to hurt like crazy, and I'm going to love you through each moment of it. Even on the days you hate me. I won't let you break this off again. Do you understand?"

chapter thirty-two

My presence at the gala ended up being short-lived. Not that we had a choice to stay. Dorian hadn't been lying when he said I squirted all over his clothes; my hair and make-up were wrecked beyond repair.

Yes, I came here to unleash my own scandal, but even I knew that showing ourselves in front of the guests like this would be taking it a step too far.

Dorian had visited this home before. Therefore, he knew how to maneuver us to the side exit, which led to the road that wrapped around the house. Carl was already waiting for us in the Rolls-Royce.

We took one step outside and Dorian jerked to a stop, his hand around my arm. "We need to get your coat."

"I didn't bring one."

He threw me a look that confused me.

Until Dorian rushed to slip off his suit jacket and wrap it around me. "It isn't summer. In fact, it's one step away from winter. You came out naked in this weather."

I couldn't help but laugh. "I'm not naked. I told you already."

He threw me an impatient look next.

"Dorian?"

I tensed at the sound of that feminine voice calling his name. Every instinct I had flared. I already knew what was coming.

Why there was a woman approaching us—approaching *Dorian*, to be exact.

He exhaled, nostrils flaring. When he turned to see who it was, his jaw hardened.

Which solidified my suspicion.

"I'm sorry. I can't talk right now. I need to get my girlfriend home." He placed a hand on my lower back and began leading me to the car.

"Girlfriend? Oh."

I guess whoever she was didn't see our kiss in the ballroom.

Carl stepped out of the car and opened the back door for us.

Despite all my warnings to myself, I snuck a glance at the woman.

Gorgeous, as they all were. Tall. Curvy. A red-head.

Because my man didn't seem to have a fixed type. His only requirement was that they were stunning. A connoisseur of women.

I had to remind myself of what happened upstairs. Of the fact that I was the only woman he'd ever claimed to love.

Sliding into the car, I wrapped his suit jacket tighter around me.

Dorian joined me in a rush. His worried expression broke my heart. He wasted no time intertwining our fingers and cupping my chin. "Are we okay?"

I had to learn to control my reactions. It wasn't fair to him if he had to walk around constantly afraid because his lovers were everywhere to be found, and I was too possessive to handle it. "We're okay."

"Home, sir?" Carl asked Dorian.

Dorian's hesitation was clear as day.

He was afraid to take me back to his place now that I'd seen those videos.

It killed me that he was right. We'd made our own memories there, but I wasn't sure if they'd be strong enough to stop me from feeling unsettled at his place. "Take us to my apartment, Carl," I said on a whim.

My boyfriend's relieved smile lit up the entire limo.

My boyfriend. It was the first time in five months that I allowed myself to think of him in that way.

My answering smile was as big as his.

"I WANT YOU TO COME WITH ME WHEN I START SEEING PLACES this week." Dorian petted Beck, who was laying between us on my bed.

He was naked and relaxed under the covers.

As if he didn't just move our relationship even further with that one comment.

I was naked under the covers, as well. He'd wasted no time ripping our clothes off as soon as we stepped foot in my apartment.

Thank God my mother wasn't home. I'd forgotten she was staying with me when I suggested that we go there.

"It makes sense," he continued, his gaze on our puppy. The more I studied him, the more I noticed how false his relaxed state was. He was only pretending to be at ease for my benefit. "You should help me pick it out and make sure it's a place you'll be comfortable in."

My breath caught.

Was he implying what I thought he was?

A strange giddiness flowed through me. Even so, I did my best to maintain a straight face. "Dorian . . . you don't think it's too soon for something like that?"

Piercing blue eyes flew up to lock on mine. Aside from that, his body remained the same, and his hand didn't pause as he continued to pet Beckham. "Do *you*?"

I should've. But the more I thought about it, the more excited I was becoming. "It's only been four months." My voice was breathless and the excuse sounded feeble even to my own ears.

His voice, by contrast, was firm. Determined. "Five months. Those three weeks we were separated don't matter. We were still together and you know it."

He was right. I did. We'd felt each other every moment of that separation, which is what led me back to him in the end. "Okay." I raised a hand to hide my burgeoning smile. "I'll go look at places with you."

"Come here." Grinning, he tugged my hand away and dragged me over for a kiss.

We were lost in each other's lips, with our puppy barking for attention between us, when a commotion outside the room pulled us apart.

It was the front door opening.

My mother's voice rang out.

But she wasn't the only one.

"Did our daughter invite you here?" my mother yelled.

"I'm allowed to come see both of you!"

I shot up on the bed, gasping.

"This is considered harassment, Stephen. And I am not in the mood for it. I don't want to see you. There's nothing left for us to say—"

My mother's sudden silence was the precursor of a heavy, strained pause.

One that was broken by my father, who had clearly stumbled upon our discarded clothes. "Do you see this? Do you see how she's behaving? She's probably back there with him doing—"

"What she's doing is none of your business!"

My mother's defense of me barely registered before my father continued.

"Or is she with someone else? What have you taught our daughter that she thinks it's okay to behave like a slut?"

Dorian was off the bed in a flash.

I whispered his name, scrambling with the covers as I tried to follow him.

He rushed over to the dresser, where he'd left some of his clothes weeks ago. I barely made it off the bed, and he was already dressed in a pair of sweats.

Yanking a white t-shirt over his head, he threw my door open and stormed outside.

Beck ran after him, barking again.

I ran to the same dresser, shaking. My mind struggled with the turmoil, and I pulled out the first item I found.

It happened to be one of Dorian's dress shirts, but I didn't have time to find anything else. I could hear my father and Dorian's raised voices.

Rushing to button it up, I took the same path Dorian just traveled. The scene I found in my living room was exactly what I'd expected and feared.

My mother was standing between Dorian and my father.

She had her hands on Dorian's chest and was urging him to walk backward.

"You will never insult her that way again. Do I make myself clear?" Dorian's voice was calm and deadly.

The way he stared at my father sent a shiver down my spine.

My father's light blue eyes—eyes I inherited—jerked toward me. When he saw what I was wearing, his lip curled into a sneer. "Do you know that I offered him the chance to make you an honest woman and he turned it down? He doesn't want to marry you, he only wants to use you."

I reeled with shock, stunned that my own father was acting this way.

I should've accepted it by now. His actions lately had revealed the dirty truth about who he was. Yet, I still hadn't fully assimilated the facts. Not when it came to him.

"That's not what happened, and you know it!" Dorian snapped.

"Did I not tell you that you could marry her and I'd give my blessing?" my father snapped back.

My mother turned to face my father, aghast. "You will not do to Dorian what you did to me for money!"

"You heard Antonia," Dorian said. "And that is between Demitra and I. It's none of your business when I decide to ask her."

Wait, what?

My knees almost buckled. I had to place a hand on the hallway wall to stop myself from collapsing.

When, not if.

Spinning.

My mind was fucking spinning.

"I suggest you leave, Stephen. Neither Demitra nor Antonia invited you here."

"I can come see my daughter whenever I want, and you will not stand in my way of doing so."

No matter how much my heart was raging, and my mind struggled to comprehend what I'd just heard, I had to take control of this situation.

If I didn't, every part of me screamed that my father and my boyfriend were about to physically attack each other.

In my living room.

I found the willpower to steady my voice and meet my father's stare head on. "You need to leave. Now. I don't want to talk to you, I don't want to see you, and frankly? I don't know when that's ever going to change. So just go. Before I call security and tell them to come escort you out."

chapter thirty-three

Being in school always turned out to be a headtrip for me. For months now, I'd felt like I was living two separate lives, and neither one seemed to meld well with the other.

It was my last year in school, unless I decided to pursue a Masters in Enterprise Risk Management.

I was undecided as of yet. I'd taken classes in Risk Management, but I wasn't sure if I wanted to go through more years of schooling.

Seated in one of the antique, classic classrooms that Columbia University boasted, I set up my tablet and keyboard on the tablet arm of my chair. I was one of the first students in class, which afforded me a few minutes to myself.

My entire degree was centered on business. However, as I thought about my possible Masters, my mind couldn't help but apply the basics of my possible future major to my current life situation.

Enterprise Risk was based on four concepts: financial risks, strategic risks, operational risks, and risks associated with accidental losses. A risk manager researched those potential risks in order to inform the leaders of a company and try to, at best, prevent them.

Or, at worse, mitigate them.

If I thought of Dorian and I in those terms, I could foresee no way of preventing the risks—i.e; potential fallouts—of our situation. It was known throughout history that women could be vicious creatures.

It was even more true among our social class, with daddy's little princesses being raised to believe that everything they wanted was their due.

While I believed Monica was truly mentally ill and a one-of-a-kind threat, that didn't mean there weren't others waiting in the trenches. I doubted they'd stir trouble to the level Monica had.

But they'd insert themselves with their flirtatious yearning and inappropriate comments.

Men had an incredible ability to forget the women they'd had one-night stands with.

Women, from what I'd seen so far, were not the same. Every woman Dorian slept with in the past seemed to remember him, whether it was one night or not.

It made me sick to my stomach to admit I couldn't blame them.

I could try to inure myself to the constant interruptions everywhere we went. I might even succeed to a certain extent, too. Yet, even the hardest of people would eventually find themselves torn down.

There were only two possible options I could foresee that might work: inundate people's consciousness with the magnitude of our connection in the hopes that most of those women would take the hint and eventually back off.

Or ride it out, let time pass. Again, with the hopes that they would eventually back off.

Getting married would certainly speed up the process.

The thought came out of nowhere and bathed me in a cold sweat instantly.

I would not go there. I would not read into Dorian's comment to my father. I would not become that girl, the one that pined for something as serious as a marriage and subconsciously pushed her boyfriend to take their relationship there.

I wasn't even twenty-one, yet, for fuck's sake. Was that something I was even ready for?

Anyway, it was on Dorian if he ever wanted that, and it would be on his timeframe. Not mine. Eleven-years separated us, so I couldn't say I was in a hur—

Someone plopped into the seat next to me. "Demi!"

My head jerked up.

Angelina had transferred to Columbia last semester to finish her final year with me, and this was one of the classes we shared together. Cheeks pink from the cold, she looked gorgeous, and excited. Her pale green eyes shimmered. "Have you seen?" She shoved her phone in my face.

It was the picture of Dorian and I that she took at the gala. She'd captured the moment when we'd first reunionited with that kiss, and no one could mistake the emotion coursing between us.

Dorian was holding me to him as tight as he could.

I'd given myself over to him completely and it showed on every line of my body.

The picture had gotten an insane amount of reactions since it'd gone up on my social media—some were positive, some were neutral, and some were downright negative.

I left my profile public in order to increase its reach. Unfortunately, that meant anyone could view and comment on it.

Studiously ignoring the comments had become a pastime of mine. I didn't want to see who was attached to them and possibly expose myself to the identities of Dorian's other ex-lovers.

But Ang's excitement was about a specific comment, one I hadn't seen, yet.

It was Dorian, and what he wrote sent an instant reaction through me.

Missing my girlfriend every second I'm not with her.

"Who would've thought he has that kind of romance in him?" Ang whispered breathlessly, and I couldn't help but smile at her exuberance.

"Dorian is actually a really romantic guy," I replied under my breath.

And I was missing him like crazy.

"It's almost enough to make me want one of my own."

I raised an eyebrow at her. "He's waiting for you to give him the chance. Remember?"

"Lucas?" She laughed incredulously. "Honey, he's even worse than Dorian was. And I can admit I'm nowhere near as strong as you are."

Was I really that strong? I'd left him for three weeks because I couldn't deal.

I brought out my phone to send him a text right as the professor walked in. The bulk of the students followed after.

Most went straight to their seats, minding their own business as usual.

Then there was the "Mean Girls" clique, for lack of a better nickname.

Sakina and Cecilia Gardiner.

Lily Goulding.

Reilly Haworth.

The first two were new money.

The last two were old money.

All of them disliked me with a passion simply because I refused to play along with them. Until Angelina started classes here, I kept mostly to myself.

Now, the foursome walked toward their own seats, all but snickering in my direction.

They knew.

About my father.

Definitely about Dorian.

The professor began class before they could say anything.

I knew the comments were coming regardless. They kept sneaking glances at me throughout the whole class.

My response? I sat up straighter. Jutted my chin proudly. Placed a mental brick wall between them and I. Shifted my focus to class and acted like they didn't even exist.

They were nothing but jealous girls. The world I was now playing in was full of jealous *women* with years of experience on those girls. It was better that I saved my energy for them.

It was my last class for the day and it seemed to last forever. As soon as it was over, however, I rushed to pack my things. Angelina didn't ask what my hurry was, which made me wonder if she noticed the looks those girls had been giving me.

I picked up my phone to put it in my bag and saw a text from Dorian.

'Waiting for you outside.' - D.

What? He was there? At my school?

I didn't stop to question it or respond. If he said he was outside, there was no doubting him.

My boyfriend was here to see me.

Again, at school.

After months of us keeping each other hidden, such a normal thing made my toes curl.

"He's outside," I told Ang, leaving it at that.

She gave me that excited smile again.

I gave her a quick wave and practically ran out of the classroom. The Columbia University campus was timeless and gorgeous as usual. Normally, I strolled through, soaking in the architecture and layout of the grounds.

Not today.

It took me less than five minutes to get outside. That was when I finally called Dorian. "Which entrance?" I rushed to say, not giving him a chance to greet me.

His smooth chuckle sent goosebumps through me. "I'm on Broadway, baby."

The main gate, then. "Coming." I hung up and headed in that direction.

The black gate was kept open during school hours, a massive entryway that seemed to lead away from New York and to a different town entirely. I was one of dozens of people heading out, while dozens more walked in. I passed the small guard booth, looking left and right—

A dark car was parked in front of a fire hydrant. Leaning against it? A gorgeous man with curly blond hair.

My man.

I all but squealed and ran in his direction.

Smiling, Dorian straightened off the car and swooped me into his arms for a kiss.

"You're here," I breathed against his lips.

"Left work early so I could come pick up my girlfriend," he responded, kissing me again.

I giggled between kisses. "And your girlfriend is extremely happy with you right now."

"Oh yeah?" Dorian maneuvered me so my back was against his front and took out his phone. "Happy enough to take a picture with me?"

It wasn't the first time we'd taken a picture together, but it was definitely the first time we'd done it out in the open.

In public.

Dorian aimed the camera and leaned down to kiss my cheek from behind.

My cheeks hurt from how wide I was smiling. The shot he captured showed my eyes and face glowing from happiness.

"There." Dorian dropped his phone into his pocket and turned to open the passenger door for me. "Now I have a picture to post on my own account."

I practically floated into the passenger seat.

It was a perfect moment. It felt well-earned after half-a-year of secrecy and so much drama.

And it was enough to make me forget about all the extra drama that was waiting on the sidelines and about to head our way.

For a little while, at least.

chapter thirty-four

The Irish pub I entered was packed for happy hour. It was one of thousands like it in the city, yet I couldn't deny that this one had its own type of charm. It was one of our popular hangout joints. Livana had no issues drinking here, or anywhere, since she was already twenty-two.

I couldn't deny that we'd chosen to claim this place as ours because of their lax ID policy.

Yes, I was aware I shouldn't have been drinking until I was legal. Although it wasn't our fault that this place assumed we were the right age.

As Ang liked to say: most of Europe set their legal drinking age at eighteen. America just hadn't caught up.

I bypassed the crowd hanging around the front and waved at the bartender who saw me pass. Searching for a familiar head of pale blonde hair, I weaved in and out of the crush. The noise seemed to grow louder the deeper into the bar I went.

Several guys turned to try and grab my attention. I expertly ducked out of their way and ignored their pretend-whining about how I was the one ignoring them. Finally, I spotted Livana near the end of the bar.

Her blue eyes were glued to the floor and she seemed a million miles away.

I didn't blame her. Knew why, too. She hadn't been the same since she left Calum in Chicago. It'd been almost two weeks since we last saw each other. It was right before my visit to Calum at his penthouse, and I hadn't had a chance to discuss what he said with Livana.

It needed to be done in person. I doubted she'd listen, but it was worth a try.

Her gaze was so focused on her drink that she didn't even notice me approaching. I walked right up to her and wrapped a hand around her arm.

Almost jumping a foot in the air, she steadied her drink and glared at me.

I ignored her like I'd done the guys who tried to pick me up.

Our table in the back, the round booth we always occupied, had just opened up. If we didn't grab it now, it would be taken in seconds by another group.

I rushed us straight toward the back where the booth was. When Livana dug in her heels and tried to pull her arm out of my grasp, I didn't pay attention to that, either, but it definitely struck me as weird.

We made it to the table and I wasted no time sliding in. The previous occupants had left their empty glasses, but someone would probably run over to clean them up in a bit.

Livana stood right in front of the table, glaring at it even harder than she'd glared at me.

I raised an eyebrow at her. "What?"

"Do we have to sit here of all places?" she asked. It was almost as if the table were spooking her, and for the life of me I couldn't understand why.

"We always sit here. What's the problem?"

She jerked her shoulder and the movement made the lights bounce of her dark purple, silk shell top. "Maybe we just need to try a new table. That's all."

She was wearing a tight leather jacket above the top. Dark blue jeans and black ankle boots finished off the outfit. She looked like a total badass, except she was acting the total opposite. "Do you see any other open tables?" I waved a hand in the direction of the packed bar to illustrate my point.

"Fine. Whatever." Liv threw back the rest of her drink and continued grumbling under her breath as she finally slid into the opposite side of the round booth. "There? Happy?"

"I'd ask what the fuck is wrong with you, except I already know the answer to that."

Hatred was too tame a word for the look she gave me.

As predicted, a bus boy ran up and rushed to clear the table. I'd never seen him before, but I smiled in greeting regardless.

Flustered, he almost dropped one of the glasses, and he mumbled hello under his breath.

Liv waited until he was gone to raise both eyebrows at me. "Didn't you get back with Dorian after forgiving him?"

I rolled my eyes. "I'm just being friendly, something you should try. And yes, I'm back with him. Have I forgiven him? It's hard to say. It happened before I met him, so what is there to forgive?"

"You're angry as fuck at him for doing it, regardless. If he hadn't been such a slut, there would've been nothing for you to see. Nothing to have thrown in your face and break your heart." She let loose a high-pitched whistle in the direction of the bar.

I was surprised the bartender, Greg, heard her above the noise of the crowd. He was at the very end of the bar and he turned in our direction at the sound.

Liv motioned to both of us, and it was clear she was telling him to get us whatever she had been drinking.

Usually, a waiter would serve us, but with the happy hour mayhem going on, it would probably be a while before one gave us attention.

Greg nodded and got right to work. If I wasn't mistaken, that was Beluga Vodka he was pouring into those glasses.

"It's fucking four," I reminded Liv.

"Some of us aren't riding on a cloud of happiness and would rather forget," she shot back.

"Yeah, that's exactly why this meeting had to happen." I left her in the booth, studying me in her confusion, as I went over to grab our drinks. "Splash some cranberry in there. Some of us aren't trying to die," I told Greg.

He laughed and did as I asked.

Returning with our drinks, I placed one in front of Livana and resumed my seat. "I'm going to talk, and for once your stubborn, damaged self is going to hear me out before you interject."

"You're the bestest friend I could've ever asked for," she faux-sang sweetly, her voice dripping with sarcasm.

I waited until her glass was at her mouth and she was swallowing to launch my first volley. "You speak of things that shouldn't have been done in the past, so I wouldn't have had to see them in the present. Then there would've been nothing to have thrown in my face and break my heart. But isn't that similar to what you did to Calum?"

Liv gagged on her drink.

"That man loves you. He's wrecked because he lost you."

"And how the hell would you know?"

Fire and fury and pure fucking brimstone was brewing in her blue eyes.

I shrank back into my seat, doubting my approach for the first time. Then again, Livana had been damaged by her ex at a young age, and it'd made her difficult to deal with. She needed a metaphorical kick in the ass to wake u—

"She knows because I told her," Calum said, appearing next to our booth.

I'd barely begun registering the shock of him being there, when he slid into the booth next to Livana.

They made a striking couple, his dark hair and hazel eyes playing off her pale blonde hair, and blue-gray eyes. My heart hurt just looking at them, at the way Calum was eating up the sight of Liv.

I didn't know when they'd last seen each other, but his expression told me it'd been a while.

"What the hell are you doing here?" Livana asked in a breathless voice as she clearly struggled to catch her breath. "Are you following me?"

"I should be," he replied smoothly, and reached across the table for her drink. He made quick work of finishing it, clearly unbothered by her indignation at his actions. "But, no. I came here for a drink . . . and the memories. Only to find you here, at our booth."

Their booth?

A light bulb went off in my head. Suddenly, Livana's aversion to the table made sense.

She'd brought him here, to our favorite hang out spot, in the past.

Not only that, but they'd clearly spent time at this booth.

"You need to leave." Liv's tone remained the same. Actually, it was smaller than before, weak, a clear indicator of what his presence was doing to her.

Calum leaned closer, one arm braced on the table's edge. "After you finally give me the time of day and let me talk."

She slapped her hand against the table. "No. And you"—she whirled on me, desperation echoing in her stare—"What does he mean that he told you? You spoke to him?"

"You really need to stop for two seconds and listen to what he has to say," I told her.

"He's not Dorian. I'm not you. This isn't something from his past that was replayed for me. He actually kissed his freaking ex."

"After having how many of your ex-lovers rubbed in his face?" I was probably being cruel, but it was for my friend's sake, as well as Dorian's friend's sake. Maybe I wouldn't give a damn how Calum was fairing, if I hadn't seen one of my closest friends deteriorating for weeks without him. "You went on a rampage against men after Corey cheated, and left trails of them in your own wake. As someone living through the mind fuck of loving a person with that kind of past, I can assure you, it's no fucking picnic. So sit the fuck down and listen to him. Just listen. And if you still don't like what he has to say, then by all means, continue running."

She blinked at me, shell-shocked.

"I love you," I told her in a calmer tone. "You're my friend. You've been wrecked for weeks and guess what? So has he. You don't need to get back together with him. I know he isn't Dorian and you're not me. I'm just asking you to listen. Okay? Can you promise me to do just that?"

Bottom lip trembling, she continued to blink back her tears, and she looked so lost, so lonely in that moment, that I wished I could just force them back together. "Fine. Okay," she mumbled in that little voice.

Calum's hand fisted on the table before curling into a fist. He threw a grateful glance my way, but it was short-lived. He couldn't keep his eyes off my friend for more than a second.

Alright. I'd done my good deed. Maybe. I hadn't expected him to show up here and interrupt my talk with her, but it was just as well.

His presence would probably have more of an impact than my words ever could.

"Forgiving them for their mistakes isn't the question. It's whether you'd be happier with or without them. Think about that." With that parting shot, I quickly exited the booth and took my cell out of my jacket.

Without looking at the couple I'd left behind, I sent a text to Dorian, warning him that I was on my way.

He was at work last I heard, but I didn't care. Seeing the pain between Calum and Liv first hand merely reminded me of everything going on between Dorian and I. I needed to be with him again. Even if it was just for a few minutes.

I'd done what I'd come here to do. Everything else but him could wait.

chapter thirty-five

T he building on East 78th was awe-inspiring. Timeless, like so many of the structures that were born out of the 18th century obsession with Classicism. Pure white on the outside, with different style windows on the top portion of the building, my jaw dropped the moment I caught sight of it.

The building itself had been here for almost a hundred years.

However, the interior had recently been gutted, one floor at a time, a renovation ten years in the making.

I stood inside the main floor of the duplex penthouse, one of only two on the upper part of the building, and this was the only one sporting the double-story, arched windows. I couldn't stop gawking for the life of me.

Dorian's old penthouse had a hell of a view.

This one was determined to outdo and eclipse that. Almost every room on this floor was its own conservatory, with views of Central Park outside most of the windows.

Sorensen International would call this one of the crown jewels in its portfolio now that the building had reopened and the new residences were up for sale.

It never occurred to me that Dorian would consider calling this home. When he said he would go apartment hunting, I never thought it would be one of the places his firm designed.

Coming up behind me, Dorian placed his hand on my lower back and nuzzled my cheek. "Someone is in love. I can tell."

As much as I loved him, I couldn't tear my gaze away from the view of this place long enough to acknowledge him.

"It truly is one of the best places to live in the city," the broker who was giving us the tour said, clearly salivating at the idea of selling this bad boy right away.

And to the owner of the company that renovated the place.

The pay cut would be astronomical. No lie.

Chuckling, Dorian led me away from the grand foyer, past one of the many sitting areas, and toward a staircase with a gorgeous balustrade that sported an eye-catching design. "If you don't mind, I think I'll tour the second floor with my girlfriend myself. I know the design by memory, after all."

Our broker had effectively been dismissed.

She wanted the paycheck too badly to object, obviously, and had no choice but to oblige.

Dorian led me up the stairs to the second floor. It was somehow even more gorgeous than the first. We passed a second sitting room, and continued down a wide hallway with a plush, beige runner. We didn't stop until we were inside what was clearly the master bedroom.

Hands around my waist, he leaned down and rested his chin on my shoulder. Together, we stood before the bed, and I knew he was waiting for me to say something.

But I couldn't. My throat was too tight. It was a struggle just to swallow.

Eventually, Dorian gave up waiting for me to talk on my own. "So? What do you think? Can you imagine it?"

"Imagine what, exactly?" I whispered. He'd hinted it, but he hadn't stated it point blank yet.

Suddenly, I really, really needed him to. Because despite all my warnings to myself not to read too much into his comments, not to dream too far into the future, or want the impossible, I was where I'd told myself I wouldn't be.

Envisioning a new phase in our relationship.

One that went so far beyond what we'd already shared.

Dorian brought me flush against him. I shouldn't have been surprised to feel his semi pressing into my ass—my man was always ready to go. We were in a room, alone, with a massive bed calling our name.

I was thinking about it.

He definitely was, too.

"You know what I'm talking about, baby." He placed a soft kiss against the side of my neck. "But since you need me to spell it out for you . . . You. Me. Here. Making this our home."

I couldn't help the gasp that escaped me at the confirmation.

He released me and stepped away.

Rooted to the spot, my mind spinning, I didn't turn to see where he went.

The bedroom door closed.

Startled, I spun to see what he was up to.

Dorian slowly made his way back to me, hands in his slacks. His erection tented his pants, and I could barely keep my eyes off it.

"Maybe you just need a bit of convincing," he murmured in a silky tone.

"Dorian . . . That lady is waiting for us . . . You haven't bought it . . ."

"Baby, I saw your eyes light up as soon as we got in here. It's practically already ours." He swept me off my feet and rushed over to the bed.

I squealed, words stuck in my throat, and next thing I knew I was on my back on the king size mattress. Spread across the luxurious, white duvet.

Dorian made quick work of my jeans, all but tearing them down my legs, ignoring every one of my weak objections. "Gotta try it out, right? See if it's the right fit?" he rasped, tugging my thong to the side.

I leaned up on my elbows, shaking from head to toe. My eyes kept darting to the closed door, expecting the broker to come through at any moment. Did he even lock it?

"Fuck. You're gorgeous. I'll never get over it," he said right against my pussy, and all it took was his breath washing over my flesh to obliterate every worry I had.

Giving into him, I slid my fingers into his curls and tugged him closer.

He didn't waste time. He never did when it came to eating me. His first lick against my clit had my back bowing off the bed.

Whimpering his name, I spread my legs wider to give him access.

Dorian wrapped his hands around my thighs, holding me open, and began eating me in that lewd way. He didn't just give me oral for my pleasure. He clearly loved eating me out, loved making out with my pussy until my clit was unbearably swollen with the need to come.

Seeing his blond head working between my legs undid me every time.

I writhed under him, fucking his tongue. In the back of my mind, I hoped to high hell these walls were perfectly soundproof.

The rest of me didn't give a damn.

Urging him on, I moaned his name, told him how much I loved his mouth on my cunt. How I wanted to ride his face every time I looked at him. How I needed to come all over his mouth and leave my scent on him.

Dorian went wild at my words, growling against me as he licked me faster. His expression was what tipped me over the edge.

The sweet, hot ache of that orgasm consumed me. When he slammed two fingers into my clutching core, I swear I saw fucking stars for the millionth time with him.

Melting onto the bed, I let my twitching legs fall open. I fully expected Dorian to rear over me and fill me with his cock. Holding out my arms, I beckoned him to me.

He came over me, but he made no move to unbutton his pants. Instead, he fisted my hair and forced me to take the thrust of his tongue into my mouth.

This kiss was just as lewd and wild as the ones he'd given me between my legs. He was forcing me to taste myself, to understand why he was so addicted. My hips churned beneath him, my pussy rubbing against his hard dick through his pants.

"Agree, Demi." Breathing harshly, he laid his forehead on mine, eyes closed. "Say you'll move in with me."

"Fuck me on this bed, and I'll agree to whatever you want."

Laughing, he shook his head and kissed my cheek. "We don't have time. We need to get back downstairs. But I need you to agree more. I don't want to be away from you and Beck anymore. You both belong with me."

Only he could bring me back to the verge of tears while leaving me dangling on the edge of lust. "You honestly don't think it's too soon?"

"Baby, we'll be together for six months in two weeks. You know I don't give a damn if anyone thinks it's too soon. You don't have to move all your stuff in right away. We can start slow. As long as you spend more of your days here in the beginning, that's enough for me. For a little while, at least."

I brushed my thumb along his lower lip. "You're a major pain in my ass sometimes, and there are some things about you that utterly break my heart. But I am madly, sickeningly in love with you. You know that?"

His answering smile was one part ecstatic, one part sad due to my comment about him breaking my heart. "You have to know by now I'll do anything to keep you."

God, I wanted him inside me so fucking bad right then. "Yeah," I whispered in a watery tone, looking into his eyes while my own threatened to flood with tears. "I'm starting to see that."

"So move in with me. Fuck everything else that's going on. This is what matters the most."

I wrapped my legs around his waist. "Okay. I'll move in with you."

His next smile damn well lit up the entire massive room.

"But only if you fuck me on this bed first. Screw the broker. I don't know why I cared in the first place."

Throwing his head back, Dorian laughed, and the sound washed over me in perfect, glowing waves.

I was moving into this amazing, jaw-dropping place with my boyfriend and our puppy.

It was going to take me years to wrap my head around it.

To believe this dream was actually true.

36

chapter thirty-six

Dorian and I stepped outside the building with the broker right behind us. The doorman gave us a half bow and wished us a good night.

We returned the sentiment. The broker—I think she mentioned her name was Paisley—stopped next to us, her face flushed and excited.

I could barely look her in the eye after what Dorian and I did in that bedroom—soon to be *our* bedroom.

"We'll have all the paperwork drawn up by the end of the week," she told Dorian.

"I'm paying for it in full. Have it done sooner."

God, the way Dorian got down to business sometimes, and the way he calmly but firmly demanded what he wanted, never failed to get me all worked up. It brought to mind memories of the two short months we worked together.

All the meetings I was a part of as I watched him do his thing.

The boardroom table . . .

Fuck. I missed that table. So many good things had happened there.

I made a mental note to visit him at the office. Soon.

"I'm sure they'll be eager to expedite the process for you, Mr. Sorensen. I'll bring it up as soon as I'm back at the office."

"Good." With that one word, Dorian ended our interaction with Paisley and guided me toward the Rolls-Royce waiting for us at the curb. Clearly, he had text Carl and informed him that we were on our way down.

We'd barely taken two steps in that direction when a man ran up to us.

The flash of a camera blinded me.

Dorian maneuvered me so that his body was covering mine. "What the hell are you doing?"

"Sorry, man. Didn't mean to scare you both. Just wanted a picture of you and the girlfriend. I work for Page Six, by the way."

"And what the hell do you want with us?" My boyfriend snapped.

Paparazzi.

My mind registered that word, along with a profound confusion. They still did things like that? I knew they still followed around and hounded the super famous, but we in no way qualified for that moniker.

His next comment cleared up any confusion I had.

And unleashed a wave of panic I'd never experienced before.

"Do you mind commenting on Ms. Adamo now that those videos were leaked?"

"*What*?" Dorian snapped.

"No offense to your girlfriend, man. I just thought one of you would like to comment on those sex videos of you and Ms. Adamo. They're everywhere and spreading like wildfire."

My knees went weak.

Horror followed close behind.

She leaked them.

That insane bitch took her copies of the videos and she fucking leaked them for everyone to see.

THE CAR WAS SPEEDING TOWARD MIDTOWN, WHERE BOTH Dorian and I lived.

He was on the phone, talking a mile a minute.

I was in the seat next to him, staring unseeing out the window, my entire body numb. I couldn't even begin to process how I felt. My mind latched onto his conversation in an effort to distract me from the impending apocalypse in my chest.

"I don't give a fuck what they say, Joey! I want her fucking arrested. I want those leaked videos traced back to her. And I want it fucking now!"

It was the angriest I'd ever heard him.

I knew why, too.

It wasn't just what this would do to his family name, his company's reputation.

He knew what this was going to do to me.

What I was already dealing with as we sat in this car.

"What the fuck do you mean they can't arrest her without proof? My copies were already deleted. Of course it was her!" Even as he raged next to me, his hand searched mine out.

I felt his fingers slip between mine, but I was too paralyzed to respond.

Dorian squeezed my hand in a bid to get me to react. "You can't be serious. What do you mean they won't even consider issuing a warrant for an arrest until they prove she leaked them? What the fuck is the law good for then?"

There was a chance she'd get away with doing this to him.

With doing it to *us*.

That knowledge sat heavy in the space between us, an unvoiced, corrosive fact.

"Listen to me very carefully, Joey," Dorian said, his voice suddenly smoothing out into a cold, unnerving tone. "I want her destroyed completely. I want her name ruined more than it'll already be with this leak. I want her company abolished. I don't give a fuck about the damage to her family, friends . . . I don't give a damn what it takes. If you aren't the man for the job, tell me now. Because I'll find someone willing."

As far as I knew now, Joey had been working with Dorian for a really long time. I'd gotten the sense that they were close. Friends, even. Yet he was threatening him as if Joey was nothing more than an uncooperative employee.

"I understand what you're saying, but her paying for this in the most brutal way possible is non-negotiable . . . Then make it happen. And make it happen fast. She's clearly unhinged and dangerous. She needs to be muzzled and controlled." Dorian ended the call, flung his cell across the seat in front of us, and spun to face me. He cupped my face, thumbs caressing me. "Talk to me. Say something. Curse me out, I don't care. Just speak."

I placed my cold hand over his; an act of comfort and assurance. I knew what he was thinking.

I'd just agreed to move in with him less than an hour ago.

Now this.

"The law might not be enough to stop her or punish her." I licked my lips as I tried to gather my thoughts. "I've only researched a little, but if they can't prove she leaked them, she can play the victim to this. Even blame you."

He gave me a solemn nod. "I have no doubt she's planning to blame me. Spin this so that the authorities focus on me instead of her."

"Then we can't just count on your lawyer, or the police to handle this."

Dorian paused, eyes searching mine. "What exactly are you saying, Demi?"

"That I'm going to end up in jail for killing that bitch if we don't get creative."

His lips twitched with involuntary amusement. He bit back his smile, focused on me as if he were trying to read my mind. "So what do you suggest we do about it?"

"You're filthy rich. My mother is even richer. Fuck the law. I mean, let them do their thing and whatnot, but maybe it's time we think outside the box. Use our money and connections to find other ways of handling this. There has to be someone we can hire to dismantle her life, isn't there?"

It took Dorian so long to respond that I started to get nervous. His expression was inscrutable as he thought it over. "What you're suggesting might be illegal, depending on who we hire."

"Okay."

He scowled at my easy acceptance. "Then I don't want you, or your mother's money, to be any part of it."

"That's non-negotiable," I said, using one of his favorite sayings. "We're together. We're in this together. If you truly care about how this is hurting me, you'll let me be a part of this." It was vengeance, plain and simple, and I was shameless enough to own it.

At that point, I didn't give a damn about right or wrong.

I just wanted that woman to pay for her craziness.

For trying to destroy what Dorian and I had together.

The seconds ticked by with us locked in a battle of wills.

"You really need this." He didn't phrase it as a question, but I answered with a nod anyway. His thumbs caressed my cheeks again and his eyes dropped to my lips. "You know I can't deny you anything you need. It's a goddamned weakness that I find highly inconvenient."

If his goal was to force a smile out of me, he succeeded. "Is that a yes?"

"If it keeps that smile on your face, then yes. We'll figure this out together. Even if I don't like it."

"I love you, Dorian," I mumbled in a small voice.

Every time his expression melted with that relief, I lost another part of my heart to him. Which was confusing, since he already owned the whole damned thing.

"I love you, too, Demi. Don't ever forget that. Even as shit gets uglier moving forward. Never forget it again."

chapter thirty-seven

Telling yourself that you wouldn't give in, or go down without a fight, was all well and good.

But when the moment came to live up to that, you had to be ready to stand up for that promise.

You were going to be tested time and time again, and you had to find the resolve not to back down.

We chose my apartment for our upcoming meeting—well, Dorian chose it.

It'd become clear that he didn't want me anywhere near his old place.

I didn't know how I felt about that. Was I upset? Was I relieved?

At least Beck's enthusiasm as soon as Dorian stepped through the door brought a smile to my face.

Dorian was sitting on my camel-colored love seat, bent over as he played tug-of-war with Beck. The puppy growled aggressively and tried to yank his tug toy out of Dorian's hand.

I allowed myself to take in the moment. To let the happiness drift over me and remind me that this was what I was fighting for. That our future would have infinite moments like this once we moved in together and got over this massive obstacle standing in our way.

What would it be like to see a little toddler running to greet him at the door the same way Beck did?

The thought hit me right in the gut. I inhaled sharply and pushed the visual to the back of my mind.

My intercom rang. I turned and headed to pick up the receiver. It was the front desk informing me that Angelina had arrived. "Yes, please. Let her up." How odd. Angelina had told me that she would be here with her new boss, Ilvia Muzio, the president of Kaur Russell Group. They were one of the most reputable public relations firms in the city.

Both Dorian and I had decided to sign with them.

When the doorbell rang, I wasted no time opening it—

"Oh."

"Yeah," Ang groused from her spot leaning against my door frame, lips pursed.

Lucas Alexander stood next to her and waved happily at me, hazel eyes shining.

That was the main difference between him and his brother, Calum. They were practically twins, except that Calum's eyes were narrower, and he was forever cloaked in that air of seriousness that followed him around. Lucas had rounder eyes and that fun-loving, *laissez-faire* aura that warned the world not to take him too seriously.

That he was only out to have a good time.

Then again, I was pretty sure he'd decided to stalk my friend to the ends of the Earth. If that didn't scream seriousness, I didn't know what did. "What are you doing here?" I asked him.

Ang pushed off the door and walked inside. "I kept asking him the same thing, yet nothing he said made sense."

"I'm here to offer Dorian emotional support as his friend." Lucas stepped inside and adjusted the lapels of his grayish-blue suit. His burgundy tie was next. "I'm also here following *your* friend."

I closed the door, amused despite myself. "You don't say?"

Dorian stood from the loveseat and met Lucas half way. He was shaking his head as the two men clapped hands. "What I'd tell you in Chicago?"

"Keep that shit to yourself," Lucas warned, following Angelina to my couch.

She sighed and rolled her eyes, but made no move to stop him as he took the seat next to her. "My boss is running ten or so minutes late. She'll be here soon."

I went back to the intercom to alert the front desk, and asked them to allow her straight in once she arrived.

Dorian sat in the loveseat once again. Beck must've run off somewhere and I made a mental note to go check on him later. Joining him on the loveseat, I watched as Ang pulled out her tablet.

"It's pretty bad." Ang's eyes flickered in my direction as she said it. "But at least it's not all over the news, bad. Just Page Six and the gossip blogs."

Lucas smirked at Dorian. "Finally a reason to be glad the world is currently such a fucked up place. A multi-millionaire architect's sex tape isn't even a blip on their rader."

Ang threw him a look that shut him up pretty quick. "That might change if she gets indicted, or word continues to spread through the gossip rags that you're pursuing criminal charges against her."

Or if our quest to find something to use against Monica bore fruit. After all, her name was tied into this scandal as deeply as ours was.

My head hurt as I tried to consider the options, the repercussions.

As I did my risk analysis and found nothing but chaos at the end of each possible road.

My doorbell rang.

Ang was on her feet before I could get to mine. "I'll let her in."

I let her do so since it was her boss at the door.

Ilvia Muzio was as fascinating as her name. She breezed inside with her brown hair flowing all the way down her back. Her light blue business suit was expertly tailored, but loose enough to not hug her body. A wide belt in the same shade as her suit was wrapped around her waist. She paired it with a sensible, plain white shirt and insanely high white heels.

We all stood as she got close.

Introductions were briskly made, hands shaken, and no time was wasted. She held out a manicured hand and Ang passed her the tablet. "You both signed the contracts, so we can just get right to it."

Lucas took his seat further down the couch.

Ang purposely sat all the way on the left.

Ilvia smoothly lowered herself into the middle, oblivious to the way that Lucas was glaring at Angelina. Her nearly black eyes did a quick scan of whatever was on the tablet. "I need to know the names of every woman you've ever recorded yourself with. The only way to mitigate the potential problems is to predict them beforehand."

My stomach dropped.

Her approach made perfect sense. It's exactly what I would do in a business setting, what I was doing in my mind.

Dorian shifted next to me. "I already deleted my copies of the videos."

It wasn't the first time I felt like asking him just how many he'd fucking made over the years.

An answer I didn't need. That would lead to me wondering how many times he watched them to get himself off—because regular porn wasn't just enough. It had to be porn featuring himself.

I wished thoughts could be controlled and I didn't keep spiraling into these ruminations. That bitterness didn't follow on its heels.

Ilvia met Dorian's stare with a blank, yet stoic expression. "And we both know she didn't. Now, do any of your other ex-lovers also possess any videos featuring you, and are any of them close friends with Ms. Adamo? Is there any chance of them teaming up against you to throw even more dirt on your name?"

The brunette in the red dress in Chicago. She was the first one that came to mind. I'd caught a glimpse of her face before she rammed into Dorian, and I remember picking up on her resemblance to Monica.

That, and I saw it for myself on the video.

Didn't need to be a psych major to realize how twisted it was on Monica's part.

Nor did I have to be a psych major to analyze just how attracted Dorian once was to her.

It took me a minute to realize the room had gone silent.

To feel Dorian's worried stare on my face.

But it was Ilvia's eyes that I focused on. "You and I can discuss your part in this right after. You're welcome to step out for this part." She said it without any inflection, expression remaining the same.

I appreciated the sympathy regardless.

Running my sweating hands across my thighs, I stood. "I think I'll go see what our dog is up to."

Dorian reached out for me. "Demi."

"No, it's okay." I ran my hand down his cheek. "Do it. You have to. I'll be back after."

"I can't promise I'll get you through this with a squeaky clean reputation. That ship has already sailed. But I can promise you that the better prepared we are, then I can navigate both of you to the best of my abilities. The quicker the focus is on both of you as a couple, and on each of you individually as you move forward in the most public, positive way possible, the quicker we get society's focus away from this mess."

Dorian ran his hand through his hair and released a frustrated breath. "Fine. Let's do this." His blue eyes met mine, and I could see how worried he continued to be.

Those three weeks I left him destroyed us both.

It's why I was still there and planned to stay no matter how bad things got.

I just needed a little space to gather my resolve once more.

Leaning down, I placed a quick kiss to his cheek, and then left the room. Maybe one day, I would have no choice but to come face to face with all the lovers from his past.

Maybe I wouldn't.

Knowing all their names would get me nowhere right now. It definitely wouldn't help our relationship move forward. It was best that I focus on what I needed to do.

Which included calling my Mom and getting her up to speed. She had some connections I was dying to get in touch with.

I found Beck in the guest bedroom. He'd tucked himself in the corner next to the bed and was busy gnawing on his bone.

I softly closed the door and dialed my mom. She answered on the fourth ring.

"Demi? Honey, is everything okay?"

"It's . . . as good as can be expected, I suppose. Listen, have you stayed in touch with the Stenhams?"

"Well, of course. Vivian has actually been keeping in touch with me during this whole mess."

Her divorce from my father.

Who was being a bigger dick by the day and swearing up and down that he was going to fight the pre-nup.

Maybe I couldn't completely block out what was happening with Dorian, but I spent an inordinate amount of hours every day blocking out thoughts of my father.

I didn't plan to stop now.

"Last I heard, they're still close with the Adamos, too."

My mother's silence was followed by a proud tone. "Good girl. You're doing your homework."

"I need to know when their next event is and if the Adamos will be present without their daughter." I was thinking the time had come for an audience with Frankenstein himself.

AKA Monica's Daddy Dearest.

And I needed it to look like a coincidence that I bumped into him.

Going straight to his office wouldn't do.

"I'll call her right away, Demi."

"Thank you, Mom. I love you."

"And I love you, my strong girl. Let's go kick some ass, yeah?"

I laughed with delight, a sound that took me by surprise. "Yeah, Mom. Let's."

38

When the Rolls-Royce pulled up in front of NBC Studios, I turned to Dorian in confusion.

Dressed in a Sebastian Cruz black suit with velvet, filigree details along the blazer, and a silver-and-black filigree tie, my man was absolutely dressed to kill. I almost couldn't look at him without having some kind of attack. He smiled at me, one of those curls falling in front of his brow, and I barely bit back the urge to push him against the seat and ride his face into oblivion. "Just a little longer, baby. You'll see."

Tonight's outing was a surprise. All he'd told me was that this would be our first outing as a couple and that we were going somewhere popular. Therefore, I should dress to impress.

And I had.

But this man had come to annihilate tonight, and I wouldn't be the only victim left slain in his wake.

The door opened, catching me by surprise.

Carl smiled and tipped his hat. His coffee-brown eyes sparkled with amusement.

He knew what my surprise was and he hadn't given me a hint,

either.

I grabbed his outstretched hand and allowed him to help me out of the vehicle. This wasn't a red carpet event of any sort, but there was still one or two paparazzi around. The flashes from the cameras caught me by surprise. Somehow, I controlled my expression as Dorian exited the vehicle behind me.

I'd chosen a gray dress made mostly of gauze from the high-waisted belt down. The slit began high like the dress I'd worn to the Goffs event, and this one also had a single strap on one side holding the tight, cupped bodice in place. My hair was piled into a messy bun on top of my head. I'd also decided to forego any jewelry since my eye makeup was done in dark, smoky shades.

I could envision the image we made as a couple as those cameras went off a few more times.

Dorian placed his hand at the small of my back and began leading me toward the entrance. It wasn't until I looked up at the NBC Studios sign one more time that it dawned on me where he might be taking me.

I whispered the name of the restaurant excitedly.

Dorian's response was a cocky smirk that only made him look ten times sexier. Especially with that scruff covering his jaw. I knew he'd left it like that for me because he knew I loved it. It threw off the entire polished look of his suit and hair, and made me that much wilder for him.

I'd been ready to go since he picked me up.

I doubted I'd make it through dinner without needing some part of him between my legs.

The elevator ride up to the 65th floor was torture. All I wanted was to plaster myself against him and thank him properly, but I knew where it would lead. And we weren't alone in the elevator. I had to settle for a kiss on the cheek and being tucked close to his side.

Seeing the dark wood wall with the golden letters spelling out the restaurant's name was surreal. I'd spent my whole life living in this city and hearing about this place, but I'd never had an excuse to come here before. We ascended the brown, carpeted steps to the bronze, art-deco hostess stand.

"Sorensen," Dorian said to the young woman behind the stand.

I gave her credit. Somehow, she stopped herself from tipping over at the sight of him. Out of respect for me, I supposed, she jerked her eyes to mine and kept them glued there.

After everything I'd gone through with his exes, I couldn't help but give her a grateful grin.

The entire silent exchange wasn't lost on Dorian. He ducked to kiss my cheek from behind. The scent of his cologne surrounded me, and I trembled. The pulsing between my legs grew more powerful, becoming almost unbearable.

A young man approached the hostess stand to take us to our table.

Arm around my waist, Dorian led me once more, and I had a feeling that he was aware of every reaction I was having.

We were seated at a table directly in front of the glass windows. The Empire State building towered, surrounded by a sea of glittering skyscrapers. Above our heads, the giant crystal chandelier dominated the circular ceiling. Tonight, the lights within those circles were glowing in the signature rainbow colors that gave the restaurant its namesake.

Dorian was seated in front of me, watching my expression as I took it all in.

Smiling gleefully, I faced him again.

His own face broke out into a smile upon seeing it. "I take it that I did good?"

Laughing, I reached for his hand. "If there were somewhere private for us, I'd show you just how good."

That smile fell off his face and his jaw twitched. Eyes darkening, he let his gaze travel over my upper body. "Don't tempt me, baby."

But I wanted to.

I wanted to crawl over this table, in front of everyone, and climb right on his lap.

Lust tightened his face even further.

No doubt he could read my mind by simply looking in my eyes. He always knew when I was ready for him. When I could barely wait another second to have him.

Dorian's lips parted with an exhaled breath. His wide chest rose and fell beneath that black vest. His eyes passed over the open space as he took it in for himself. "It's gorgeous, isn't it?"

"It is," I agreed, my stare locked on him.

A waiter stopped at our table with a bottle of wine. "The 2008 Bordeaux you requested, sir." He held the bottle out for Dorian to see for himself. After a quick inspection, Dorian nodded his approval. The waiter poured it into our glasses with perfect, controlled movements, then left the bottle on the table for us.

"Pre-ordered?" I asked Dorian, clinking my glass against his when he held it up.

He tilted his head. "I told them to be prepared." Watching him lick his lips after drinking made me cross my legs under the table. My clit wouldn't stop throbbing, and the incessant pounding was messing with my concentration. "As I was saying . . . this place? It's nice enough to hold an event here, isn't it?"

That enigmatic way he was studying me screwed with my thoughts even more. I wished I could read his mind the same way he seemed to be able to decipher mine. "Yes, and they do. They rent this place out for parties and weddings. Don't they?"

Dorian's lids dropped over his eyes, hiding the piercing blue irises behind his dark lashes. "And St. Patrick's is right next door. Perfect for a wedding. Yeah."

My body went numb with a speed that almost made me drop my

glass. Fighting to hide my reaction, I lowered it slowly to the table.

His gaze shot up to laser in on me.

Looking through me.

Trying to rip more secrets from my mind.

And I had a feeling that the one he was after was the same secret I kept refusing to acknowledge. No, not a "secret". An unspoken desire. A yearning powerful enough to nearly overcome my common sense.

I turned my head away and got lost in the nighttime view of New York City from sixty-five floors above street level.

God, what exactly was he talking about? Was it what I thought it was? I wanted to ask outright, like I'd done when he hinted at me moving in with him, but I was afraid of his answer.

I'd never say no.

But I couldn't say yes right now, either.

We'd just begun dating like a normal couple after nearly half-a-year of secrecy. Dorian wasn't in a relationship when we began sleeping together, yet for months I'd felt like his side piece—a secret that couldn't see the light of day. A secret that could never be accepted by society and my loved ones.

I hadn't even realized how much I wanted to have a normal girlfriend-and-boyfriend experience with him until the possibility was dangling within reach.

"Demi . . . baby, should I be worried about how pale you are?"

I turned to face him. "Should I be worried that this isn't just a regular date?" I tried to insert a little bit of flirtatious humor into it.

There was no telling by Dorian's expression how he took my question. He was careful to not let me see if it affected him or not. Sitting back in his seat, he ran his fingers up and down the stem of his glass. The fact that he wouldn't stare into my eyes while doing it gutted me. "I see . . . so you'd be opposed to the idea."

Jesus. Just thinking that he might have a ring hidden in one of his pockets broke my fucking heart. "Absolutely not."

Finally, that brought his attention back to me. "No?"

"I'd just be opposed to it so soon . . . I . . ." Couldn't believe we were actually discussing this, without saying the term "marriage" outright. "I love you. Of course I'd want that one day. But we just agreed to move in together."

We were still in the middle of sorting the scandal of those sex videos out.

Maybe he wasn't as much of an open book as I was, yet when something hit Dorian hard, it was pretty obvious. His relief every time he realized he wasn't on the verge of losing me, for example, would change the air around him. As if his aura were beaming.

It was like that now.

His muscular frame relaxed and he smiled again, his happiness growing by the second. When he reached for my left hand, he enveloped it with both of his, and his grip was tight. Possessive. "You want us to live together for a bit before we go there, yeah?"

The way he was massaging my hand and fingers melted me on the spot. "And do more of this. You know." No need to elaborate. He nodded as soon as I said it, understanding what I meant.

"It was rough for me, too, at first. I knew immediately it wasn't just sex. The only reason I hid you back then was because of your father. We both cared what he would think at the time."

And Monica hadn't gone batshit crazy over the idea of losing access to his body.

His touch on my hand, and the fact that we shared the same thoughts on this situation, infused me with a wave of love.

A feeling that was dangerous when he was massaging me the way he was, and he looked the way he did tonight.

Dorian focused on my hand and began working on my left ring finger.

I lost my breath all over again.

"One day, though, you'll be wearing it . . . and I'm going to fuck you wearing nothing but that."

My heart tripped.

My walls rippled.

My skin burned with sudden heat.

And our waiter decided to come at that moment to take our order.

Dorian let go of my hand and sat back with a self-satisfied expression that would normally annoy me.

God damn, it looked so good on him, though. Especially while he was in that outfit.

He ordered something for both of us, but I couldn't hear what it was above the roaring of blood in my ears. The waiter walked away and I blurted out, "I don't think I can focus on eating."

Dorian licked his lips. "Well, baby, you need to. It's our date night, remember? And I need you well-fed before I get you home tonight. I plan to fuck you as many times as possible. You might have to climb on top at some point, but I'll do my best to maintain my stamina for the first four rounds, at least."

I swallowed heavily. "Four?" We hadn't broken that kind of record yet.

"At least," he repeated smoothly with a wink.

I hoped to God that man wasn't kidding.

Because he had no idea what he'd just unleashed upon himself tonight.

chapter thirty-nine

Dorian managed to keep me off him—well, mostly off him—in the car on the ride to his place.

I'd fully expected us to go to his condo in Midtown and I didn't even care by the time dinner was over. Didn't give a damn about his bedroom and the memories of those videos.

I just needed him.

Badly.

It felt like I needed him worse than I'd ever needed him before.

Instead, the car ride took even longer than I could've imagined. When the car came to a stop, I saw we were outside our new building.

Our new home.

I nearly tackled Dorian against the car seat once more. "You closed on the place?"

"Uh huh. And demanded they leave all the furniture for us. There's a bed we didn't finish trying out." He lunged for me, pinning me against the seat, tongue tangling with mine. I fisted his hair with a groan. Tilting my head, I slanted my mouth against his to deepen the kiss further.

He didn't let me.

Rearing back, Dorian fumbled with the intercom button. "I've got it, Carl. No need to open. Enjoy the rest of the night off."

"Will do, sir. Thank you," Carl replied through the speaker.

The door was flung open after.

Dorian all but climbed over me. Once outside, he reached back for me, but I was already reaching out for him.

The walk to the front door passed in a blur. I knew that the doorman greeted us, but I couldn't see past Dorian. We made it into the elevator, which was blessedly empty. He slid in his key for the penthouse floor.

That's when I finally tackled him.

His back slammed into the wall.

I dragged his lips back down to mine.

Shameless, burning for him, I palmed his erection as our tongues connected. Dorian jerked in my grip, and the way he moaned in his chest left my pussy clenching. The feeling of emptiness was too much to bear.

Dorian palmed my ass and thrust against me. Every bit of his body was hard, taut. He vibrated with barely leashed restraint as he rolled his hips and ate at my mouth.

Whimpering, I struggled with his belt.

"What—"

I didn't let him finish, kissing him frantically as I ripped his belt open and almost broke off the button of his slacks. The ache in my pussy was deep, painful, and my crotchless panties did nothing to contain how wet I was.

"*Baby.*" Dorian threw his head back to keep his mouth away from mine. "Cameras. Not here."

The elevator opened on our floor.

I practically yanked him out into our foyer.

That's as far as I let him go.

Pushing him against the side table, I fell to my knees right there, on our new penthouse's marble floor, and brought his cock out to play.

He had enough time to reach for the table behind him and grab on for support.

Then, I took him straight to the back of my throat, uncaring of how thick he was. How it blocked my ability to breathe. Dorian's thighs shook and he bit out a harsh curse.

"You're wild. Holy fuck, baby."

He hadn't seen anything yet.

I worked his cock with my mouth, going as deep as I could each time. In between, I somehow found enough concentration to finish getting his pants down his hips. I released my hold on his dick with a breathless gasp. A trail of saliva connected my mouth and his plush, swollen tip.

His entire length was dark pink, the veins along it enlarged from the blood flow.

His gorgeous balls were drawn up and tight.

Just how I wanted them.

I spit on his dick one more time, leaving it nice and soaked, and jerked him with a tight fist. Leaning lower, I tongued his balls and sucked gently on them, alternating between licks and sucks.

"Oh, God. Yes." He cupped the back of my head, pressing my face deeper into his balls. "Lick them, baby. Just like that."

"I want you to come on my face," I moaned, jerking him faster. His dick was already on the verge, I could feel it about to explode in my grip. "Come all over me, Dorian."

His pained expression, dark blue eyes glittering, and that drawn out moan undid me. "That's what you want, my little cockwhore?"

I bit my lip and nodded. "Do it. Come for me, baby."

His head fell back, neck bulging. "Fucccccckkk."

The first hot spurt landed against my cheek.

I gave him no mercy. No pause. I jerked him through that entire orgasm, even as he twitched and trembled. He lost his voice halfway through, but I could tell he wanted to beg me to wait.

To stop.

Instead, I pumped his cock until he had nothing left to give me.

By the time he was done, cum was dripping off my cheeks and onto my chest. I had no doubt that my bodice was covered in it, and I loved every bit of it.

Dorian's chest shuddered with a breath. He leaned into the side table and forced his eyes open.

I waited until our gazes connected to swipe my finger along my cheek. As I stared into his eyes, I slid that same finger into my mouth and hungrily sucked his cum off it.

His expression darkened. His dick twitched. "I know you don't want me to ask you now, but just so you know, you're so fucking marrying me one day."

I broke into surprised laughter, even as my heart skipped like twenty beats in a row.

DORIAN CLEANED ME IN THE KITCHEN, HIS TOUCH GENTLE AS HE wiped me down. I could tell he was working through something in his mind, and it was the only thing that stopped me from mounting him on the nearest surface.

After, he served us some more wine, and I was pleasantly surprised to see he'd had our new kitchen stocked as well. He was planning multiple steps ahead, perhaps too many steps ahead, yet it made me appreciate him that much more.

He led me outside onto our terrace. It was as gorgeous as the rest of the home, and the original wood-and-white cushioned furniture had been left as well. There was an eight person dining table also done up in white on the far left. Large candles burned on the ground, adding to the atmosphere.

I was leaning against the parapet, my arms braced on the concrete surface, glass of wine in my hand.

Dorian was wrapped around me from behind. He nuzzled my now clean cheek and placed a small kiss on my throat. "You blew my mind back there."

I giggled, leaning into him. He was already hardening against my ass again, even though it'd only been like ten minutes since we finished in the foyer. "That was the point."

"*Mmmm.*"

I shivered at the feeling of that moan vibrating against my throat.

He tongued my pulse and his hands slid down my exposed thighs. I couldn't even feel the chill in the air with all of his heat around me, and he knew it.

Trembling, I tilted my head to give his mouth more access. The glass in my hand nearly slipped.

Without missing a beat, Dorian took it from me and placed it on the parapet. When he turned me around to face him, I was ready for him. I saw a flash of his tight expression, that sexy intent that always took over his face when he was ready to fuck me, before our lips met again.

I hadn't come for him yet. I'd been primed for him all night. I lost control as soon as our tongues touched, my frantic whimpers filling whatever space was between us.

"God. You were made to be fucked by me," Dorian groaned into my mouth. In a swift move, he lifted me off my feet and wrapped my legs around his hips.

I ground against him and kissed him harder.

I don't know how he was able to concentrate enough to move us, but he made it over to one of the couches and sank into the huge, plush cushion.

A tremor shook my core as he released his dick once more.

Dorian reached for my bodice.

I reached for his erection.

As I was working him inside me, his tip gliding along my soaked pussy, he managed to get my tits free.

"Fuck yeah, baby. Ride that cock."

He didn't need to tell me twice.

"Open your shirt. I need to feel your skin." He was ragingly aroused, his body giving off heat, and I was dying to feel it.

Dorian bit his lip, hips twitching with impatience to get deeper inside me, and almost tore through his vest.

I rushed to help him loosen his tie as he pried the buttons of his shirt free.

As soon as his muscular, flexing torso was bared, I sank down on his dick with a cry.

He gritted his teeth, massaging the hard tips of my nipples. "Tight, baby. Perfect. Always. I love your pussy so much."

"I love *you*," I mewled, leaning down to take his mouth again.

Gripping my desperately bouncing hips, Dorian let me eat his mouth and ride him at my pace. When I took him to the hilt and ground my hips, he let out a breathless cry that I felt everywhere.

Tongues dueling, I ground on him harder. His thick cock stretching me, my swollen clit rubbing against his groin . . . the way he rolled my tight nipples as our tongues mated frantically . . . "I'm almost there, baby. Almost. Going to come so fucking hard on your cock."

"Fuck. Fuck. You feel amazing." He jerked me closer and ducked to take my nipple into his mouth.

Game fucking over.

Just seeing his tongue playing with the tip, while he expertly rolled the other, detonated me.

Unable to stop it, I climaxed with a strength that left me wide-eyed, unseeing, air struggling to make its way into my lungs. My pussy pulsed around him, each move sending a new hit of pleasure to my core.

Dorian snarled, losing his rhythm beneath me, and began pounding me with all he was worth.

I saw flashing lights in my vision as my orgasm extended. He rammed me with his dick, forcing me to take every bit of sensation.

Pumping his cum into me, he came with a ragged groan. His arms tightened around me, trapping me, and I hugged him to me just as tightly.

"I love you," he rasped against my collarbone.

"I love you, too. You know that," I said into his curls, breathing in his scent.

"Nothing is taking this away from us, right?" His lips moved on my skin as he spoke.

Leaning my cheek on his head, I stared off into the night, at the city we would have to face come morning. "No. It's too late for that. You're stuck with me now."

"Good. Because it's exactly what I want. You know that."

After what he'd said in the foyer? The hints he kept throwing around? Yeah. Yeah I did. He was all mine, and I wouldn't let anyone take that from me.

chapter forty

I sat at the kitchen counter, in our new penthouse, and watched the tablet screen in horror.

One would think I'd be used to it by now, the sinking feeling in my stomach. The acrid disappointment that overwhelmed every cell.

"Antonia Kastellanos Davis had no comment to give today as she walked into the building where her lawyers' offices are located. A stark contrast to her husband, Stephen Davis, who has had much to say in the last two days."

The shot switched to one of my father standing outside the Aelius Tower, where SD Interiors, Sorensen International, and Agathen Designs—Calum and Lucas' architectural firm—were located. "All I can say is that I have done everything in my power to prove to my wife how sorry I am. It was a horrible mistake, but I wish she wasn't tearing our family apart over it. In the end, if she wants to leave me, she's welcome to do so, but I built this company from the ground up and I won't let her just take it from me to appease her scorned fury."

"Is he fucking kidding me?" I shouted, slamming my glass onto the counter.

"Keep watching," Ilvia murmured, nodding at the tablet.

I almost didn't want to. How much worse could this get?

I was about to find out.

The shot changed yet again, and it was a slideshow of images of me and Dorian.

The shot from my social media at the Goffs' event.

The picture Dorian posted the day he picked me up from school.

Us outside NBC Studios.

Even the night that paparazzi for Page Six harassed us outside this building—the first night we saw the penthouse.

"The Davis family has had its fair share of scandal lately, and it's propelling them into the spotlight in a way they haven't been in over a century. Maybe more. Demitra Davis, Stephen and Antonia's only child, is embroiled in a torrid love affair with her ex-boss. Who happens to be knee-deep in a sex tape scandal that's quickly taking the internet by storm. It's not every day that a rich man's intimate history is leaked this way, and can I just say what a great multitasker the guy is? No really, this kind of stuff is usually only seen in scripted por—"

I hurried to shut the tablet off.

Ilvia Muzio, Ang's boss and our official "PR Person", raised an eyebrow at my outburst. Aside from that, she maintained her composure. "Luckily, that's a talk show. Not the five o'clock news."

"That'll come next," I whispered miserably.

"And that's why we're here to discuss the situation." She reached for the tablet and brought it back to life. "From what I understand, Ms. Adamo was given until today to address the warrant that was issued for her."

There was no sense of satisfaction at those words. No vindication. Only the never-ending dread that kept multiplying.

I wanted her to pay. Of course I did. Maybe this would finally get her to back off—although she'd already dealt the maximum damage possible.

Then why did my body go cold as I thought about it?

Because this would add another layer to the scandal. Point another spotlight at the situation and draw more eyes in.

"You're going to have to harden yourself against this somehow," Ilvia commented.

"How? How does someone forget those videos and ignore the situation? While my father is being a fucking jackass and publicly fighting my mother on her *well-deserved* right to divorce him?" Sick didn't even begin to describe how I felt.

"Well, you decided to stay with Dorian and even move into this new place with him. So you focus on that decision and stick to it no matter what."

I was going to. That was a given. I wouldn't be leaving Dorian again over this. We'd been through too much.

I just couldn't wait for this bullshit to finish blowing over.

Ilvia snapped her fingers. "And, you bring your focus back to this conversation and what you need to do next."

"Which is what? Exactly."

"Well, right now you're just a young twenty-year-old girl that attends college, happens to be the daughter of parents who began what will certainly be a bitter divorce, and you're dating your ex-boss, who is eleven years older than you and is in the middle of a sex tape scandal. We've got a lot of naive, victim vibes floating around, and it isn't going to help Dorian look any better in the end."

She was right, and it was an insecurity that had been bugging me for months. Even before the whole Monica thing blew up, I'd been wondering what I wanted with my future. I had a passion for my chosen degree, but how would I apply it?

It's why I hadn't gone back to work with Dorian.

Why I'd entertained the idea of taking the position Keith's dad offered.

I wanted to make my own way, build a name for myself. "I have a year left before I finish my degree. And even then, I'll need years of experience before I can branch off and do my own thing."

Ilvia got a contemplative look on her face. "What's your major again?"

"Business with a focus on Risk Management."

"And where are you working as of right now?"

I told her the name of the publishing company where I'd taken an administrative position after Sorenson International.

Ilvia's red lips pursed as she mulled it over. "It's going to be hard to convince any company to give you advancement opportunities until this is in the rearview mirror, so to speak."

Another blow.

I really was in the weakest position of everyone involved. Imagining a reality where I had to remain a regular administrative assistant while I finished school and the world watched me on Dorian's arm shouldn't have bothered me.

But I had my own ambitions. Always did.

"What do you suggest, then?" I asked Ilvia in a low voice.

"We want people to focus on the positives of your relationship with Dorian, on the positives of his future projects, and on your own prospects as an individual. Give me a little bit of time and I'm sure we can come up with something."

MY CONVERSATION WITH ILVIA WAS STILL WEIGHING HEAVY IN my mind as Dorian and I arrived at our next event together. We'd been invited to an exclusive art exhibit at the New York Public Library's Schwarzman Building.

Well, Dorian was invited on his own.

I was supposed to be my mother's Plus One.

She was here somewhere, but I'd decided to arrive with him, instead.

So many heads turned to watch us walk into the Gottesman Hall that it was impossible not to notice. I did my best to pretend I didn't, though. There was no point giving them the satisfaction.

And I wouldn't stumble for their avid gazes, either.

My man and I were here together to showcase our relationship, and to enjoy our date night. If that bothered them, they could all collectively kiss my ass.

At least, that's the attitude I tried to adopt. It was easier said than done.

A lot of people kept their distance, which helped make the start of the night easier. Dorian and I were free to roam around the massive, marble columned hall and take in all the art on display. Despite my tension at the people analyzing us, I almost got lost in Dorian, and we managed to have a great time.

More than once he nuzzled my cheek, taking my scent into his lungs.

Each time, I offered him my mouth for a quick kiss.

PDA was never a big thing when it came to our social class and these types of "refined" events, but I didn't care. I loved him, and I wanted everyone to see it.

I didn't spot my mother at all despite searching her out in the crowd. After sending her a quick text to check on her, I allowed Dorian to lead me toward one of the windows, and the marble bench beneath it.

Everyone here knew I was only twenty, so drinking in front of them wasn't an option. Much as I probably needed a slight buzz to calm me down.

Dorian motioned toward the bench. Once I was seated, he bent to kiss my cheek. "I'll find us something without alcohol to drink."

I grabbed his hand before he could leave. "You can drink. You don't have to hold back for me."

He gave me this small smile that hit me right in the heart, and ran the back of his fingers down my cheek. "No. I'm good. Trust me."

I kissed his hand in response.

Once he was gone, I looked around the hall for any signs of my mother.

Found Livana heading my way instead.

Surprised to see her there, I waited until she was sitting next to me to greet her. "Hey. What are you doing here?"

"Came with Calum. It was supposed to be our official first date as a couple, but then we remembered you and Dorian are here. And we kind of don't want to steal your shine, you know?" Tonight, she'd styled her blonde hair in big, loose curls that framed her delicate face, and she flipped those curls over her shoulder as her blue eyes widened. "Oh my God, but maybe we should. What do you think? Cause a scandal of our own and take the attention off you guys!"

I laughed at the mad glint in her eyes. "I take it this means you guys are also back together."

"Yes. Thank you." Expression soft, she placed her hand on my forearm. "I needed that verbal kick in the ass. I'm glad you did it."

"Oh, thank God," I mockingly sighed, placing my hand on my heart. "I was convinced you'd hate me forever."

"Bitch, you're never getting rid of me."

We shared a wide grin.

"I also take it this means you told your parents you're with Calum. Are they okay with it?"

"*Pffft*. They're fucking pissed. Like about to disown me type pissed. I've had enough of their shit, to be honest. They haven't teamed up or agreed on anything in ages, but suddenly this is the thing that unites them. So what if Dad married Calum's *second* cousin. What the fuck does that have to do with us?"

It was true, yet we both knew that in our social circles, the older generations were still old-fashioned about certain things. They were more than likely going to make a huge stink about this, and sadly, they weren't the only ones.

"I'm sorry, Liv," I murmured.

"Ugh, it's whatever. I'm quitting Dad's company and taking Mikael with me."

"Where are you guys going to work, then?"

Livana shrugged. "I've actually been considering starting my own thing, you know? I have a ton of money in the trust fund that Dad can't take from me, because Grandma knew her son can be a pain in the ass sometimes. I might use that money to start from the ground up."

My ears perked up at that. "And do what? The same thing you were doing with your Dad?"

"Yup. My own branding company. Maybe even grow big enough to be Dad's competition one day." Her mischievous smile was contagious. She was like a little elf plotting some evil deed. "Take all his clients that absolutely love me . . . okay, well, just the women who are obsessed with Mikael. I think there's like five of them plotting how to turn him straight."

We burst out laughing.

"How serious are you about this?" I asked.

"Why?"

"Well, I'm wondering if you'll be in need of someone with a business major and a focus in Risk Management."

Her eyebrows shot toward her hairline and she turned to face me on the bench. "Tell me you're serious."

I looked her in the eye. "I'm so serious."

"Then this is really happening. We're freaking doing this."

Disbelief filled me, and for the first time in days, it was the good kind. This was such an unexpected twist, but it was the perfect solution for what I'd been pondering.

Why not do it?

And why not ask my mom to help out also? She would. That was a given. Unlike my father, she had my back no matter what, and as long as I presented her with a well-thought out business plan, she'd be game to invest. "We are so doing this," I said under my breath, nearly vibrating with excitement.

Liv bounced in her seat, and she was adorable in her own excitement.

Something caught her attention and she turned.

Calum was ahead of us, across the hall, surrounded by a group of men.

"Excuse me." Liv threw a saucy wink at me. "I have to go steal your thunder and all that."

She was gone in the blink of an eye.

I watched her sashay her way over to the group in her silver Louboutin's, her hips swaying in her oversized, cream sweater dress.

Calum turned in surprise when he saw her coming.

She didn't stop, either. She kept on going until she was plastered to him.

Then, in front of everyone present, she dragged his head down to give him a thorough kiss.

Considering I'd done the same at the Goffs event, I couldn't fault her for it. Attention was instantly locked on them, and as Liv predicted, would probably help detract from what was happening with Dorian and I.

I finally saw him in a circle of other men. They were standing next to one of the columns on the right. We caught each other's eye and smiled.

Dorian held up a finger, signaling that he would be right with me. When he turned to one of the older men talking to him, I wondered if that was someone he worked closely with.

Bringing out my phone, I sent him a quick text to let him know that I'd gone to look for the bathroom. Once out of the hall, I turned left and wandered aimlessly. It took me a while, but eventually I stumbled upon a door with the universal restroom sign on it.

Walking inside, I saw three stalls available, and headed toward one of them.

The door opened behind me.

Assuming it was just another woman in need of the bathroom, I kept going.

"Girl. We need to talk."

The voice was unfamiliar, but clearly this person was addressing me. No one else was in there with us.

Curious, I spun around—

It was her.

Not Monica, but the woman that was nearly her fucking twin. The one that threw herself at Dorian the night of the design festival in Chicago.

The one that had been riding him in that video.

"What the hell do you want?" I snapped, my temper igniting too quick to be controlled.

That woman, whose name I didn't know and didn't want to fucking know, seemed amused at my outburst. Her perfectly straight, black hair, and tanned skin made her seem exotic to me. Foreign.

Which she was.

Monica's family were of Italian descendancy.

Judging by this woman's accent, she was as well.

Her lips parted in a cold, unamused grin, and her teeth were shockingly white compared to her skin. "I told you, girl. We need to talk."

chapter forty-one

I stepped out of the bathroom and into the hall once more.

That woman—Viola, as I now knew her name was—had left as soon as she was done saying what she had to say.

I'd remained in the bathroom for a while after, trying to wrap my head around it.

My head turned to the side—

Dorian was storming down the hall in my direction. "There you are. You weren't answering your phone."

I scowled at his expression. "What's going on? Is everything alright?"

He stopped in front of me and brought me in for a hug; his heart was hammering, which worried me even more. "I'll tell you in the car. Let's go."

The questions swirled through my mind, followed by another hit of anxiety. What happened now?

How much more could we both handle?

All of it. That was the answer. We had to get through each bit of this hell until we made it through to the other side.

With his hand on my lower back, Dorian led me through the

building and out the main doors. We took the stairs down onto Fifth Avenue, where Carl was once again faithfully waiting by the curb.

Once inside the vehicle, Dorian turned to face me. "Why were you gone so long? What happened?"

I considered telling him about my conversation with Viola, but whatever he was dealing with seemed to be more pressing. "You first. What's going on?"

His jaw pulsed as he brought out his phone and typed on the screen. When he handed it to me, I saw the paused video, who was on it, and my whole body flushed with anger.

"She did a press conference?"

"Answered questions outside the police station today when she finally showed up about the warrant," Dorian responded in a tense tone. "Just watch it."

I grabbed his phone with shaking hands and pressed play.

The video began with Monica exiting the station alongside what must've been her lawyer. As always, she looked gorgeous, and well-put together, as they headed down the short flight of stairs.

"Ms. Adamo! Do you have any comment on the charges against you?"

Both Monica and her lawyer stopped in front of the reporters. When her lawyer opened his mouth to speak, Monica held up a hand to silence him. "Of course I do. I am cooperating completely with the authorities and in due time my innocence will be proven. I would've never leaked such an intimate moment on the internet."

"What about the rumors that you also sent a video to Dorian Sorenson's girlfriend in retaliation?"

Monica laughed, and I wondered if anyone else could see how fake it was. "Retaliation for what? Dorian and I weren't in a relationship. I simply sent her what she asked me to send her, because she wanted to see for herself if her doubts were unfounded or not."

My sharp intake of breath was loud in the car.

Dorian snatched the phone from me and closed the webpage with the video. "I'm so sorry." He grabbed my hand.

"She's trying to make this a she-said she-said situation. Her word against mine. Because how the hell could I ever prove that I *didn't* ask for those videos?"

He pinched my chin lightly to bring my focus back to him. "We'll find a way. I swear we will."

My eyes widened as I remembered what had occurred in the bathroom. What Viola said. "You asked me why I was gone so long . . ."

"Something happened. I knew it."

"The other girl in that video with you followed me into the bathroom. Viola." Even saying those words killed something inside me. I wanted to find some kind of magical potion that could forever erase what I'd seen.

All I could do was pray that the passage of time would be able to dull the memories, and the feelings that came along with them.

"Fuck! What the hell did she want? What the fuck is wrong with these women?"

I placed my free hand on his arm. "She didn't approach me to start anything," I told him softly. "I'm not sure I can believe her or not, but she actually wanted to offer her help."

EVEN I COULDN'T TAKE VIOLA'S OFFER TO HELP US WITH THIS situation seriously. Dorian surely didn't.

Could we trust her or not?

She'd told me bluntly: this was becoming a huge inconvenience for her and it needed to stop.

In Italy this probably would've blown over much faster.

Here, as well.

But with Monica's stubbornness to not give in, this would probably drag on forever.

We walked into our penthouse and Beck immediately came running to greet us. Dorian bent to give him some attention, but I could tell his mind was a million miles away. He straightened and Beck immediately ran to me. "I'll talk to Viola."

I scratched behind Beck's ears absentmindedly. "I wish you didn't have to speak to her at all," I mumbled, although it was a ridiculous and immature feeling.

"Trust me, once this is over, I have no intention of staying in contact with any of the women I fucked again. I wish I would've known women can be this irrational and jealous."

"It's ancient knowledge, Dorian. We're wired to compete with each other. Especially over a man like you." A man who took sex to a whole other level.

"What are you talking about? Right now I'm wondering why you're even still with a man like me." He left it at that and walked in the direction of the living room.

I assumed he was heading out to the terrace to contact Viola.

Hated it, but it benefited me in the end. I had my own phone call to make. We didn't get a chance to bump into my mom at the art exhibit, and I really needed to touch base with her.

I made sure to fill Beck's bowl with some dry food. Once he was happily munching away, I headed up the stairs to the master bedroom. I closed the door gently, although the chances of Dorian hearing it from outside were impossible, and quickly dialed my mother's number.

"Honey! I'm so sorry, I'm running late."

"It's okay, Mom. We already left."

"Why? Is everything okay?"

I proceeded to inform her how *not* okay things were. "Mom, I really need a chance to 'bump' into Monica's dad. Unless you've been able to hear any gossip about what he thinks of all this? She's bringing bad publicity to his company as well. As much as people say he spoils her, this can't all be kosher. Right?"

"As far as anyone can tell, Alessandro and Maria have withdrawn from social life for the moment. Alessandro seems to be focusing on work, and that's it—"

"And I can't show up at his company without causing legal issues for myself and Dorian. Monica will use it as proof that I'm the one harassing her," I said miserably, dropping into a seated position on the bed.

"You didn't let me finish, Demi. There is one event he absolutely can't bow out of, and I happen to have an invite."

I closed my eyes in relief. "Mom, if I could hug you right now, I would."

"I just hope you're making the right choice."

"What other choice do I have? I have to try. She's not backing down, and Dorian pressing charges seems to have escalated her." I left out the part where Viola, another of Dorian's exes, offered her help to prove that Monica was lying and get her to stop already.

I still didn't quite believe it was true.

And I had been too shocked to ask her what kind of proof she was speaking about.

"Alright, well, I don't see the harm in you attending this event with me and 'bumping' into Alessandro. Nor is there harm in casually speaking your mind when you do."

"Thank you so much for helping me with this, Mom."

My mother sighed. "I hate this for you. I truly do. I can't wait until it's all over."

"I know, Mom. Me too."

"I'll pass by with my driver to pick you up tomorrow. It's an early start, so be ready by three."

"Okay, Mom. Will do. Thank you again."

"Don't thank me, yet. We have no idea how this is going to play out."

chapter forty-two

I slid into the car alongside my mother. Dressed in a gorgeous metallic A-line gown, my mom greeted me with a light kiss on the cheek.

"Is that the Naeem Khan gown?" I asked, recognizing it.

My mother smiled mischievously. "Decided to polish it off and take it for another spin."

Although the thought of my mother out on the prowl, or anything akin to that, bothered me, I was proud of her all over again. "You look fantastic. So, where are we heading?"

"It's the Urban Design awards. Smaller scale, but Alessandro was invited."

I wondered why Dorian hadn't been. Or had he, and he simply hadn't told me? Not that it mattered. Him not being there was the only reason I had a shot at getting away with this. I didn't tell him my plan.

There was no way he'd be on board with this.

As a matter of fact, I was probably batshit crazy and desperate for trying this.

Alessandro's daughter and her fucked-up antics were to blame.

"Wait a moment." I turned back to my mother, confused. "How are we getting in?" My mother, although she owned a massive amount of shares in SD Interiors, was not actually involved in the running of the company, or the actual architectural designs.

"Your father was invited. Therefore, so was I. We're lucky they sent the invitations for each of us separately."

"Are you telling me that I'm crashing this event?" As if I needed more attention upon arriving there. "If you're his plus one, then I—"

"Relax, Demi. I'm taking your father's place; you're taking mine." She reached into her wristlet and took out a compact mirror.

"How is that possible?" I asked, although I had a sinking suspicion how.

"I asked him to do this for me."

"Oh God. What did he ask in return?"

My mother opened her pocket mirror and reapplied her lipstick with neat swipes. "I promised I'd sit down and 'negotiate' with him."

"He's going to try to get back with you, Mom," I groaned.

"Perhaps. But no one said this meeting with him is actually going to take place." She closed her compact mirror and slid it back into her wristlet.

Stunned, I sat there in silence, eyebrows raised.

She winked at me with a smirk. "If he wants to play dirty, I can too. Especially if it helps our daughter sort through her situation."

My throat tightened. "I really don't know how to thank you, Mom."

Placing her hand on mine, she gave it a squeeze. "Pull this off. Then, date Dorian for a longer time than I dated your father before you marry him. Make sure he's truly worth it."

"No one mentioned anything about him marrying me," I mumbled in a small voice.

My mother gave me a dry stare. "Demi, that man is moving you into his penthouse. He's going to propose."

Nothing more was said on the ride to the event.

I SAT THROUGH THAT AWARD CEREMONY, CHOKING ON MY nerves the entire time. There was no telling if the Adamos had noticed that Mom and I were there. All I knew was that Alessandro Adamo was never on his own, and finding a spot to encounter him, where I could deliver my message without prying ears, was starting to seem impossible.

I'd told Dorian I was meeting up with the girls.

When he texted me to see how my night was going, and I had to lie to him about it, my anxiety only grew worse.

The longer I was there, the greater the chance that I was either spotted by someone he knew, or I ended up on someone's social media in the background of a photo.

My mind spiraled with paranoia, yet I didn't dare remove my focus from Monica's father and mother. Perhaps my best shot was with her, if she walked away from him to head to the women's bathroom, but according to the rumors, she didn't hold any real power in the family.

Alessandro did.

Monica bowed to him. Or, at least, she used to. I refused to believe her father signed off on her stunt with the sex videos.

Alessandro accepted his award for the night and finally separated himself from the crowd of people surrounding him. He left his wife holding the award and walked out of the main hall.

I wasted no time following him.

It wasn't until we were halfway down the hallway that I realized that I was being too impulsive. Too impatient. There was no way I could pretend I was bumping into him accidentally if he caught me following him this blatant—

Alessandro turned around.

I jerked to a stop, heart in my throat.

He stared me up and down slowly, a semi-disgusted perusal that made me want to shrink into myself. "I see that my daughter is right about you cornering people at events."

I had two options at that moment: give into the anxiety and back down . . . or plow forward with this rash plan and meet him head on.

Jutting my chin, I did my best to act unaffected by his critique, and stared him in the eye. "I won't get into the fact that she went to the Goffs' event knowing that she couldn't get within five-hundred feet of Dorian—"

"Do you enjoy this? This mess you've created, little girl?"

There was no faking the indignation that went through me at his questions. It sandblasted through my fear within seconds. "Your daughter just leaked sex videos of her and Dorian because she can't get over the fact that he's done with her. I think you need to reanalyze where you're placing the blame here."

Was that surprise I saw on his face? Or more disgust? It was hard to tell, yet it was clear that I was ruining my entire endgame by letting my temper take the wheel.

I opened my mouth to apologize.

Alessandro adjusted the cuff of his tuxedo, his movements unhurried. A man pretending he was calm; I suspected he was anything but. "Had you never come along, my daughter would've never had an excuse to act out like this."

My mouth remained open as I tried to digest what he'd said in a way that actually made sense. "Do you understand what you're saying? If it wasn't me, it could've been someone else. Or . . . did you expect Dorian to eventually settle down with her, or something?"

He dropped his arm and didn't respond.

Which was a response in and of itself, wasn't it?

"Oh God, you thought he'd marry her."

"Or perhaps marry no one."

"And, still, he would've kept sleeping with her. You're . . . you're . . . ." An enabler. The worst kind. It shouldn't have come as a shock, since everyone knew he'd spoiled his daughter to the point of ruining her.

"Did you follow me just to hound me with your thoughts about my daughter?"

"I wanted to speak with you because I thought there was no way you'd be okay with all this negative attention she's bringing your family, and your company."

"Ah, so you want my help to end the mess you helped create."

This man was unbelievable. Utterly unbelievable.

Just like his daughter.

This was clearly a waste of my time. I'd miscalculated when I thought he would want to help end this drama.

There was a part of me that was starting to believe that he approved of his daughter's tactics.

"I hate to remind you of this, but I'm not the one leaking those videos. And, sadly for your daughter, we have proof that she was willing to share them."

"As I said, you want this. You want to have my daughter arrested in order to appease your childish jealousy—"

"Jesus Christ, you're sick. Your whole family must be sick. Your daughter is the one who can't handle her jealousy. Unless you find a way to reel her back in, she's giving us no choice but to continue pursuing charges. It'll be the only way to stop her." Appalled by this man's way of thinking, I turned to leave.

"If I were to . . . say, get my daughter to leave you two alone, does that mean you'd stop using the law as a means to control her?"

I closed my eyes and took several deep breaths. This man was one-hundred percent responsible for how his child turned out. Forget the rumors of him spoiling her. One conversation with him, and it was undeniable. "We have to 'use the law', as you put it, because she won't back down and just leave us in peace."

Dorian wanted Monica and her family crushed for what she'd done.

I wanted that, too.

But not as badly as I wanted to just leave all this behind us. Move on with my life and focus on my time with Dorian. Enjoy the fact that we'd moved in together, and whatever the future brought us, without this bullshit hanging over our heads.

"So you're saying that if I get my daughter to back down, you will withdraw charges and convince Dorian to leave her alone in response."

I faced Alessandro Adamo once more. "Fine. Just get her to fucking stop and to back off. *Permanently.*"

"Demi!"

The sound of Dorian's voice startled me hard enough to make me twitch.

When I looked over my shoulder, I saw him storming in my direction.

Somehow, he'd been alerted to my presence here.

And, as I predicted, he was furious about it.

"What are you doing?" he snapped, stopping next to me and placing his hand on my waist. "Let's go."

"Wait. Dorian."

"She was offering me an intriguing deal. But now I see you aren't in agreement with it, therefore this has been a waste of my time."

Dorian glared at Alessandro. "We don't need any deals with you."

"Dorian, damn it. Wait!" I pushed his arm lightly to get his attention. "He says he can get Monica to back off and leave us alone."

Dorian didn't take his gaze off Alessandro. "Let me guess. In exchange for me not dragging your daughter through the courts, and your company as well, as I break every single contract between us."

"Don't be a fool," Alessandro snapped. "You want to explore this young thing at your leisure—"

"Watch it," Dorian growled.

"As I was saying," Alessandro calmly spoke over him. "Most of the contracts between us are already well underway. Even if you have legal standing to end the contracts, it will set you back years and millions of dollars. Not to mention the property owners that hired us to work together worldwide. And the last thing you want right now is more bad publicity as you attempt this thing you have going with the girl."

I'd approached him to find a solution, but he had been clearly thinking this over on his own for a while. As much as he wanted to defend his daughter, he was ready to save his company first.

And her, as well. If she didn't face legal consequences, then she wouldn't be punished for what she'd done anymore.

"Monica deserves what's coming to her," Dorian gritted through his teeth.

I placed my hand on his shoulder.

That was all it took for him to turn his head in my direction, although I could see how much it cost him. "We need to end this." *I* needed it to end. Something I didn't have to convey to him. He knew it as much as I did.

Dorian stared into my eyes, and I could see the wheels turning in his head. There was a moment of quiet, where I could almost hear him internally coming to grips with the loss of his vengeance, before he forced himself to address Alessandro. "I'd need some kind of legal guarantee that you will keep your daughter away from me."

"Done. We can have our lawyers draw up the papers. My daughter will be informed. If she ever approaches you, or your little girl, again she will be sent out of the country to get whatever treatment she needs to finally get over you." He spat that last part with utter disgust.

He was talking about institutionalizing his adult daughter.

The same one he was defending at first.

Monica clearly needed the help, but I couldn't wrap my mind around how that man's thought process worked. How he could flip so easily from one extreme to the other.

"Fine," Dorian responded with the same amount of vehemence in his tone. "But I'm not withdrawing charges until then. And I will demand every copy of the videos she holds is destroyed. I'll have my lawyer contact yours." He dismissed Alessandro and grabbed my arm. "We're leaving."

chapter forty-three

Silence reigned in the back of the Rolls-Royce.

Dorian hadn't said a word since we got into the car; I wasn't inclined to bridge that quietness first. I kept going over the end of our conversation with Alessandro in my head, and doubts crept to the forefront of my mind.

Could he truly control his daughter?

She was an adult. I was sure she had to have her own money stashed away.

Would Dorian be signing some kind of legal agreement with the head of the Adamo family for no reason?

Joey wouldn't let Dorian sign something that wasn't ironclad. It was the only consolation I had.

The event had taken place downtown. As the car made its way through traffic on its way uptown, minutes stretched on endlessly.

I clutched my hands together in my lap.

Out of the corner of my eye, Dorian shifted on his seat. I sensed him turn toward me, but he made no move to touch me.

"Why didn't you tell me?"

His voice was low, calm, curious more than anything. I expected more anger, and was beyond relieved when it seemed like he had none to give.

"I didn't think you'd be open to it. I know it was wrong to hide it from you, yet I had to try something."

"Look at me, baby girl."

I could never resist him when he called me that, let alone when he used that tone.

Turning to him, I was surprised to find him staring at his lap with a worried expression. "Dorian?"

He pulled my hands apart and held my right one in his own. "I'm glad you did it. As much as I wanted to take this all the way and destroy her, this might be the quickest way to end everything. If he isn't lying, and he actually has that kind of control over her."

It never failed to floor me each time we ended up on the same wavelength. The sweet relief that followed left me almost weak as all the adrenaline drained away. I reached for his hand with my other one, clasping it between both of mine. "You want it to be over already as well."

Dorian's lashes lifted along with his gaze. For all the relief I'd felt seconds ago, his scrunched brow and tensed frame triggered ripples of unease. "Yes, for your sake. Mine? I don't care, I wanted to see her burn. Literally. But . . ."

"But?" I urged, heart pounding.

"Remember when you asked to be a part of the plan? To perhaps dig into her and find dirt?"

"Yes . . ." I braced for whatever was coming, because it was clear he was on the verge of delivering news he knew I wouldn't like.

"I'd already hired someone weeks ago to dig into her. And, aside from the sex videos with me, she seems to be squeaky clean."

I ripped my hands away from his as if burned. "I-I don't understand. Why didn't you tell me the moment we agreed to work together even more? Why hide this from me?"

"Listen to me, I fully expected to involve you. I was actually planning on sitting down with you and talking about this in the next few days. Things have been crazy, and when they aren't? It's fucking amazing coming home to you every day. To Beck. The few minutes we get at night to just be together, and forget all the shit, mean everything to me."

He seemed so sincere and earnest—desperate to not piss me off.

I took a slow breath, urging myself to calm down. We'd had enough fights thanks to this Monica mess, and I wouldn't allow this to devolve into yet another one. "Explain this to me in a way that makes sense."

Dorian nodded, a curl falling over his forehead. For the life of me I would never understand how such an intensely masculine man could look so young and adorable at times. "I was making moves from the moment she began threatening me. Okay, not really. My first moves involved keeping you in the dark."

The reminder wasn't appreciated, and I knew he could tell.

He hurried to explain himself faster. "Once things got too serious, I immediately got Joey onboard. He couldn't offer me much help at first. I had to wait for her to strike first in order to have the law on my side. Obviously, that didn't sit well with me because I didn't want this to come out and break your heart. I didn't want to lose you. So I hired a private investigator to start digging."

"Still don't understand why you didn't tell me this before."

"I was going to. It's just that . . ."

I let my head fall back with a sigh. "*Dorian*. I can't, literally *can't*, handle anymore anxiety."

He grabbed my thigh over my dress and squeezed. "I'm sorry, okay? I'm sorry. For this, for not being a hundred percent upfront."

"About what?" I all but snapped, on the verge of losing my temper.

"I didn't just hire an investigator. I took other measures, in the event that Monica would slip up, or would approach you on her own."

Taking pity on him, since he was clearly nervous as hell, I kept my lips shut as he gathered his thoughts. Even as my entire body rebelled with the possibility that he was about to say something that would break my heart.

"I installed cameras in the boardroom to capture the meetings leading up to the design festival."

Meetings that Monica would be a part of.

Why would me knowing that worry him? "And did you capture anything worthwhile?"

"Not. Not the boardroom cameras. Well, aside from her staring at me like an unhinged psycho during those meetings, but that's hardly illegal."

"So . . . what?"

"I didn't just install cameras in the boardroom. I was afraid that she'd do something in Chicago. I fucking knew it after our last meeting ended. I'm a fucking idiot for even convincing you to go with me there, when every instinct told me she'd do whatever she was planning during the conference."

"She was going to send me that video regardless," I told him. "Even if I had stayed behind."

"True, but I still believed she wouldn't be dumb enough to risk sending it electronically. I truly thought she would corner you somewhere and do it in person. I also had my hands tied because I couldn't get into your laptop, or phone, to install tracing software in case she did. I should've asked for your passwords and told you why, but I didn't want to take this mess there."

"I need you to just spit it out. Now. What did you do?"

"The night you went out with the girls, I placed hidden cameras throughout the hotel room."

This man could seriously trigger the worst of me at times. "So while you were busy arguing over text with me, you were once again putting your multi-tasking skills to use."

"Damn it, Demi. I wanted video proof in case she cornered you there."

"You recorded us having sex that night." That's why he was worried. Why he was so scared to confess.

"Yes," he admitted without preamble.

It wasn't the first time, although we'd never recorded anything too long. Usually, it was him recording me with his phone while I sucked his dick.

It used to turn me on.

It still did.

But my arousal was tinged with a sickening horror that couldn't be denied. I sat back in my seat, staring at the front of the car—at the closed privacy screen. "Dorian . . . do you have a porn addiction?"

"Fuck this," he hissed, and leaned forward to yank my face toward him. "I have a *you* addiction. Period."

"You keep recording yourself having sex with women so you can watch them later on and jerk off to them. That's porn addiction. Possibly sex addiction, now that I think about it."

"I'll admit I've always been wild about sex. But there's no way you'll ever get me to name it an addiction until I met you. Before I used to do my thing, either with them or alone, and forget about it during the day. I liked to watch the videos to jerk off to, but I swear to you I wasn't fixated on it all day. I got my nut off and kept it moving. With you, though? Demi, it's all I fucking think about. All day, every day. I can't work. I barely sleep well unless you're next to me, and even then I wake up with wet boxers, or wet sheets, because you're in my fucking head even while I'm sleeping. You know that part is true."

I did. I'd been there in the middle of the night, or in the mornings, when he woke up with wet cum spots in his boxers.

My body flushed at the reminder, an inconvenient, yet heady

reaction that I couldn't control.

"Baby girl, I can't help what I did with others in the past, and I am so sorry you found out about it, but I swear to you on everything I am, no one ever worked me up like you do. I told you this because I wanted you to understand why I'm not mad you hid your plans from me."

"It's not on the same level," I said softly as he caressed my face with drugging strokes.

"I'm aware of that."

"What else are you hiding from me?" My lids grew heavy. Each stroke of his fingers along my jaw sent warm pulses through me that relaxed and aroused me against my will.

And he fucking knew it, as always.

His own lids lowered to half-mast and he drew me closer. "You won't understand. And there's no videos of that, either, so you'll never have to see it."

"You're right. Then I don't want to know." I could guess what it entailed, and I'd had enough details to last a lifetime.

"I've done some crazy shit when it comes to sex in my life. Now I wish I hadn't." He had me right up against him, one move from being on his lap. All he had to do was lift me. His other hand fell to my waist, fingers flexing as if he intended to do just that.

I placed my hand on his chest to stop him. "Are you going to expect me to do that stuff at one point?"

"I'd never share you," he snarled in a low voice, fury at the thought tightening his features.

"I'd kill you if you ever tried to bring anyone else into our sex life. You know that."

Dorian licked his lower lip and smiled. "I'm glad we're on the same page."

"How about other stuff?"

He began easing me onto his lap. I shouldn't have let him

distract me, yet resisting him was nearly impossible. "I would never do anything you don't want. But, please, by all means, experiment with me in any way you ever see fit."

The images unleashed by that statement left me so wet that I couldn't help but tremble on his lap. "Stop trying to distract me with sex."

"But we're so good at it together."

And he'd captured it on video. Like he'd done with so many others before. "Dorian, those videos. I won't tell you to get rid of them, because I won't deny a part of me likes you watching it if you aren't with me. But I don't think I can watch them with you anytime soon."

"Then I won't force you. Just know that we're so fucking hot together. Hotter than anything I've seen or done in the past."

I crossed my legs tightly at his hungry tone, my pussy pulsating to the beat of my heart. "You've watched them?"

"How else do you think I survived those three weeks without you, baby?"

God, he was delicious and I just wanted to eat him alive. Even when I shouldn't. "I told you: stop trying to distract me with sex."

"Baby, I can almost smell how much you want sex right now," he groaned, staring hungrily at my lips.

"I'm serious. We have enough shit going on. We need to communicate moving forward. And, yes, that includes me."

Dorian pressed his lips to my chin, teasing me without mercy. "Does part of me communicating include me telling you that my dick is practically leaking for you right now? You need to be fucked in this dress."

He'd *never* had any problems communicating when it came to that. "Dorian! I'm serious."

"No more secrets, baby. I swear. But I'm serious, too. Let me at least make you come in that dress. I'm fucking dying for it."

44

I'd gotten used to Jocelyn's annoying, nasty mug greeting me from the reception desk every time I walked into Dorian's office on the fortieth floor. Seeing someone new in that chair threw me off.

I came to a stop near the sitting area.

The young man at the desk turned. His brown eyes lit up with recognition at the sight of me. "Ms. Davis, good afternoon. How are you?"

He knew me?

Or at the very least, he knew my name.

Seeing my confusion, he offered me a sheepish grin. "Mr. Sorenson informed me of who you are in case you visited."

My heart warmed at Dorian's thoughtfulness.

At the fact that he'd replaced his female receptionists with a male, as petty as that might sound to some.

And I was glad that he'd had to introduce me to his new employee. It meant the scandal of what was happening with my family, and my relationship, hadn't become national news. Many people were aware of it, but clearly not everyone.

"Hi." I walked to his desk and extended my hand. "Demitra Davis. As you already know. Nice to meet you."

He shook my hand quickly. Professionally. "Brentley Baur. It's a pleasure. Mr. Sorenson spoke highly of you."

"Did he now?" I looked toward his closed office door. "Is someone in there with him?"

"He's actually in a meeting with the board."

My first thought was the boardroom and that dark wood table we'd fucked on.

Yet, my stomach tightened right after. Turning back to Brentley, I asked, "The board? Why is he having a meeting with them?" It was nearly the end of the day. I didn't remember them ever convening so late in the past.

Brentley didn't give me a reason for the meeting; not that I expected him to. He simply said, "They should be done soon."

So there would be no waiting for Dorian at the entrance of the boardroom.

Nervous, I wandered over to the seating area and dropped into one of the cushioned chairs. Perhaps another twenty or thirty minutes passed. My leg bounced faster and faster. Brently was probably staring at me out of the corner of his eye and wondering what was wrong with me.

I didn't care.

I wasn't lying when I told Dorian a few days ago I couldn't handle anymore anxiety. The unknowns that still lay before us were taking me time to get used to. When I saw the first man in a suit exit from the hallway leading to the boardroom, followed by a few others, I knew the meeting was over.

When their eyes cut in my direction, and another ten people in suits came behind them, gazes also on me, I knew what that meeting must've been about.

The problem with being the head of a publicly traded company?

The board had final say in almost everything.

If you were the CEO and happened to bring bad publicity to the company? They could decide you were more trouble than you were worth.

Glued to my seat by dread, I watched them head toward the elevators. I took their stoic, yet slightly disapproving glances. Prayed to everything out there that I was wrong and it wasn't what I thought it was.

If Monica cost Dorian his position at this company . . .

If Dorian lost it because of his relationship with me . . .

It didn't bear thinking about.

Alessandro Adamo's company was still a private company. They could withstand more of the scandal without him being in jeopardy of losing what he'd built.

Once the last board member was out of sight, I shot out of the chair and began heading straight to the boardroom. It wasn't the first time I walked that path—I walked it many times during the two months I was interning here—and even if it had been, Dorian's pull was too strong. It could lead me anywhere.

I found him inside the boardroom. He was still sitting in the chair at the head of the table. His head was in his hands.

The sight brought me to a stop. Without thinking twice about it, I whispered his name in a small tone.

Dorian's head shot up.

His eyes widened at the sight of me and he rose from the chair. "Demi? What are you doing here, baby?"

I waited for him as he walked closer. "What happened? I saw the board members exiting as I was waiting."

He stopped before me and his chest rose and fell with a slow breath. "I think you know what."

"They're going to remove you as CEO?" I gasped, my entire body freezing.

Dorian hurried to grab my hands. "Not quite . . . not yet, at least. But they needed to flex their muscles and throw around their threats. That's all, baby." He reached up to run his finger across my brow. "You always get so pale when you're scared," he mumbled softly. "Please stop worrying. It's going to be okay."

"It's hard to stop," I admitted in a low voice, trying to do as he asked and calm myself. "Every time there's hope that this is going to end, something new happens."

"Come here." Enveloping me in a hug, he kissed my temple and placed his chin on of my head. "Whatever happens, it's going to be alright. *We're* going to be alright. I don't want to lose the company my dad built, but he decided to go public against everyone's advice, and I decided to be an irresponsible idiot. Now, here we are. Either way, I have enough money. And Calum's company is still private. I'll head over and beg for a spot."

I snuggled into his hard chest, soaking in his heat and scent. "I don't want you to have to do that, though. You built it up twice as much as your dad since you took over." A little fact I'd figured out during the months I was trying to ignore my attraction to him.

My idea of "ignoring" it had been to research him like some lovesick psycho.

Dorian's hands dropped to my lower back. His fingers flexed against me and he brought me even closer. "Hmmmm." That hum shot through me, bringing every sense to life. "I told you, it's going to be perfectly okay. No matter what happens. You know why?" He nuzzled my cheek and worked his way down to my neck. His breath ghosted across the sensitive flesh, sending goosebumps through me. "Because we're together now. You live with me. And nothing is separating us again. So everything else is workable."

I struggled to think past the desire thrumming through my veins. The last time I'd been in this boardroom, Dorian had just returned from his four week trip to France. He'd devoured me on its surface, reminding us both who I belonged to. "I don't want you to lose anything because of this. That's all."

"I told you"—his lips caressed my neck as he spoke—"I have everything I need if you're with me."

Emotion overwhelmed me, took control of my impulses. I tugged his face away from my neck and pressed my lips to his. His tongue slipped inside, connecting with my own.

His groan was echoed by my needy whimper.

Proof that we'd both been on edge.

Aroused.

Possibly thinking about the same thing: the last time he fucked me in here.

It was the most foolish thing to do. The board had just left here, after apparently castigating him on his choices and how they reflected on the company. Cooler heads would've decided against this. Would've parted and waited till they got home.

Not us.

Not ever.

This thing between Dorian and I would always be too hot, uncontrollable. A bomb always one hair trigger away from going off.

Dorian squeezed me to him, fucking my mouth with his tongue.

His hard cock pulsed against my belly.

I kissed him back with everything I had, grinding against his hardness. My senses zeroed in on every aspect of him. The feel of his muscular, hard body vibrating with need against me. His scent. His taste. The pained, small groans that echoed in his throat as our movements grew more frenzied.

Dorian tried to pull back. He pressed small kisses all over my jaw, my face, as if he couldn't quite put that distance between us.

Of course he couldn't. He was on fire for me. Desperate to have me coming around his cock. Dying to thrust into me and empty himself inside me once more.

"We can't," he groaned, straightening to his full height. "Not here. The cameras—"

He thought I'd forgotten about them.

I hadn't.

And although the thought of sex videos still brought to mind everything we'd gone through lately—everything I'd seen—I was also on fire for him.

Aroused beyond logic.

He took me there every time. Dragged me into that sexual darkness that made me want to do almost anything, try almost anything, with him that would make both of us hornier.

I stepped out of his embrace, and turned to the boardroom doors. Without looking at him, I pushed them closed.

"Demi?"

I dropped my trench coat on the ground and grabbed the hem of my sweater. Yanking it over my head, I let it join the coat and faced him.

His shock was written all over his face.

So was his arousal.

I fucking loved seeing him turned on. He was literally like a fallen angel of a man, with his blue eyes and those blond curls, too beautiful for his own good.

Desire only heightened his appeal. That tightly leashed aggression that lived inside him was dying to break free.

He fucked me until I almost passed out on that table last time.

This time, it was going to be my turn.

Walking up to him, I tugged his head back down for another kiss.

As our mouths connected and our tongues intertwined, he tried to talk between kisses.

"Baby, wait. The cameras—"

"I know they're there." Pushing on his chest, I led him until his ass met the edge of the table. "You're going to lay back and let me have control this time. While they're recording. Aren't you, baby?"

Eyes flashing, he cupped my ass and groaned. "Fuck. Are you serious?"

"Yes. Get on the table, Dorian."

Uncertainty warred with lust on his features, and he hesitated a second too long for my liking.

Grabbing his straining dick over his pants, I gave it a rough tug. "This is mine, and you don't get to deny me. Get on the table so I can grind on your cock and come all over it."

His lids fluttered. "Fuckkkkkk. You're so fucking sexy." He yanked my hair and kissed me. "You know I love feeling your pussy gushing all over my dick."

"I know. I'm practically gushing now, that's how wet I am," I confessed breathlessly as we kissed. "Get on the table and I'll give it to you."

One last kiss, then he wasted no time doing as I asked. Lifting himself onto the table in a seated position, he slid backward a bit, then proceeded to lay down.

A big, sprawled feast of a man with a swollen cock.

I took a moment to ingrain the image of him in my head—

Then climbed onto the table with him, ready to give those cameras a show.

chapter forty-five

I climbed onto the boardroom table's surface. Dorian watched me with hooded eyes the entire way. "Why are those jeans still on your body?"

"For the same reason that your pants are still on yours," I responded, easing closer on my knees. He was still dressed in his business suit, a classic black one tonight, and my mouth watered at every inch of his body. Dorian filled out suits like only few men could. His crisp, white button down framed his trim waist perfectly.

Beneath his black belt, his cock raged inside those dress pants.

"Demi, as much as I love your eyes on me, you need to climb on top of me. Now."

Dorian's voice was another part of his appeal that was impossible to deny. I'd never forgotten the rush of seeing him in person as I was growing up. I think I had a crush on him as a young teen, my heart tripping every time I'd seen him come over to our home for events and whatnot.

Then I'd walked into his office the day of my "interview" for the intern position. It had been informal, more of a reacquainting than an interview, but my first glance of him behind his desk had left my legs liquified.

My blood on fire with lust.

My pussy clenching with the need to be fucked hard and fast.

When he'd stood to shake my hand and said my name…

I could've come for him right then and there.

"Demi?"

"Dorian," I breathed his name, leaning over him but not touching quite yet. "What did I say about letting me take control?"

His hands twitched as his sides. "Baby girl, I'm all for letting you have it, but I need you to touch me." His dick jumped in his pants at the words.

Smirking, I sidled closer and began working on his tie. I was careful not to touch him aside from that. "What you need is to come. As usual."

"In you. Your mouth. Your cunt. Your ass."

It wasn't the first time he'd let it be known he wanted that, and I'd be lying if I said it didn't excite me.

Once his tie was loosened, I made quick work of unbuttoning his shirt. I had no plans of fully removing it, or his blazer. Part of the excitement was the reminder that we were here again, in this boardroom, and there was the risk that we might be caught if someone walked in here this late at night.

Dorian's flexed, delicious torso came into view. I took a second to bask in the sight of it, his gorgeous abs, then reached for his belt.

"Finally," he groaned, hips shifting impatiently.

I kept my cool, although inside I was already a quivering mess. All it took was me lowering his zipper and his dick throbbed as it was exposed, practically falling out of his pants. He was so hard he'd slid through the opening in his briefs.

I lost my breath at how swollen and beautiful he was.

That moist tip called to me—to my mouth.

"Stay right there. Just like that," I demanded in a hoarse voice.

As dangerous as it was, one of us was going to have to be naked for this.

I didn't know where he'd placed the cameras, but I suspected there had to be at least one on the ceiling, aimed right at the table we were on.

I stood on the table long enough to slip out of my pants and panties. They landed on the floor somewhere behind me, and my bra followed.

Dorian licked his lips, eyes on my waxed pussy.

Fuck, I was dying for that tongue on me, licking me again.

So I did just that.

I eased down and turned around, my mouth facing his dick. When Dorian realized my intentions as I raised a leg over his head, he moaned in the back of his throat.

"God, we haven't sixty-nined since Chicago. Get that pussy over here." His hands landed on my ass, kneading the cheeks and guiding me.

So much for letting me have control.

Not that I cared as much anymore. My eyes were glued to his straining dick.

I spread my legs and lowered myself over his gorgeous face. His warm breath washed over my needy clit. I wrapped my hand around his erection and brought it to my mouth.

Dorian hummed, tongue massaging my clit with perfect expertise.

I answered him with a hungry hum of my own, and let my tongue flick out to circle his tip.

"Fuck, baby," he growled against my pussy. "Ride my face while I fuck your mouth."

Didn't need to tell me twice.

I gave myself up to the sensation and slid his length into my mouth, taking him as deep as I could go. My hips churned in his grip, pussy riding his mouth. His own hips thrust off the table, impaling my mouth with his dick each time.

My mind flashed to how it must've looked to the cameras—my ass in the air, his hands spreading me wide.

As much as I wanted to make it last, blood rushed to my clit, the tension building. Dorian leaked pre-cum into my mouth, the bite of salt leaving me desperate for another taste. The intensity with which he was eating my pussy registered on every level.

Every damned time.

I was near combustion, ready to drench his mouth with my orgasm.

He reached up and thrust his index finger into me.

I moaned around his cock, circling my hips to fuck his finger.

But he didn't let me for long.

He slid it out of me and upward. Suddenly, he was right *there*, circling my ass.

I couldn't even be shocked. He was eating my pussy out too good, groaning at the taste, and the tingles of sensation his finger was causing blanked my mind entirely. All that existed was him. The pleasure. The brutal need to come that was building each second.

His large hand cupped the back of my head, holding me in place for his fucking. "That's right, baby. Drench my tongue. I can't wait to be inside this cute ass of yours." He sucked my clit into his mouth softly.

He worked his finger into my ass.

Fucked my mouth harder, faster.

Convulsions shattered through me. It was the first time I was coming with something in my ass, and the added sensations left me writhing, absolutely wild on top of him.

My body fell limp, even with his throbbing length in my mouth. Ripe for him to fuck, manhandle.

The thought must've gone through his head as well.

Suddenly, I was lifted off his cock and face. My back hit the surface of the table. I blinked up in surprise and found Dorian rearing over me. "Sorry, baby. I know you wanted control but I can't stop myself."

My legs were spread fully open unmercifully. The head of his cock brushed my soaked, swollen pussy. I tensed, desperate for that invasion, that perfect, unbeatable feeling that always came with that first thrust.

Dorian opened me even wider. His chest heaved. "That orgasm left you so tight. You're hungry for it, can't wait for me to fuck your ass." He nudged his tip into me, fighting past the tight muscles. "Jesus. Christ. Baby, relax for me. Let me in."

I wanted nothing more. Couldn't think past the need to have that beautiful dick exploding inside me. "Don't worry, baby. Just give it to me. Come in my pussy."

"Fuck, yes. Give me every goddamned inch of that beautiful cunt." He surged inside me, impaling me to the base. Lowering himself over me, he pushed my breasts together and took turns laving each nipple with his tongue.

"Dorian!"

"Tell me who owns this pussy."

I was pounded into the table on his next thrust. My teeth chattered from the force. "Y-you. Oh, God. You."

"Yeah. I do. I'm going to own it forever." He lifted my legs over his shoulders, bending me in half, and rammed into me. The sight he made, half-undressed in his business suit and fucking me like a deranged beast, left me trembling on the verge again. "You're mine. Forever, Demi. Say it."

His glittering, delirious eyes drilled into me. Invaded me. Commanded me.

He wasn't on his knees with a ring proposing, but there was no mistaking what he was demanding. What he was telling me.

"Motherfuck." Fingers digging into my thighs painfully, he adjusted me and ground his dick into me. "Admit it, baby. You're marrying me one day."

"*Oh God oh God oh God*," I mewled, startled by the strength of my second orgasm as it flooded me out of nowhere.

No, not out of nowhere. It had been because of him.

What he'd just said to me.

"Holy shit. Look at you. Exploding around me at the thought. Fuckkkkk." His hands squeezed my thighs to the point of pain. His expression broke as his cocked jerked wildly in my pussy.

Spasms rocked his body.

His own orgasm seemed to last an eternity. He released his hold on my legs and collapsed on top of me, breaths racing.

I wrapped my arms around him, stunned. At a loss for words.

So fucking in love with him that I couldn't see straight.

Even so, there was a tinge of alarm. I adored him. I wanted to be his wife.

There, I'd admitted it.

But I thought we'd come to an understanding that it would happen later once we had time to settle down and date.

Once I finished school.

Once this scandal was behind us.

Just as quickly, that apprehension faded. Because it didn't matter in the end when it happened, only that he wanted it as much as I did. So fuck it. If he asked again, I was going to say yes. Screw the timeline.

But he didn't. Eventually, he raised up on the table to rain kisses across my face.

Giggling, I offered my mouth.

We kissed languidly for long, drawn out minutes, basking in that sense of connection. "Let's get you dressed, and then back home. I want to spend all night fucking you all over the penthouse."

It was Friday, so we were free to do just that.

On shaky legs, I eased off the table. Dorian handed me my panties first, followed by my jeans.

He buttoned his shirt as I slipped on my sweater.

I shrugged into my trench coat and went over to him.

"I smell you on my mouth. You know how much I fucking love that," he rasped, as I smoothed his blazer.

"I love you," I responded simply, smiling.

His answering smile did things to me that I couldn't describe. "Ready? Let's head home."

"Let's."

We turned toward the doors.

They burst open and I saw a flash of dark hair.

My heart fell to my feet as recognition sunk in.

Monica stormed into the meeting room, fury vibrating off her form. She took one look at me and her tanned skin flushed dark pink. "You. You fucking bitch. You went and turned my father against me?"

chapter forty-six

Dorian shoved me behind him.

Normally, I'd be disinclined to hide from Monica and would face her on my own.

But her expression had stuck with me.

The unhinged way she'd stared at us.

"You idiot," Dorian said calmly. "You goddamned idiot."

The cameras were recording this.

I had no idea how she got up here, how she evaded security and Brentley, but it'd happened. She was once again violating the restraining order and this time it was being captured on film.

"Fuck you, Dorian! How dare you let this bitch get into my father's head?"

So her father had confronted her in the end. Instead of corralling her, it'd pushed her to act in an even crazier fashion.

Either way, it benefitted us. Something I knew Dorian was also aware of.

"I didn't let my girlfriend do anything. She's her own woman, and well within her rights to approach Alessandro and ask for his help in controlling you. Clearly, someone has to."

Monica practically screeched at that comment. "You'd let her fucking ruin my standing in his company, in my family, just because she can't handle seeing the truth! She can't handle seeing that she isn't special, that you fuck all of us the same way."

Her words . . . I fought to not let them affect me as she intended, but after seeing those videos, it was *hard*. I'd done so well the last few weeks, had pushed those memories so deep into my mind that they barely surfaced.

Yet what she said had rung a bell too loud to be ignored.

I couldn't help the insecurity that blossomed and threatened to suffocate me.

"You've never seen how it is with Demi, and you never will. But stop making an ass out of yourself and assuming shit you know nothing about. Clearly, I belong to her now, when I haven't belonged to anyone before her. The reality is that you're the one who was never special, and you can't deal with that. If it were up to me, she'd be wearing my ring already, and she knows that."

Monica's sharp intake of breath drowned out the sound of my own.

I couldn't believe the ease with which he admitted that; bubbles of euphoria rose from the pit of my being all over again. The tingles of excitement, of *happiness*, were undeniable.

Eye-opening.

What I needed to refocus my attention in that moment.

Dorian truly was ruthless when he needed to be, and the impact of his words was exactly what he'd been aiming for.

"You fucking bitch. All you do is ruin everything," Monica growled, and it was clear she was addressing me.

Everything seemed to go into slow motion.

I looked around Dorian's body to see Monica rooted to the spot, staring at him as if *he* were the insane stranger. Even as her body trembled with hatred for me.

The doors behind her burst open.

Brentley. "Sir! She ran past me. I already called security—"

He didn't get to finish because Monica took off in our direction.

Not ours. She was gunning for me, and didn't care if Dorian stood in her way. Unbeknownst to her, the cameras were capturing all of this.

Dorian shouted something at her, but I didn't make it out. My priority was my sudden, impulsive plan. He tried to lead me around the boardroom table, all while covering me with his body.

I broke out of his hold. Whirling, I saw Monica slam into Dorian as he caught her and tried to keep her away from me.

She didn't even attack him in return. All she wanted was to get her hands on me.

Good.

"I had to speak to your father," I yelled over the noise of multiple people shouting at once. "You don't know what to do with your feelings about Dorian and you're clearly out of control." I'd never played a role to this extent before, yet I was achingly aware of the cameras.

Of how this would benefit us as long as I aimed the right words at her.

"You will fucking stay away from my father!" she screeched like a bat out of hell. "This has nothing to do with feelings. You ruined everything. You couldn't be a grown woman that could handle him as he really is. No. You had to be a clingy little girl and convince him to be monogamous." She spit that word out with a level of disgust that disturbed me.

What had her father done to her? No, really. Just what did it take for someone to end up as twisted as her?

Not my business. Brentley said security was on their way up. My job was to finish pushing her over the edge before they got here.

"Listen to yourself, Monica," I said, striving for the calmest, coldest tone I could muster. "You're throwing a fit because you can't fuck him when you want anymore. You can't share him with me like you did the others. Do you realize what that means? *You* are the clingy one. You're needy. I told you: you're too sick to understand love, but you fell for him. You fell so desperately that you settled for having scraps because you knew deep down *you* could never have him for yourself."

It was worse than her reaction to Dorian's words; her form went limp, her hazel eyes widened, and all the fight left her.

Even Dorian had gone still at my words.

I drove the nail home with my next statement. "That father that you're so desperate to appease must've fucked you up really bad. You have no concept of emotions, of affection. Of love. But you're also a lost idiot. You call me the little girl, but you don't even recognize what that possessiveness you feel means. All that work to be the most gorgeous, the most successful, yet you wasted almost ten years of your life waiting for my man to focus solely on you. Yet you were clearly never enough."

Predicting what came next was easy. I'd chosen my words with a specific goal in mind. I knew it was going to hurt, yet it was the only way to finally finish this.

And Monica didn't disappoint.

Taking advantage of Dorian's momentary distraction, she ran around him and practically flew at me.

I let her catch me.

When she pulled my hair to hold me in place and land a hit on my face, I let her do that, as well.

I could've fought back—God knew I wanted to more than anything—yet I had to go for maximum effect for the sake of the footage.

That meant playing the weak victim and lifting my arms up to cover my face in defense.

The only flaw in my plan was Dorian's reaction to Monica's physical attack on me. I caught sight of him rushing toward us—

Shouts sounded out, what seemed like two new men running inside. They got to us before Dorian could and had no issue manhandling Monica off me.

Her screams were like that of a wounded animal as they carried her out of the boardroom.

Dorian was suddenly in front of me, hands on my shoulders. "Baby, are you okay? Look at me."

I wiped my cheek where'd she hit me. The skin was hot from the blow, but otherwise it was fine. "I'm okay. I swear I am."

He jerked me into his arms. "Holy fuck, when she got her hands on you."

I could still hear Monica screaming as they dragged her down the hall. There was so much I wanted to say to Dorian, but I wasn't sure if he was allowed to edit those videos before handing them over to the authorities. It was bad enough they might see us having sex on there. I didn't want to give away what I'd done on purpose while in this boardroom. "Take me home, Dorian."

His chest rose and fell beneath my cheek. "I need to speak with the cops once they get here to pick her up. They might want to ask you questions, too."

He also needed to download the video and have it ready to go, yet neither of us was going to discuss that in this room.

"Okay. We'll stay." As much as I hated the idea, he was right. It was necessary. Plus, my face was probably red from where she'd struck me, and it'd be great if they saw that themselves.

Dorian's hand circled my neck and his thumbs kneaded the tense muscles there. "I'm sorry, baby. For all of this. We'll leave as soon as we can.

I accepted the kiss he gave me gladly, then let him lead me out of the boardroom.

Brentley was waiting for us by the door, practically vibrating with anxiety. "I'm so sorry. I should've done more to stop her."

"It's fine, Brentley. She was out of her mind. Don't worry too much about it," Dorian said as we turned left to walk down the hall.

When we got to the reception area, Monica and the security guards were nowhere in sight. I figured they'd taken her to the actual security area where they would hold her until the police arrived.

"Come. Let's wait in my office. I'll tell reception to let the officers up here."

I nodded, too afraid to hope that this was actually the end, yet praying for it regardless.

If this is what it took to finally get her under control, so be it. I could accept it. As long as Dorian and I could face tomorrow with all of this behind us.

Dorian's arm came around me, his hand gripping my shoulder.

I reached up and clutched that hand, letting him lead me one last time.

chapter forty-seven

I would've preferred to never have to see her again.

Dreams were rarely attainable, though. And getting rid of all traces of Monica Adamo from our lives might take much longer than I would've liked.

At least today was another step in that direction. Thank God for small miracles.

What she did to us that night was more than the violation of a restraining order. It was, by the legal definition of the term, a physical assault.

Exactly what I'd counted on. What I'd planned to happen.

She only got a single slap in, which meant she couldn't be charged with either a Class D felony, nor the more serious Class B felony.

A misdemeanor is all she could be threatened with.

But it was in addition to the criminal contempt of court for violating the restraining order, and the revenge porn charge.

They were finally able to trace the log in to Jocelyn's email.

It had been from Monica's laptop.

We could never truly prove where she got the password from,

but Dorian and I knew it had to be from Jocelyn herself.

Monica was facing thousands in fines, a maximum of about three years jail time.

Alessandro's company stood to lose a whopping total of seven-point-six *billion* dollars if Dorian went ahead with the breach of contract filing and sued him for profits lost.

I had no idea what kind of wrath her father aimed at her—because, let's face it, the threat of the legal and financial repercussions had clearly not been enough to control her—but Monica finally agreed to give it all up.

In exchange for us dropping the charges and Dorian not pursuing the lawsuits.

At least, that's what her father claimed. He was here, sitting across from Dorian at the table, and Monica was seated a few seats down.

But she wasn't engaged. She just stared blankly at the wall while her father did all the talking.

"To recap, Sorenson International agrees to finish off the pending contracts with your company, and no further obligation is owed on Mr. Sorenson's end. In return, Ms. Adamo will be legally bound to stay away from all job sites, from Mr. Sorenson and Ms. Davis, and no further attempts at communication will be made. Failure to follow that instruction will be considered an immediate breach of contract and we will be forced to proceed with our lawsuits against your company," Joey reiterated from his seat next to Dorian.

He was on his left.

I sat to Dorian's right.

As studiously as I was trying to ignore Monica, her father was doing a hell of a job of pretending I didn't exist. Perhaps he was trying to make me feel inconsequential, but truthfully, I preferred it this way.

"That was already agreed on," Alessandro responded evenly, his

332   THE ALLURE SERIES

jaw twitching.

Ah. So he didn't like the reminder of what he stood to lose if he didn't keep his creation on a leash.

Good. I hoped it weighed on him forever.

God knew that Monica would always be a phantom I fully expected to return. I would learn to live with it, to be prepared. To never be anxious again. Yet the reality was what it was. Multiple futures lay in the balance, all subject to the whims of one insane woman.

Thankfully, this meeting would assure that no matter what happened, Dorian would win in the end.

"Yes, well, after Ms. Adamo showed such blatant disrespect for the laws of this state, and the restraining order set in place, it needed to be repeated."

Joey was awesome. As nice as he seemed on the surface, once he knew the law would be on his side, he transformed into a no-nonsense attorney, ready to bring down the hammer on anyone he needed to.

"We have also been given messages between Ms. Adamo and Ms. Beninato"—Viola had come through in the end—"where Ms. Adamo confessed that she was planning on sending those videos to Ms. Davis in order to cause chaos in her relationship with Mr. Sorenson. Not to mention we were able to trace the email, sent from Mr. Sorenson's employee's email, to the Wifi of the hotel room your daughter was staying in during the design conference."

"We get it." Alessandro's nostrils flared slightly with his next breath. "Just give us the damned paperwork to sign."

Alessandro's lawyer—whose name I had already forgotten—placed his hand on Alessandro's arm.

A signal to calm himself.

Dorian and Joey exchanged a look, and that was it. The pile of contracts was slid across the table to Alessandro.

When he snapped his fingers to demand his daughter's attention, my lips parted in shock.

Her only response was a blank stare, and she turned like an obedient little soldier to take the paperwork handed to her. There was no expression on her face as she signed where the attorney told her to sign, and initialed in other places he motioned to.

She didn't even stop to read what she was signing.

Her hair was brushed and fell in a straight curtain down her back, but aside from her black business suit, she wasn't wearing any makeup.

She was the blandest I'd ever seen her.

Practically dead while still breathing.

I refused to feel bad for her after everything she'd vindictively done. That didn't mean that the questions weren't swirling through my head again.

Had Alessandro abused Monica in the past?

Clearly, he did in the emotional sense. But something about their relationship, about the byproduct of Monica's broken psyche, left me wondering what exactly happened under that family's roof as she was growing up.

I couldn't spend another second thinking about it. The very air in that office was stained by the Adamo family's aura. I just wanted to be as far away from them as possible.

Alessandro signed his parts, Dorian signed his, and then the paperwork came around to me.

Dorian had insisted I be here today.

That my name would be on the contracts.

That I signed in front of them.

He wanted to drive the point home that I would be as untouchable as he and his business were.

I appreciated it, but I wish I didn't have to be there today.

The rest of that meeting went by in a blur. I knew I had signed where I needed to, I just didn't fully remember doing it. I retreated to the back of my mind and didn't pay attention to anything else that was said.

Dorian gripped my hand and pulled me gently to my feet. Next thing I knew, we were outside in the hallway, standing by the wall of windows.

"You know what I'm going to ask you," he murmured, ducking his head until our eyes met.

"I'm okay," I whispered back, soaking in his closeness. "Just can't wait to leave."

"Carl said it should be no more than ten minutes. Traffic got a little congested and he had to go around the block." Outside the windows, snow was falling faster and faster.

It was November in New York, and winter was finally in full swing.

Some years the first snowfall happened as late as Christmas.

This year, it hit right before Thanksgiving.

I nodded at Dorian and walked into his arms. The warmth of his body enveloped me instantly and I almost forgot where we were.

What we'd come here to do.

Out of the corner of my eye, I saw a tall form walk past, bearing regal and his trench coat matching his dark hair.

Monica's father.

Alongside him, his attorney.

I closed my eyes and blocked the sight of him out. Didn't need the reminder. Or any reminder.

Dorian's arms tightened around me.

Forever connected to me.

Forever attuned to my needs.

I hugged him tighter as well and pressed my face to his neck. "I love you," I mumbled into his skin.

He nuzzled my face with a hum. "As I love you."

A mirthless laugh jerked us apart.

That dead version of Monica stood behind me, and that empty expression was somehow more frightening than her psychotic possessiveness of Dorian had been.

"Enjoy it while it lasts. His need for variety has always been legendary. Lie to yourself all you want," she said impassively, her eyes fixed straight ahead. "It's only a matter of time."

I had absolutely nothing to say. Would I always live with that fear? Of course. But I'd chosen to put my faith on Dorian.

I could see on his expression that he did have a lot to say, but Monica walked away before he could. I watched her head down the hall in the direction her father and his lawyer went.

He didn't even wait for her.

She was also wearing a black trench coat, ebony hair falling down her back, and she struck me as a supremely lonely figure as she got further from us.

I hoped it was the last view I ever had of her.

I really did.

"Demi." Brow furrowed, Dorian turned back to me. "Ignore her. She's just—"

I placed my hand on his chest. "It's okay. She clearly needs to believe that. It doesn't matter. I think . . . let's just hope this is over."

He pinched my chin tenderly. "I need to know you trust me."

"For the most part. And I will do everything in my power to make that trust absolute."

"*We* will do everything in *our* power to make sure you end up trusting me. Fully."

That man was everything. He truly was.

I made myself my own promise: I'd do everything in my power to make sure I proved that to him.

Somehow.

Joey joined us finally and Dorian's phone vibrated with a

notification.

Carl was outside waiting for us.

Holding hands, Dorian and I walked besides Joey as we headed toward the elevators…

And toward a new life.

At least, I hoped so.

I was so ready to move forward with my man and get to the important stuff.

Like hopefully planning a wedding soon.

DORIAN

dorian

EPILOGUE
epilogue

9 months later

I stood in the rooftop garden next to St. Patrick's Cathedral and took in the beauty of it.

It really was going to make the perfect venue.

For the wedding, that was.

The reception would take place in the restaurant—as I'd discussed with Demi that night almost a year ago. This location would've been amazing for a wedding, as well, but I had my heart set on the original image I'd envisioned that night.

Of course, my soon-to-be fiancé would have to agree with my vision.

I'd cross that bridge when I got there. First, I had to officially pop the question.

Which is why I'd paid to have the entire rooftop garden shut down for the night. It would be just her and I up here, surrounded by the night lights of the city. It was almost August, and thankfully not too hot, which made the atmosphere even more perfect.

I'd hired a chef just for us.

Our table was set feet from me, in the middle of the grassy walkway. Candles were lit on top thanks to the lack of wind tonight.

I stared at my watch.

If everything went according to plan, Carl should already be dropping Demitra off downstairs. She'd be here shortly.

My heart raced, but not with fear. Excitement. Lust. Desperation? Yes, all of that. It'd taken every ounce of self-control to get to this point, to wait this long to ask her, and I couldn't believe the day had finally arrived.

Demi graduated college yesterday.

She turned twenty-one four months ago.

For almost a year, she'd thrown hints at me, letting me know I didn't need to wait. That she wanted this as much as I did.

And, somehow, I'd found the strength to hold off.

Why? In the end, her original logic had won out. As we finally settled into life together, without the unnecessary drama that Monica brought us, I'd come to realize that Demi had been right.

We didn't start off normal.

We didn't get to date until after all the bullshit had begun.

We didn't get to enjoy each other the way we should've since the beginning.

Demi deserved all of that, and more.

Not only that, but she deserved to finish school, settle into her new business venture with Livana Payne, and focus on that for a bit before I brought the wedding into the picture.

It also gave us some time for the original drama of her parents' divorce to blow over. Stephen fought tooth and nail, and in the end all it did was hurt his cause even more.

He lost everything but the company.

Demi's mother took pity on him and let him keep it, but she took everything else with her when she was done with him.

My phone vibrated in my pocket. One look at it, and the

excitement slammed back into me. Carl had just alerted me that Demitra was on her way up.

Maybe she'd come to think that I didn't want this anymore. Maybe she'd given up hope at some point that I'd ask her someday. A possibility that had torn me apart, yet I'd been convinced I was doing the right thing.

Finally, here we were.

I turned to face the entrance to the rooftop garden, and had to slide my hands into my pockets to contain myself. The impulse to rush over and scoop her into my arms the moment she walked in was undeniable.

She came into view wearing a cream, satin dress that draped her body like an indecent curtain. The slit—her and those goddamned sexy slits—rose to her hip this time.

Her motherfucking hip.

Was she wearing any panties under there?

Every nerve burst into flames at the thought that her bare pussy was uncovered. Ready for my mouth. My cock.

Her hair was curled at the ends, a style she'd kept ever since we got back together, and her baby blue eyes glittered with happiness at the sight of me.

My heart punched into my ribcage. *Jesus.* That was my wife right there. She had to be. She better not even think of saying no now that the day had come.

Throat dry, I wondered if she'd subconsciously known what tonight would end up being. Was that why she chose that satin dress in that color?

She had to be suspecting something now that she was here. Her eyes kept darting between me and the church at my back. I could see the wheels turning in that pretty head of hers.

Demi couldn't keep her gaze on the surroundings for long. Eyes heavy-lidded, she took in my outfit. Her little tongue peeked out as she wet her bottom lip.

My cock knew that tongue very, very well, and had no problem reacting to it as soon as I saw it.

"Hi," she said in a saucy, cute tone.

"Hi, yourself," I murmured, hands fisted in my pockets.

If she looked at me like that one more time, I was going to make it down to my knees alright, but not to propose.

To slide one of those thighs over my shoulder and make her scream so loud all of Manhattan heard her.

I could taste her pussy already.

Shit. The heat spread through my body in vicious waves. I had to wrap a hand around the ring box in my pocket to steady myself.

Demi walked up to me, hips swinging in that barely decent dress. "There is just something about you in an all-black suit . . ." She pressed her body to mine, hands sliding up my chest, and I couldn't hold back my moan at the sensation. "That does it for me so hard. Especially with the collar unbuttoned." Leaning into me, she pressed her juicy lips to my chest.

"Shit, you're looking to be fucked," I growled, wrapping my hands around her shoulders to ease her back.

She giggled. "When aren't I?"

Get through this. Get through this, I reminded myself. Besides, as much as I'd paid to have this rooftop all to ourselves, there was no guarantee that we wouldn't get caught if I devoured her up here.

Which begged the question: how the hell were we going to make it through dinner?

Shaking my head, I tried to dispel the fog of lust she always bombarded me with and took a step back.

Demi watched me, brow furrowed with her curiosity.

Before she could distract me again—or I lost my nerve all together—I looked her in the eye. "You were right that night."

"Huh?"

"The night we went to the restaurant and you assumed that I was about to do what you thought I was hinting at."

It took a few seconds, but eventually I saw the light click on in her eyes.

I reached into my pocket and brought out the ring box. Then, I lowered myself to one knee in front of her.

Her breath left her in a rush.

"I've been holding onto this since that night, almost a year, just waiting for the right time. And you were also right that it wasn't the right time back then. We had so much to still experience with each other before we could get to that point, and I wanted to give you some time to settle into your new life, too."

Tears welled in her light eyes, and she whispered my name in a watery voice. "Dorian."

My heart beat harder than it ever had, a violent, distracting sound. I opened the ring box, letting her see the engagement ring I bought her almost a year ago. "I love you, Demi. I love you with everything I am. I think I loved you the moment you first walked into my office all grown up to do that interview for the internship, and I was just too stupid to realize it. You're everywhere inside of me. You're everything I want and need. And I need you to marry me as soon as possible, and do it in that church back there. I need you to agree to give this city the biggest spectacle possible so that every damned person still rooting against us is forced to see and hear about it. It'll be the biggest wedding this city has seen in a while, and I want it with—"

"Dorian." She closed her eyes, two fat tears falling down her cheeks. "Stop talking and get the fuck up here."

It was my turn to blink in confusion. "Huh?" That wasn't a yes. Why wasn't that a yes? She hadn't said yes, yet. What was going on?

"Dorian, get the fuck up here, so you can put that ring on my finger, and then I'm going to do things to you that might possibly traumatize you."

A laugh burst out of me as I processed her words. "Wait. That's a yes, right?"

With a small growl, she grabbed my blazer at the shoulders and tried to drag me to my feet. "It's a damned yes, a definite yes, a *hell fucking yes*, and if you get up here right now, I'll be saying it all over again with your dick inside me."

It shouldn't be possible to love anyone as much as I loved her.

Laughing, I got to my feet and let her bring me down for a kiss. It blazed out of control instantly, with my girl eating my mouth and clawing at me like she planned to climb me right then and there.

Digging deep into my core, I found the self-control to break that kiss and grab her hand. "Wait. Wait. It's not on your finger yet."

"Well, hurry then!"

Have you ever been so happy that the feeling overwhelmed you with madness? A delirium that nearly robbed all your common sense and left you stumbling in its wake.

I slid that ring onto her finger, where it was going to stay for the rest of our lives, and I swear I felt my own eyes watering.

Demi took maybe a second to look at it. "It's so beautiful. Come here." Wild, uninhibited, she pulled me back to her lips.

The way she kissed me . . . I wasn't lying when I said that I didn't remember any of the women before her. Not that I had amnesia, but more like the sensations had been erased. The experiences had been dwindled down to nothing more than visual replays, because I couldn't recall what anyone felt like prior to her.

I snarled into that kiss, trying to remind myself of where we were.

All while Demi began tugging me toward one of the benches. That gorgeous body writhed against me, encased in silk, and I knew I was a goner.

I would always be a goner for her.

There was nothing she could ever ask for that I wouldn't give her, especially if it was my cock she was demanding.

"Baby," I whispered roughly, gripping her ass. "We might end up in jail if we do it up here."

Her response? "Okay. Get inside me. We can pretend you're my husband already and we're on our honeymoon."

Hearing her call me her husband undid me. Remade me. Fucked me up only to fix me all over again. Everything about me seemed to spin on its axis.

This girl was everything to me.

She'd been everything to me since the day she came into my office.

"That's a fucked up way to end the night of our engagement, isn't it?" I asked, lifting her up into my arms regardless.

"It'll be one for the story books. That's for sure. We'll call Joey. He'll fix it."

We shared another laugh, lips meeting again, the wildness of our connection obliterating my common sense.

My caution.

My self-preservation.

My entire identity.

As it always would.

Because we'd proven that we were never going to let each other go.

No matter what came, or what happened, this was how it'd always be.

I was a lucky motherfucker and I was never, ever going to forget it.

The End

Review Team

Want to join my official review/hype team and get free reader copies, goodies, and more?

Come on over, then!

Go here to sign up: https://bit.ly/nibelites2

Want exclusive teasers to all my upcoming work?

Join my Facebook reader group: Haus of N.

ABOUT *the author*

N. Isabelle Blanco is the *Amazon Bestselling Author* of the Allure Series, the Need Series with K.I.Lynn, and many others. At the age of three, due to an odd fascination with studying her mother's handwriting, she began to read and write. By the time she'd reached kindergarten, she had an extensive vocabulary and her obsession with words began to bleed into every aspect of her life.

That is, until coffee came a long and took over everything else.

Nowadays, N. spends most of her days surviving the crazy New York rush and arguing with her characters every ten minutes or so, all in the hopes of one day getting them under control.

Sign up for the newsletter at https://bit.ly/NIBsignup to be the first to know how all these arguments turn out :)

ALSO BY

a isabelle blanco

Ryze Series
(Dark Paranormal Romance)
Lust
Silence
Vengeance
Cursed
Hunt
Sacrifice
Light (Coming Soon)

Allure Series
(Contemporary Romance)
To Want You
To Have You
To Lose You

Retaliations Series
(Romantic Suspense)
A Debt Repaid
Damage Owed (Coming Soon)

Siege Series
(Dark Romantic Suspense)
Twisted Heartbreak (Coming Soon)
Twisted Rage (Coming Soon)

Need Series (Co-written w/ K.I. Lynn)
(New Adult Angst)
Need
Take
Own

Made in the USA
Columbia, SC
10 March 2025